Blood an

JD Kirk lives in the north of Scotland with his wife, two children, and a number of sturdy umbrellas. He loves the Highlands, crime thrillers, and cats.

# Also by JD Kirk

## DCI Logan Crime Thrillers

# JD KIRK

# BLOOD
## AND
## TREACHERY

🄲 **CANELO**CRIME

First published in the United Kingdom in 2019 by Zertex Crime

This edition published in the United Kingdom in 2024 by

Canelo
Unit 9, 5th Floor
Cargo Works, 1-2 Hatfields
London SE1 9PG
United Kingdom

A CIP catalogue record for this book is available from the British Library.

Paperback ISBN 978 1 80436 818 3

Cover design by Tom Sanderson

Cover images © Shutterstock

Look for more great books at www.canelo.co

Printed and bound in Great Britain by Clays Ltd, Elcograf S.p.A.

I

# Chapter 1

The call had come in the night before, just as Fulton had been settling down to read Carrie her bedtime story. The book was some nonsense about a magnetic cow, but she loved the pictures, and they'd always take time to point out all her favourite bits whenever she came to stay over.

Truth be told, he probably looked forward to it more than she did.

It had been years since they'd had a wee one in the house, and while he hadn't been expecting to become a grandfather quite so soon, there was no denying that the adorable wee bugger had been a blessing. She'd fairly put the bounce back into his wife's step, and had been just the kick up the backside he'd needed to avoid sliding gracelessly into a late middle-aged spread.

They'd just brushed her teeth, given Granny a kiss, and were heading up the stairs when the call came. Missing climber. Helicopter en route. All hands on deck.

That had been... what? Fourteen hours ago? He was sure they'd have found him by now, but no such luck. Still no sign.

From the car park, he could see most of the summit of Buachaille Etive Mor, aside from a few areas where the cloud clung to the peak like a wrap of cotton wool. There were two teams engaged in the search—Glencoe

Mountain Rescue, and their neighbours from Lochaber—and he occasionally caught glimpses of them as they crisscrossed over the Buachaille, searching for the missing man.

The Coastguard chopper had been forced to return to Inverness for refuelling a few hours back, and some sort of collision in the Moray Firth was going to keep it busy for the foreseeable, which meant the only way they were finding the guy was on foot.

Even assuming all the information on his location was correct, it was a big mountain to cover. If he'd changed his mind and ventured elsewhere—one of the Three Sisters, maybe—then their chances of finding him were virtually non-existent.

Fulton wasn't thinking about any of that, right at that moment, though. He was thinking about his stomach, which was loudly rumbling, and felt like it was twisting itself in knots.

He unwrapped the porridge oats bar he kept in his kit and took a bite. It had the same amount of oats as a bowl of porridge, apparently. Pity it tasted like a lump of lightly-sugared cardboard.

His radio squawked at him, forcing him to chew faster. The dry, grainy oats put up a good fight, but he was eventually able to swallow the claggy lump down.

'Aye, go ahead,' he said, using a pinkie to fish a stray wad of porridge out from between his teeth and gums. 'Any sign?'

The voice on the other end belonged to Gary Rigg. He was one of the younger members of the team, though more experienced than many. His exhaustion weighed down his words as they tumbled from the radio.

They'd been up there for hours now, battling the cold, the rain, and the mountain itself. It had been dark for most of it, and Fulton knew from experience how effectively that particular combination of factors could strip away all your energy, taking most of your optimism with it. Lose that hope, and the drive to push through the pain all but evaporated.

They were good lads, though. They'd keep going for as long as they had to. They always did.

'Any word on the chopper coming back?' Gary asked. 'We could do with the support.'

'Not yet. It won't be any time soon,' Fulton told him. There was no point sugar-coating it. None of them would thank him for it. 'We're on our own for now.'

There was some swearing. Mostly good-natured, but not exclusively.

'Aye. Fine,' Gary responded. 'I've sent Chris back down. His knee's giving him gyp. Thought you could check him out.'

Fulton winced. 'He'll no' be happy about that. What way's he coming?'

'Your way. Down past the SMC hut. You'll probably see him soon.'

Fulton's gaze flicked across to the white stone building with its roof of local Ballachulish slate. Sure enough, he could just make out a figure limping forlornly down the slope behind and to the right of it. He'd known Chris long enough to judge his body language, and as a result, could well imagine the actual language currently coming out of his mouth.

Chris was one of the old guard. He'd have wanted to see it through, and would not take well to being benched.

'Aye, I've got him,' Fulton said. 'I'll let you know if I hear more about air support. Stay safe and keep in touch.'

Gary grunted a sign-off, and Fulton watched Chris make his way closer. He was still a good few hundred yards away, just approaching the footbridge that crossed the River Coupall.

Chris had just stepped onto the bridge when he stopped, turned, and backtracked. He took half a dozen paces to the left, squatted down, and peered at something on the ground.

Fulton watched him, his tongue exploring inside his mouth for any last crumbs of the porridge bar. His stomach grumbled in complaint when no hidden caches were discovered between his teeth.

Over by the bridge, Chris knelt down and brushed at the ground in front of him. His movements were slow and wary, like he was clearing away a large cobweb and was worried something eight-legged and angry might pounce on him at any moment.

'OK...' Fulton muttered, still watching. He leaned forward and squinted, trying to get a better view.

Chris's next movement was sharp and sudden. He sprang to his feet, his age and all concern for his long-suffering knees forgotten. His retreat was a series of hops, one hand held in front of him as if for protection from whatever he'd seen.

Fulton saw the older man grasp for his radio. His voice came out as a thin crackle through the speaker. He almost sounded calm, and had Fulton not just watched his performance, he might even have fallen for it.

'Hello? Fulton? I've found something.'

'Aye. I noticed,' Fulton replied. He swallowed, his mouth suddenly dry. 'What is it?'

4

There was a pause. Not a long one, but long enough to disguise an unwelcome shake in a voice.

'It's a body,' Chris said.

Fulton heard him exhale. At the same time, he saw him look up, and both men locked eyes from opposite sides of the river.

'But I don't think it's the fella we're looking for.'

# Chapter 2

An hour or so before the body was found, and a hundred-odd miles away, DCI Jack Logan sat face-to-face with a monster.

There had been a change of staff at Carstairs State Hospital since he'd last been in. This wasn't any great surprise. It wasn't the sort of place that people settled into for the long haul. Admin staff, in particular, came and went so quickly they were given stickers instead of name badges, their tenure at the hospital often as temporary as the adhesive on the back.

Still, his warrant card, a few white lies, and what could generously be described as some 'persuasive charm' had got him through security. Had got him here. Now.

With him.

Owen Petrie, the man behind the 'Mister Whisper' child murders of over a decade ago, sat back in the padded chair beside his bed, directly across from the Detective Chief Inspector. A vague, half-there sort of smile tugged idly at the corners of his mouth, and he hummed quietly but tunelessly, as if trying to remember a song he'd once known.

He looked healthier than the last time Logan had seen him, which was a bit of a kick in the teeth. In all the years he'd been coming to visit Petrie, Logan had taken a perverse pleasure in watching the bastard getting smaller and more shrivelled, like the life was being drained out of him, drop by filthy drop.

Today, though, he looked stronger. Younger, even. Someone had given him a shave recently, so only a suggestion of stubble shaded his chin. His hair, too, had been trimmed and combed down the left side of his head. Anyone standing on that side of him would have seen the profile of a respectable-looking older guy. A bit glassy-eyed, maybe, but normal enough.

From the other side, it was a different story. The fall Petrie had sustained while being brought to justice had caved in part of his skull, and caused the brain damage that had left him in a state just a couple of steps above 'vegetable'.

At least, that's what he wanted everyone to believe. Logan, unlike everyone else, hadn't fallen for it.

From his temple up past his ear was a mess of ridges, dents, and scar tissue. The odd clump of hair sprouted here and there like bushes in the desert, but otherwise, the damage was laid bare for all to see.

'You're looking well, Owen,' Logan told him. 'Feeling better, are we?'

Petrie's smile broadened. He shuffled in his chair, adjusting himself, but said nothing.

'Sorry I've not been in to see you for a while, Owen,' Logan continued. 'Truth be told, I don't really waste much time thinking about you these days.'

That was a lie, of course. A big one. No way was he letting the bastard know that, though.

'Have you missed me?' he pressed. 'You missed our wee chats?'

Logan's own chair creaked as he shifted his not-inconsiderable weight forward in it. 'Is that why you've been phoning me?'

He watched for the reaction on Petrie's face. Scrutinised it, searching for some minute change in expression that would give him away. There was nothing, though. Just that same empty stare, and the same half-aware smirk as always.

'Because it is you, isn't it, Owen?' Logan said. 'I know it's you. You've been the one calling me.'

This time, the change on Petrie's face was almost immediate. His brow twitched. His eyes tightened focus a little, like he was now looking at the DCI rather than through him.

'On... the phone?' he asked, struggling to form the words.

'Aye.'

'I've n–not got a ph–phone.'

'See, I think you have, Owen,' Logan said. 'I think you do have a phone, and I think that—for whatever reason—you've been using it to call me.'

Logan stood up suddenly, and the man in the chair flinched, drawing back. That seemed to shrink him again, and the detective took a moment to savour Petrie's panicked expression before pulling open the plastic drawers of the room's one and only storage unit.

'N–no, don't,' Petrie pleaded.

The drawer was filled with socks and underwear. Logan rummaged through it, ignoring the stammered objections from the monster in the corner.

Fishing down at the bottom of the drawer, he found something wrapped in a plastic bag.

'Oh-ho, what do we have here, Owen?' he asked, shooting a look in Petrie's direction.

The bag came out with a couple of firm yanks, ejecting a few black socks and several pairs of baggy off-white underwear onto the floor.

Petrie squirmed in his chair, his face a rictus of horror, his voice deserting him. He looked away as Logan unwrapped the bag and peered inside.

It wasn't a phone. Far from it. Sitting at the bottom of the bag was an open pack of incontinence pads, half of the contents gone.

Reaching into the bag, Logan gave the packaging a squeeze, still hoping he'd find a handset tucked away in there. No such luck.

In his chair, Petrie's cheeks burned red. His eyes were down, his fingers knotting and twisting together. One leg bounced, shaking the floor beneath Logan's feet.

Tossing the bag onto the floor, Logan went back to rummaging through the drawer again, pulling out underwear by the handful and casting it aside.

'Where is it?' he demanded. 'I know you've got a phone here somewhere, Owen. So where the hell—'

'What on Earth is going on?'

Logan recognised the voice without turning. That doctor. The new one who'd started a few months back. Logan had crossed swords with him on his last couple of visits. What was the name again?

'D-doctor Ramesh,' Petrie said, and the relief in his voice was palpable. 'Doctor Ramesh.'

'It's OK, Owen. Nothing to worry about,' the doctor said, stepping into the room.

He was shorter than Logan, but held himself with a level of authority that added a couple of inches. There was a suggestion of an Indian accent right at the edges of his voice when he spoke, but only if you were looking for it. Mostly, he sounded what Logan always thought of as 'rich English'—a sort of generic, upper-middle-class brogue that had been sandpapered smooth through years of expensive private education.

'Well, Mr...' Ramesh waved a hand vaguely. 'Logan, isn't it? I asked you a question. What on Earth do you think you're doing?'

'I'm conducting an interview,' Logan told him, although the handful of y-fronts he held in each hand didn't really lend any weight to the statement. 'I have reason to believe that Owen here has been—'

'Frankly, I couldn't care less what you have "reason to believe", Mr Logan,' the doctor snapped. 'You have no permission to be here. None. You are endangering the health of my patient, not to mention intimidating and harassing him unlawfully.'

Logan deposited the underwear back in the drawer and turned to Ramesh, using his height advantage to loom over the smaller man. Ramesh, to his credit, didn't miss a step.

'You will leave the premises now. Either of your own free will, or I can have security escort you. That's your decision, but you *are* leaving,' the doctor said. 'And I'll be reporting this immediately to your superiors. If they won't take action, I'll escalate to the press, if I have to.'

Logan snorted. 'Oh, aye. That'll be a scoop. "Police question convicted child murderer". Imagine the scandal.'

'"Police illegally threaten man with mental disability", would be how I'd frame it, personally,' Ramesh said. He reached into his coat pocket and produced a phone. 'Now, are you leaving, or am I having you thrown out?'

For a moment, it looked like Logan might go for the second option. But then, he jabbed a finger in Petrie's direction, muttered a warning about how this wasn't over, before barging past Ramesh and out into the corridor.

By the time Logan was passing reception, he could hear Petrie humming.

By the time he was halfway across the car park, his phone was ringing.

He glanced at the screen, grunted, then looked back at the building as he pressed the handset to his ear. 'Christ, have you got a camera on this place or something?' he asked. 'That's twice you've phoned me at this exact spot.'

'What the hell do you think you're playing at?' spat the voice on the other end.

Detective Superintendent Gordon Mackenzie—known as 'the Gozer' to most of the Scottish constabulary—rarely sounded happy. In grumpy-old-bastard terms, Logan's former superior was second only to his present superior, Detective Superintendent Bob Hoon, who had successfully turned contempt into a legitimate art form.

Today, though, the Gozer sounded like he might be angling to take Hoon's title from him.

'I've just had a phone call, Jack,' the Gozer barked. 'Do you want to guess who from?'

'Postcode Lottery?' Logan guessed. He winced, instantly regretting the smart-arsed remark.

He took the phone away from his ear while he tapped the button on the door of his Volvo and climbed inside. By the time the phone had connected to Bluetooth and started playing through the car's speakers, the Gozer's angry outburst was on the wane.

'—I'll fucking "Postcode Lottery" ye!' he bellowed. 'You know full well who it was from. You've been in seeing him again, haven't you? Petrie.'

'Aye,' Logan admitted, figuring there was no point in trying to conceal the truth.

'And what the hell did you do that for? I thought you were done with him. In fact, what are you even doing down here? You moved! I thought we got rid of you!'

Logan pushed down on the clutch and tapped the button that started the engine. 'I have reason to believe that Owen Petrie has been calling me from Carstairs,' he said.

He practically heard the sneer of ridicule down the phone. 'Oh, aye? And what reason's that, Jack? Paranoid Schizophrenia?' the Gozer asked. 'The man's a bloody cabbage. He's no' phoning anyone.'

The dash display finished its animated boot-up sequence and settled on the map screen. It showed a little triangle inside the big grey square that represented the hospital's car park. Logan's eyes drifted idly to the clock in the top right-hand corner while he considered his reply to the Gozer's rant.

He opened his mouth to speak, then hesitated. His gaze flicked from the clock to the watch on his wrist.

'Shite,' he muttered, giving his wrist a shake. The second hand ticked on a few notches, then stopped again. 'Shite!'

'What's the problem now?' the Gozer demanded.

Logan grabbed for his belt, snatched up his phone, and hovered his thumb over the screen as he wrestled the strap across his chest.

'Sorry, sir, we'll have to continue this another time,' he said.

'*What*?!' the Gozer hissed. 'We'll talk about it now, Jack. Not when you decide. We'll talk about it—'

Logan tapped the red phone icon on the screen, then tossed the handset into one of the Volvo's storage dookets.

A moment later, he picked it back up again, dialled another number, and listened to the ringing tone come burring out through the speakers.

'Come on, come on,' he whispered.

There was a click from the earpiece. He sat up straight, watching the screen like he might be able to see the person on the other end of the line. 'Hello?' he said, then he tutted when a synthesised computer voice replied.

'The number you have called cannot be reached at the moment...'

Another thumb-jab aborted the call. He wasted a few seconds typing out a text message—'On my way'—then chucked the phone, checked his mirrors and, with a roar of an engine and a spinning of wheels, went racing out of the car park.

# Chapter 3

She had left by the time he arrived, an empty coffee cup, cold to the touch, the only indication that she'd ever been there.

'Bollocks,' Logan declared, drawing a few raised eyebrows and worried looks from the Kelvinside pan-loafers sitting sipping their Lady Greys around the neighbouring tables.

The tea room's clientele had looked alarmed enough when he'd come stumbling in through the front door, out of breath, sweat sticking the shirt to his back. Now that he'd started ejecting random obscenities at an empty table, some of them looked like they might be heading for an attack of the vapours.

'Can I help you, sir?'

Logan turned to find a young man in a black shirt and white apron eyeing him apprehensively, a tray of assorted scones balanced expertly on one raised hand.

'Aye. Maybe. There was a girl… a woman here. Short brown hair. About your height.'

'Maddie. Yes,' the waiter said. 'She left.'

'Well, I can see that. When?'

'Twenty minutes ago, maybe.' The waiter's gaze gave Logan a quick once over, while his free hand went into the pocket of his apron. 'She asked me to give you this.'

Logan accepted the crisply folded napkin he was offered. He could feel all eyes in the place on him as he opened it up and read the short message scribbled just under the cafe's printed logo.

*Thanks a fucking bunch, Dad.*

Refolding the napkin, Logan pulled together some semblance of a smile. 'Thanks,' he told the waiter.

He looked around at the Kelvinside hoi polloi, with their flared nostrils and their judgemental looks. For a moment, he wanted to shout, to lash out, punish them for his own bloody stupidity.

Instead, he said, 'Sorry to have bothered you,' and marched out the door without another word.

–

She answered on his third try, the phone having been diverted to voicemail twice, and the three text messages he'd sent having gone unanswered. Her voice barked at him through the speaker of the Volvo, amplified by the echo of the car's interior.

'What?'

Logan flinched. It was just a single word, yet it had sounded dangerous. Locked and loaded, like a bomb that might blow up in his face if he prodded it in the wrong place.

'Maddie. It's me.'

'I know who it is. Your name comes up. *What*?'

'Look, I'm sorry, sweetheart,' Logan told her. 'My watch stopped. I lost track of time.'

'Your watch stopped?' Maddie shot back. Her pitch went up half an octave. *Tick-tick-tick went the bomb.* 'Seriously? Is that the best you can do?'

'Seriously, aye. I know it sounds… well, I know how it sounds, but I'm telling the truth. It must need a new battery or something. I can send you a photo. I thought I had plenty of time, but then I realised, and…' He sighed. 'Look, where are you? Why don't you come back?'

There was no response. That was promising. Maybe he'd be able to avoid an explosion, after all.

'Or, I could come to you. We could go somewhere else.'

*Somewhere that's no' full of stuck-up arseholes,* he added in his head.

'I'm supposed to be heading into work,' she replied.

Not a 'yes,' but not a 'no,' either. It was time for his big play. He was cutting the red wire.

'You can spare your old man half an hour, surely?' Logan urged.

He stopped talking, left the silence hanging there for her to fill.

'Twenty minutes,' she countered.

'Deal,' Logan said, not daring to push his luck. 'I'd make it this end of town, though. Getting across the M8 was a nightmare on the way in from Carluke.'

He regretted it the moment the words left his lips.

There was another silence. This one felt heavier, more oppressive than before.

'Carluke?'

*Tick-tick-tick.*

*Shite.*

'You were in Carluke?' she asked.

'Aye,' Logan said. 'I was… it was a work thing.'

'You were in seeing *him*, weren't you?' Maddison asked. There was no detonation. No big bang. She didn't even sound angry. He almost wished she did.

'It was—'

She sighed. It was sad, disappointed, and weary all at once.

'I should've known. God. You'd think, after all these years, I'd have remembered.'

'What are you talking about, sweetheart? Remembered what?'

Her voice cracked, just a fraction. If he didn't know her, he wouldn't even have picked up on it.

'Who comes first.'

'Hey, come on. What's that supposed to mean?' Logan protested. 'You know that's not—'

'Listen, Dad, I better get to work.'

'No, but I thought—'

She cut him off. Her voice was rock-solid now. She sounded like her mother.

'Safe trip up the road.'

There was no point trying to convince her. Nothing he could do would change her mind. He'd blown it, good and proper.

'Right. Aye. Well, maybe I can give you a shout next time I'm down?'

'Aye,' she said. 'Maybe.'

And then, the low electronic buzz that had accompanied the call stopped, and her name disappeared from the screen in the Volvo's dash.

Logan bumped his head against the padded headrest and gripped the steering wheel, his fingers tightening as if he could strangle the thing. Or better, strangle the whole bloody world.

*Petrie. This was Petrie's fault*, he told himself. And, not for the first time, he almost managed to believe it.

The phone rang again, blasting out of the stereo system. The surge of hope he felt faded as soon as he saw the name on the display. Ben Forde.

Logan sighed, took a moment to compose himself, then tapped one of the buttons on the underside of the steering wheel. 'Ben. What's up?'

'All right, Jack? How are things going down there?'

'Fucking awful,' Logan replied. He had known the Detective Inspector too long to bother mincing his words.

'The usual, then,' Ben replied. 'You still heading back up the road today?'

'Aye. Shortly. Why?' Logan asked, although he could hazard a pretty good guess.

'You're going to have to make a stop in Glen Coe on the way. We'll meet you there,' Ben told him. 'Something's come up.'

To his shame, Logan felt a moment of something not a million miles away from elation. Relief, maybe. This, he could deal with. This, he could do.

He pulled on his belt. With a jab of a button, the Volvo's engine purred into life.

'Text me the details,' he instructed. 'I'm on my way.'

# Chapter 4

There had been a bit of snarl-up of traffic on the approach to the car park, mostly caused by drivers craning their necks to try to see what all the flashing lights and fuss were about.

A couple of Uniforms had moved to intercept the Volvo as it had rumbled up the uneven track leading to the cordon, then had waved and stepped aside when he'd given them a flash of the blues.

A helicopter was circling overhead when Logan stepped out of the SUV, low enough that the whumming of its rotors kept altering the pressure in his ears. There were three polis cars and a van in the car park, as well as a few civilian vehicles and a Land Rover with Mountain Rescue livery on the side.

Near the Land Rover, a couple of guys in outdoor gear were sharing their flasks with three officers in high-vis jackets. The younger of the men said something into a radio and the chopper began to climb, then banked in the direction of the mountain that loomed over the scene.

The lightest suggestion of drizzle whispered through the air, the drops not so much falling as floating on the breeze, never quite reaching the ground. Logan had been living in the Highlands for a good few months now, and had been constantly surprised by the sheer range of precipitation the place had to offer. He'd encountered at least twenty distinct varieties of rain, from misty haze to pishin' doon. Often all in the same day.

A uniformed sergeant got out of the van and started making his way over to Logan, feet alternating between crunching and squelching on the uneven ground. Logan dug his warrant card from his pocket and offered it up as the sergeant drew closer.

'DCI Jack Logan. MIT.'

'Aye, I know, sir,' the sergeant replied. 'We met briefly before. On the missing boy case. Connor Reid.'

He offered a hand. 'Sergeant Jaffray. Greig.'

Logan tried to feign recognition, but clearly didn't do a very good job of it.

'At the initial scene. You… you asked me to get rid of a sheep.'

'Christ. Aye,' Logan said. 'They made you a sergeant?'

He hadn't intended to sound quite so surprised, it just sort of happened. Here was the man, after all, who had tried to physically pick up a sheep in order to remove it from a crime scene. The man who Logan had accused of winning his job in a raffle.

A sergeant. A bloody sergeant.

What was the world coming to?

'They did, sir,' Greig confirmed. If he'd picked up on the DCI's shock, he wasn't showing it. 'Been… what? Three weeks now, is it?'

'Are you asking me or telling me?'

Greig smiled awkwardly. 'Ha. Telling you, sir. It's been about three weeks.'

'Right. Well, good. Well done,' Logan said. He gestured to the tent that had been erected on the opposite side of the river that ran along the car park's edge. It sat like a tumour on the otherwise unspoiled wilderness. 'What have we got?'

'Oh. Aye. Sorry,' Greig said. 'It's a body, sir.'

Logan eyed him expectantly.

'A… a dead one.'

*A sergeant.* God help them.

'Right. And?'

Greig's gaze tick-tocked between the DCI and the tent. 'Well, I don't really know, sir. Mountain Rescue called it in. One of their boys found it, half-buried.'

'An accident, then? Hill-walker?' Logan asked.

'No, he doesn't think so. I didn't get too good a look, myself. We were told just to protect the scene and wait for the cavalry. I'm guessing that's you.'

'Looks like it,' Logan conceded. 'CID not been round?'

'They're on a training course,' Greig said. 'In Elgin, I think.'

'Right.'

'Nice place, Elgin,' the sergeant continued, almost absent-mindedly. 'They've got the cathedral.'

Logan pursed his lips and raised his eyebrows. He kept his face that way until the message got through.

Sergeant Jaffray cleared his throat. 'Anyway, they've said to keep them posted, but reckoned it was more of an MIT thing, so Jinkies… uh, I mean, Chief Inspector Pickering, got in touch with Inverness, and…'

Logan's expression still hadn't changed. Greig cleared his throat for a second time, and had another go.

'Do you… do you want to take a look at the body?'

'Aye,' Logan said, already striding past the uniformed officer. 'I mean, I did come all this way. Be a shame not to.'

Greig watched the DCI go marching across the car park in the direction of the Land Rover. 'It's, uh, the body's over that way, sir,' he called, indicating the white canvas structure that had been erected by the footbridge. 'In the tent.'

Logan stopped and turned. 'Right. Maybe you could keep an eye on it, Sergeant, while I go talk to the Mountain Rescue guys. Could you do that for me?'

'Keep an eye on the tent?'

'Exactly. Make sure nobody goes in.'

Greig glanced around at the empty wilderness, then he straightened, stopping just short of firing off a salute. 'Right you are, sir. I'm on it.'

'Good lad,' Logan told him.

Then, with a turn on his heel and a roll of his eyes, he continued on over to the knot of men gathered by the Land Rover. Hands were shaken, introductions were made, and an offer of tea was politely declined.

'There's going to be an accident on that road if people don't quit their rubbernecking,' Logan told the Uniforms, indicating the snarl-up of slow-moving traffic on the bend approaching the car park. 'Go and sort it out, will you?'

'Yes, sir.'

'On it, sir.'

Logan waited until they'd scurried off, then got down to business with the two members of the rescue team. One of them, who'd introduced himself as Fulton Randall, did most of the talking. He was in his late-forties, Logan guessed, and had the same no-nonsense air about him as most of the mountain rescue guys the DCI had met.

Aye, sure, they were usually up for a laugh, and most of them could've drunk him under the table, even during his worst pre-teetotal days, but when it got down to the subject of life and death, they were the type of lads you wanted on your side.

The other man was older and less forthcoming. Chris O'Hare. He'd been the one who had found the body, and the only one of the two to have actually seen it.

'Once Chris realised what we were dealing with, we thought it best not to go trampling all over the place and compromise the scene,' Fulton explained.

'Aye. Good,' said Logan. He shot a look in the direction of Sergeant Jaffray. 'I'm sure my lot could manage that all by themselves.'

'It was a bit of a pantomime watching them put up the tent, right enough,' Fulton said. 'Thought they were going to take off at one point.'

'Great. The Scene of Crime boys will be delighted to hear that,' Logan said.

He looked up at the helicopter. It was currently buzzing around the top of the closest mountain, like a bee sniffing eagerly around a flower.

From the road, the mountain had looked big. Here, closer to where it rose steeply up from the ground, it was a giant of a thing, imposing itself against the mottled grey sky.

And to think, people climbed the things for fun.

'Someone lost, I take it?' Logan asked.

Fulton nodded. 'Call came in via you guys last night. No sign of him, though. We're actually starting to think it might've been a hoax. Some of the details they gave on the phone don't really stack up. The number they left goes nowhere. Most likely someone on the wind-up.' He puffed out his cheeks and shrugged. 'Still, got to check, haven't you?'

'Bastards,' Logan said, which was about as close to a show of empathy as he was likely to get. 'But aye. I suppose you do.'

'Anyway, Chris was coming back down. Knackered knee. He's not as young as he used to be,' Fulton said.

'Oi. Fucking watch it,' Chris warned. His accent was from Northern Ireland, but mellowed by a bit of a Highland lilt. Not a born-and-bred local, then, but he'd been here a while.

Fulton smiled, but ignored him. 'He was about to cross... why am I telling him? Chris. You saw it.'

Logan's gaze shifted to the older man. He squirmed a little, his eyes darting away. Either he wasn't one for speaking up around strangers, or he had something he was hiding.

'You were coming down the hill,' Logan prompted, leaving the rest of the sentence hanging for Chris to complete.

'Mountain,' Chris corrected. 'It's not a hill.'

'Mountain. Sorry,' Logan said, although he didn't really see what difference it made. 'What then?'

'Well, like this shitebag was saying, I'd just got to the bridge and something caught my eye. Like, I didn't see anything, as such. Not the body, anyway. But the way the ground had been messed with, I thought there was something buried under there.'

He shot a look in the direction of the tent, and the lines of his face grew thin and tight. 'I thought maybe it was a Geocache, or whatever. You know, the boxes folk hide for other people to find?'

Logan had absolutely no idea what the man was talking about, but it didn't feel important, so he nodded. 'Sure.'

'So, over I goes to check it out. I brush some of the dirt away, and that's when I sees it,' Chris continued, his voice dropping to a whisper like he was telling a ghost story around a campfire. 'An *ear*.'

A crease formed on Logan's forehead. 'An ear? What, on its own?'

'No. Attached to a head, like,' Chris clarified. 'I mean, I didn't know that right away. I just saw the ear at first, but then I clocked the rest of him. Poor bastard.'

'Male, then?' Logan asked, taking out his notepad.

Chris nodded.

'Age?'

'Well, I don't know. Sure, I didn't ask to see his driver's licence.'

'Approximately,' Logan urged.

Chris shrugged, glanced shiftily between both men, then shrugged for a second time. 'Twenties, maybe. I'm not sure. I didn't exactly get a good look at him, what with him being ninety-percent underground and everything.'

'Right. Fair enough,' Logan conceded.

'Based on what I did see, though, I reckon he's only been there a few days,' Chris said. He offered up an answer to Logan's next question before he could ask it. 'You do this job long enough, you get to see a whole lot of dead people in all kinds of states. You ask me, this one hadn't been kicking around too long. Of course, Fulton would know better than me.'

Logan raised an inquisitive eyebrow in the other man's direction.

'Oh. GP. Or, I was. Retired now. Had enough of the budget cuts,' Fulton said.

An upbeat Salsa number began to play from one of the pockets of his bright red jacket.

'Sorry,' he said, peeling back the Velcro and unfastening the zip. He glanced at his phone screen for a second, frowned briefly, then put the phone to his ear and turned away from the other two men. 'Hello? Hannah? Can you…?'

He shot the screen another quick look, then tried angling himself in another direction. 'Hello? Yes. Got you. Aye. What's—'

Although he was a few feet away, Logan heard the panic in the voice on the other end of the line. He couldn't make out the words that made up the long garble that followed, but this Hannah, whoever she was, was worried.

'Whoa, whoa. Slow down, Han… you're breaking up. I can't… hello? Hello?'

Fulton checked the screen again, then cursed under his breath.

'Everything all right?' Logan asked.

'Hmm? Oh, aye. It's nothing. It's my daughter's boyfriend. Fiancé, sorry. He's been away for work for most of the week and was supposed to come home last night. We had the wee one staying over.'

'And he didn't turn up?'

Fulton shook his head and checked his phone again, but the signal had died away to nothing. 'No. She can't get hold of him on the phone, either. She hasn't heard from him in…'

He stopped talking then, the words shrivelling and dying somewhere at the back of his throat. His gaze fell on the tent, and his feet started shuffling him forward as if of their own free will.

'Oh no. No,' he whispered. 'Please God, no.'

Logan was too slow to react. His hand brushed against the sleeve of Fulton's jacket, but the Gortex material

26

slipped through his fingers as Fulton set off at a lumbering sprint.

'Oi! Wait!' Logan spat, giving chase. The ground was equal parts uneven and slippery, though, and his shoes were far from ideal.

With his well-worn walking boots, Fulton was off like a shot, clattering across the bridge before Logan could build up any sort of momentum.

'Wait! Stop right there!' he bellowed, slipping and sliding on the muddy ground.

Fulton was having none of it. Logan could only watch, helpless and slightly off-balance, as the mountain rescue man pulled open the flap of the tent. He had the sense not to dive inside. That was something, at least. Instead, he just stood there, one hand on his mouth, the other leaning on the tent's frame for support.

One of the Uniforms came clumping up at Logan's back. 'Want me to get him, sir?'

Logan nodded and waved the officer ahead. 'Aye, go,' he wheezed. 'Go.'

He watched the officer go scurrying across the bridge. Over by the tent, Fulton took a few stumbled steps back and sunk to his knees, his legs no longer able or willing to support him. He buried his face in his hands, and even at that distance, with the chopper churning the sky overhead, Logan heard the sob.

'Ah,' he muttered to nobody in particular. 'Shite.'

# Chapter 5

'You're back, then.'

Moira Corson stood behind the front desk of Fort William police station with a look on her face that suggested someone had just trodden dog shit into the carpets. She peered at Logan over the top of her narrow glasses, clearly waiting for some sort of response.

'Aye. Well spotted,' Logan said, not bothering to hide the sarcasm. Good enough for the old cow. He pulled on the handle of the door that led through from reception into the station proper. The door thunked against the frame, but otherwise didn't budge.

With a sigh, Logan shot Moira an expectant look. 'Well? Are you going to let me in?'

'I'll need to see your ID first,' Moira told him.

'Bollocks you do. You know full well who I am. Open the door.'

Moira flipped up the rectangular hatch at the bottom of the glass screen that separated them. 'ID,' she reiterated. 'It's procedure. You might have no regard for the rules, but some of us still do.'

Muttering, Logan fished in his pocket, then slapped the wallet containing his warrant card down on the counter. Moira regarded it with a slight flaring of her nostrils. 'You have to—'

Snatching the wallet back up, Logan wrestled the card out of the holder and slid that through the gap on its own. 'There. Happy?'

Without a word, Moira took the identification, held it up to the light, and spent several long seconds scrutinising it. Logan tried very hard not to look annoyed. He wasn't going to give her the satisfaction.

The trip she made to the photocopier to run off a copy of the card almost pushed him over the edge, granted, but he held his tongue until she finally slid the card back through the slot, and he manhandled it back into its tight plastic covering.

'Right, is that us? Can I go through now?' Logan asked.

Before Moira could answer, the door was opened from the other side, and a cheerful-looking older man with thinning hair and a firmly established paunch made a beckoning motion in Logan's direction.

'There you are,' said Detective Inspector Ben Forde. 'We thought you'd got lost.'

The Incident Room hadn't changed much since the team had last set up shop there, and it quickly began to feel familiar as Logan watched DS McQuarrie set up the Big Board. Caitlyn had a real knack for keeping the board—and, by extension the team—fully organised and up-to-date, and it only took her a few minutes to pull together all the information they currently had.

Mind you, all the information they currently had consisted of a name, a photograph, and a very brief statement, so it wasn't exactly a big ask to gather it all in one place.

Something wasn't quite the same as last time, though, Logan thought. Something about the whole thing was just ever so slightly different.

It took him several seconds before he could pinpoint what it was.

'Are you singing?'

Caitlyn, who had most definitely been singing quietly below her breath, stopped immediately and turned from the board.

'Uh, no. I mean, aye. Sorry, sir.'

Logan shook his head. 'I mean, it's fine. If you want to sing, you go ahead and sing. It's just...'

'You're usually such a crabbit bastard,' DI Forde concluded. Caitlyn smiled briefly, then turned back to the board as Ben handed Logan a mug of hot tea. 'We could've met you down there. At the scene.'

Logan accepted the mug, set it down on a desk, then shrugged off his coat.

'Tyler was quite excited about it. He's never seen Glen Coe. Have you, Tyler?'

At a neighbouring desk, Detective Constable Tyler Neish looked up from his phone, hastily tapped a button on the side, then shoved it in his pocket. 'Boss?'

'I was telling Jack. You've never seen Glen Coe.'

'How can you have never seen Glen Coe? Weren't you brought up about sixty miles away?'

'Aye, but we always did the A9. When we were going anywhere. Glasgow, or whatever,' Tyler explained. 'Down the A9, onto the M9 at Stirling, M80 turnoff—'

'All right, all right. I wasn't asking for your travel diaries,' Logan told him. 'Don't worry, there'll be plenty of opportunity for us to get down there. Scene of Crime are giving it a going over now, and we can go take a look when they're done. I've asked them not to move the body until we get a look at it.'

'Nice one!' Tyler beamed. He caught the looks from the others. 'About seeing Glen Coe, I mean. Not... not the body part.'

'What body part?' asked DC Khaled, appearing in the doorway of the office at the back of the room. 'Someone hacking them up again?'

'Not *body part* as in parts of a body,' Tyler began to explain, but then he gave a shake of his head. 'Forget it. It's nothing.'

Hamza appeared completely nonplussed by this, but then shrugged and indicated the office behind him with a tilt of his head. 'Fine. Router's working again, by the way. Just needed a reboot.'

'Good work there from the I.T. Bitch,' said DC Neish, firing Hamza a thumbs-up.

'I've changed the password to "Tyler is a fanny", all lowercase,' Hamza countered. 'I'm assuming everyone's fine with that?'

'I might use that for all my passwords going forward,' said Ben. 'Nice and easy to remember.'

'Right, we're ready, sir,' DS McQuarrie volunteered. 'Floor's all yours.'

'Thanks, Caitlyn,' Logan said. He gulped down a quick mouthful of tea before approaching the board and tilting his mug to indicate the headshot the DS had pinned up. 'Brodie Welsh. Age twenty-two. Local lad. Found dead this morning at the foot of...'

He pointed to Ben.

'Buachaille Etive Mor,' Ben said.

'Aye. There,' Logan continued.

'At the foot? So, what? Did he fall?' asked Hamza.

'Had a helluva nasty landing, if he did,' Logan said. 'I couldn't see much, but from what I could tell, his teeth have been knocked out.'

'Could've happened in a fall,' Tyler suggested.

'Possible,' Logan conceded. 'Less likely he'd bother to bury himself afterwards.'

'You think the teeth were done on purpose? Someone didn't want him identified?' Caitlyn asked.

'Aye, maybe. We'll see how he's doing finger-wise. Either way, it didn't work. Unfortunately for whoever killed him, his fiancée's father was part of the mountain rescue team that found the body. Fulton Randall. He recognised him right away. Poor bastard.'

'Which one?' Ben asked.

'Take your pick,' Logan said with a shrug. 'He didn't take it well when he saw the body.'

'Considering some of the sights those guys see...' Caitlyn said.

'Aye. And he's a doctor, too. Retired. Still, different when it's someone close to you,' Logan pointed out. 'Fulton and his wife had been looking after their grand-daughter the night before.'

'The victim's daughter?' Ben asked.

'Aye. She's still there now. I had someone take Fulton home. He's going to talk to the wife, then they're going to go break the news to the daughter. I offered to do it, but he thinks it'll be better coming from them. I've asked to be there, though. Framed it as me being on hand to offer support.'

'But you want to see her reaction,' Ben finished.

'Thought it wouldn't hurt,' Logan said. 'Although, given the condition and remote location of the body, unless she's built like a brick shithouse, I doubt she's involved.'

He motioned to Hamza. 'Check them both out, though. See if either of them has any previous.'

'Worth looking for any domestic violence reports, too,' Caitlyn added, and Hamza scribbled down a couple of notes on the brand-new desk pad he'd sourced from the stationery cupboard in the small office while he'd waited for the router to reboot.

He had a bit of a thing for stationery—there was little better than an unused notebook and a new pen—and the cupboard had turned out to be a bit of a goldmine.

'How long has he been in the ground for?' Ben asked.

Logan made a non-committal sort of grunt at the back of his throat. 'We'll know more once forensics are done and pathology has had a look.'

'The body'll have to go to Inverness. There's nobody local at the moment,' Ben said.

'Aye, fine,' said Logan. It was an inconvenience, but one he could cope with. He knew he could count on Shona Maguire up at Raigmore to do a thorough job. 'Fulton's already provided a visual ID. Just as well, if my theory's right about the killer trying to hide the ID.'

'I don't get it, boss,' Tyler said.

'Surprise, surprise,' Ben remarked, but Tyler pressed on.

'If someone was trying to hide his identity, why dump him just up the road? Why not put him somewhere else? Further away, like.'

'I've been wondering the same thing,' Logan said. 'Shallow grave, not far from a public footpath. It was only a matter of time before someone found him.'

'Inept, maybe,' Hamza said.

Logan considered this for half a second, then shrugged. 'Aye. Maybe. We'll see.'

He checked his watch, then drained the last of the tea from his mug.

'Right. I need to head and talk to the victim's wife. She lives in... Kinloch something?'

'Leven, maybe? Kinlochleven,' Ben said.

'Aye, that sounds about right,' Logan confirmed, reaching for his coat. 'Far?'

'Twenty-five miles, thereabouts,' Ben told him. 'Feels like longer, mind you. Horrible winding bastard of a road once you take the turn-off.'

'Great,' Logan grumbled. 'I'll swing by the scene after I've spoken to her, and find out where we are with forensics.'

'You should take Tyler,' Ben suggested.

At the mention of his name, DC Neish sat up straight. He looked irritatingly eager, which always rubbed Logan up the wrong way for some reason.

'Why would I want to do that?' the DCI asked.

'Well, so...' Ben sucked in his bottom lip, trying to come up with a legitimate reason. 'Just so I don't have to put up with him,' was the best he could do. 'I've had him all week. It must be someone else's turn by now.'

Logan let out an exaggerated sigh that was solely for DC Neish's benefit. 'Fine. Tyler, on your feet, you're with me.'

'Nice one, boss! You won't even know I'm there,' Tyler promised.

'Aye, well,' said Logan, pulling open the door and ushering the younger detective out. 'I'll believe that when I see it.'

# Chapter 6

Ben Forde had not been exaggerating about the route. After turning off the A82, the road leading to Kinloch-leven became twisting and narrow, meandering down along the side of a loch one minute—Loch Leven, Logan assumed, given the name of the place they were headed to—then snaking through woodland the next.

With its traction control, the Volvo was equipped to handle all the twists and turns. DC Neish, on the other hand, was not.

'Jesus,' he muttered, gripping the handle above the side window and locking his eyes on the road dead ahead. 'I think I left my stomach on that last bend, boss.'

Logan shot Tyler a sideways look. Almost all the colour had drained from his face, leaving only the faintest tinge of green.

'Don't you throw up in my car,' the DCI warned.

'I won't. I'm not going to—'

Tyler clenched a fist and held it against his mouth for a few seconds, before continuing.

'I'm not going to throw up,' he said. 'I'm just a bit—'

The road banked up, then sharply down again. For a moment, the Volvo seemed to be suspended in mid-air.

'Christ!' Tyler grimaced, clutching his stomach. 'Are you doing this on purpose?'

'Oh, aye. Because that's just what I want. You chucking your guts up all over my nice new car,' Logan snapped. He eased off the accelerator pedal and the Volvo dropped to a more sedate pace. 'There. That better?'

Tyler swallowed a couple of times, then risked a nod. 'Aye. Cheers, boss.'

They continued on for a mile or two in silence, Logan lost in his own thoughts, Tyler trying to keep the contents of his stomach in place using sheer willpower alone. It was only when Logan heard the younger man give a groan and shift uncomfortably in his seat that he decided to deploy distraction tactics.

'How's Sinead doing? After everything that happened?'

PC Bell was made of stern stuff, Logan knew. After what she'd gone through recently, though, she was bound to be feeling it. He'd been through similar situations himself over the years, and it always left a mark. Like it or not, put on as brave a face as you wanted, it always left a mark.

'Aye. She's not bad, all things considered,' Tyler said. 'She was signed off for a couple of weeks, but she's just itching to get back, really.'

'She needs to take her time,' Logan said. 'No point rushing back in until she's ready.'

'She says she is ready.'

Logan gripped the wheel and gazed ahead. 'Of course she does. But she isn't. She won't be. Not yet.'

'Maybe you should tell her that, boss. You'd probably have more luck convincing her than I—*Fuck!*'

The car zig-zagged along a series of sharp bends, then swung a right until it was curving alongside the loch. Despite them crawling along at thirty, the series of sudden movements were enough to test even Logan's normally rock-solid constitution, and there was a 'hwurk' as Tyler threw up in his mouth.

'Don't you bloody dare!' Logan warned, stomping on the brake and swinging the Volvo onto the shallow embankment at the side of the road.

Tyler had his seatbelt off before the car had fully stopped. He fumbled with the door, leaned out, and everything he'd eaten that morning was hastily ejected onto the damp grass.

The smell billowed back up into the car. Scowling, Logan tapped a button on his door and his window rolled all the way to the bottom. Beside him, Tyler heaved again, giving the grass a generous second helping.

Another car passed at speed, the driver's stomach evidently conditioned to handle the twists and turns. The wind from it gave the Volvo a shake, eliciting another spectacular response from DC Neish's gag reflex.

And then, with some groaning, mumbling, and a fair amount of spitting, Tyler gingerly eased himself back into a sitting position and pulled the door closed. He placed the back of his head against the headrest and closed his eyes, pulling himself together.

'Better?' Logan asked him.

Tyler swallowed. 'Aye. Bit better. Sorry.'

'Happens to the best of us, son,' Logan said. The moment of empathy was so unexpected that Tyler opened his eyes and looked over at the DCI.

'Cheers, boss.'

'No problem,' Logan said, clicking on the indicator. 'But just so you know, if any of it has landed in the car, I'll be wiping it up with your face.'

The house that Brodie Welsh had shared with his fiancée was a decent-enough looking semi-detached just a couple of minutes' walk from the local school. Logan had been given the impression that the area was pretty rough, but he'd seen nothing yet to back that up. The neighbouring houses had all been painted in the last couple of years, and while none of the gardens were exactly huge, they were well-kept.

'That the mountain rescue guy?' Tyler asked, as a man in a Gortex jacket stepped out of a large Renault and gave them a wave.

'Fulton. Aye. That's him,' Logan said, unfastening his belt. Tyler moved to do the same, but the DCI stopped him. 'You wait here. No point us both piling in. The lassie's going to have enough on her plate without you chucking your guts up all over her carpet.'

'I'm feeling much better, boss,' Tyler said, although this wasn't entirely true, and so he didn't lean too heavily into the protest.

Instead, he suggested that he take a walk around the village. Not that he expected to come across anything relevant to the case, but he needed a blast of fresh air before he could even contemplate the return journey.

'Don't go far,' Logan instructed, as they both got out of the SUV. 'Scene of Crime's expecting us shortly, and I don't want to have to listen to them whinging at me if we're late.'

'No worries, boss. I'll just take a wander round the block,' the DC said. He said it to Logan's back, though, as the DCI had already set off to meet Fulton beside the front gate of Hannah's house.

Fulton didn't bother with pleasantries. He looked too drained to even attempt them. His hand shook as he placed it on the top bar of the wooden gate, and while he may have been looking in the direction of the house, Logan couldn't help but notice how he studiously avoided glancing at the windows, like he was afraid he might make eye contact with someone inside.

'Are you sure you're up to this, Mr Randall?' Logan asked him. 'If it's easier, I can do it.'

Fulton swallowed. 'Aye. Aye. That would be easier,' he admitted. 'Thank you.' He took a breath, held it for a while, then let it out in one big blow. 'But, no. No. I have to be the one to tell her. She should hear it from me.'

He seemed to commit himself to the decision then. Pushing open the gate, he marched up the path, took a second to compose himself at the door, and was just about to enter when it was opened for him from the other side.

A woman—a girl, practically—stood in the narrow hallway, her face acutely conveying how sleepless a night she'd had. She was tall and skinny, with copper-coloured hair tied back in a loose ponytail.

Her face was an irregular pattern of pale brown freckles, like someone had flicked a loaded paintbrush at her from close range. They made her look younger still, and if Fulton hadn't already told him her age, Logan would've sworn the girl was in her mid-teens.

'Dad? Where's Carrie?' she asked. Her wide, worried eyes went from Fulton to Logan, then out to the street beyond before returning to her father again. 'What is it? What's happened? Have you heard something?'

'Come on away inside, Hannah,' Fulton said, stepping over the threshold and placing a guiding hand on her arm. 'Come on away inside and we can have a chat.'

Hannah started to let herself be led, then stopped. She twisted free of her dad's grip and turned to Logan. 'Are you the police?'

'Hannah, let's go have a sit-down and—'

'Are you?' Hannah demanded. 'Are you the police?'

'I am. DCI Jack Logan, miss. Like your father says, I think we should maybe—'

'He's dead. Isn't he?' Hannah asked. 'Brodie, he's dead.'

'Hannah, sweetheart—'

Fulton tried the hand on the arm again. The calming voice. The suggestion of a sad smile. None of it worked. Fury flashed behind Hannah's eyes, instantly changing her from a girl to a woman.

'Just fucking tell me!'

Fulton's intentions had been noble enough. Completely understandable. He'd wanted to tell her, to be the one to break the news. In the thick of it all, though, when it came right down to the moment, the words wouldn't come. His voice deserted him, and he could only gaze imploringly at Logan. Desperate. Pleading for him to end it. To do what needed to be done.

'Miss Randall, I'm sorry to have to inform you that Brodie was found dead this morning,' he said.

And, like that, the woman was gone, replaced once more by the scared, uncertain girl. She fell against her dad, while simultaneously trying to pull away from him. She shook her head as tears weaved between the freckles on her cheeks.

'No. N-no, no, no. He's not. He's not. No. Brodie. *Brodie!*'

Her breathing became louder, more frantic and wheezing. She didn't resist when Fulton put an arm around her. It was possible that she didn't even notice.

'Come on, sweetheart. Come away inside,' Fulton suggested.

'Carrie. What am I going to tell Carrie?' she whispered. 'How am I going to tell her that her daddy's not coming back?'

Fulton swallowed. Tears blurred his eyes, and Logan had the good grace to glance away.

'We'll think of something,' Hannah's father told her. He opened a door behind her and gave her shoulder another squeeze. 'Now, come on. Let's go and get a seat and we can talk about it.'

Logan hesitated outside the threshold for a moment, and took a quick look at the neighbouring houses. A net curtain twitched across the street, but he could still see the outline of a woman on the other side. Short and frail-looking. Pensioner, probably. Worth having a word with later, maybe. Often, a copper's best friend was the nosy old bugger across the road.

There was nobody at the other windows. Nobody he could see, at least. That was something to be grateful for. Fulton had managed to get his daughter inside just in time. Any more raised voices and one of the worst moments of her life could well have been turned into a spectator sport.

Logan was about to turn and head inside when he spotted a man in a tan coloured military-style jacket and baseball cap. He was standing at the corner of a house a little way back down the road, leaning a shoulder against the wall and making no bones about the fact that he was watching the events unfolding at the house.

He was too far away for Logan to shout to him without having to really belt it out, but close enough that the DCI could get a decent enough impression of him. Average height, but heavily built. From that distance, he couldn't say if it was fat or muscle, but he guessed the latter.

They regarded each other for a while, then Logan stepped inside the house, took out his phone, and rang Tyler's number.

'Boss?' came the reply after half a dozen rings.

'Where are you?' Logan asked.

'I'm just...' Tyler began. 'God knows, actually. It's a confusing place, this. I think I'm just down from the school, though. Why, you ready to hit the road?'

'No. But get back up here. There's someone lurking about. Halfway back along the road, right-hand side as you're heading towards the house. Tan jacket. Red base-ball cap. I don't like him. See what you can find out.'

'No bother, boss. On my way,' Tyler said.

'Be quick,' Logan instructed, then he tapped the icon to hang up the phone, slipped it into his pocket, and headed through to face the grief of Hannah Randall.

## Chapter 7

There was an old-fashioned cuckoo clock on one wall of Hannah Randall's living room. That was the first thing Logan noticed. It was so out of place amongst the Ikea furniture and pastel-blue walls that his eyes were drawn to it immediately.

The fact that it was a noisy bastard of a thing with a tick like a metronome also helped it stand out.

Hannah was already sitting right at the middle junction of a leather corner couch when Logan entered, her dad sitting right in close to her, one of her hands clutched in his. The other hand was kneading a wrinkle in the leather, pulling and twisting on it, like she was trying to determine if it was real.

The room was small, but well-cared for. The only mess was over in one corner, which had clearly been designated 'the play area'. Some attempt had been made to arrange the dolls, cars, and teddies into a neat stack, but the toys were having none of it and had toppled over onto the floor.

There were thirty or more framed photographs on the wall. Mostly, they charted the growth of a baby into a toddler, but there were a good number of family snaps in there, too. Logan recognised Brodie Welsh in several of them. He and Hannah were together in a few of them. They looked like a nice couple. Happy.

43

A far cry from how Hannah looked now. Fulton was still holding one of her hands. The other was now thrust into the gap between the sofa cushions, and hooked under the one she was sitting on, like it was the only thing anchoring her in place.

She looked up and blinked when Logan closed the door, regarding him with a detached curiosity he'd seen on too many faces, too many times.

'Miss Randall, I'm Detective Chief Inspector Logan. Jack,' he said. He'd told her already, but reckoned a reminder probably wouldn't go amiss. 'I'm very sorry to have to be the bearer of such bad news.'

'What happened?' Hannah asked, the words almost choking her. 'To Brodie. What happened?'

'They don't know yet,' Fulton said. He flashed Logan an apologetic smile, which the DCI dismissed with a subtle shake of his head.

'We're still working on it,' Logan said, taking over. 'We have a team at the site now trying to determine exactly what happened.'

'"The site",' Hannah repeated. Her voice was flat and hollow, but he could almost hear the quote marks around the words. Logan couldn't tell if she'd said it for his benefit or her own.

He waited to see if she was going to say more before he continued. The clock on the wall ticked loudly in the temporary silence.

'I won't pretend to understand what you're going through, Miss Randall. I can't. What I will say is that we will do everything we can to find out what happened to Mr Welsh.'

'Brodie. He didn't like being called Mr Welsh.'

'Brodie. Right,' Logan said.

'Do you know who did it?' Hannah asked. She looked at him with hope in her eyes. It was tentative, but unmistakable. 'Do you know who killed him?'

'We don't know for sure yet that Brodie was murdered,' Logan told her. 'We'll be able to determine that in the next day or two.'

Hannah's movements became brisker, more agitated. 'What do you mean? What else could've happened?'

She yanked her hand free from her dad's grip and stood up suddenly. Her eyes, which had been filled with hope, now blazed angrily. 'Are you saying he killed himself? He wouldn't. No way. Not with… Not with…'

Her gaze crept over to the toys in the corner. Her legs seemed to buckle, and she found herself back on the couch. 'He wouldn't do that,' she whispered. 'He wouldn't leave Carrie. He loves her too much. He wouldn't do that.'

'I'm not suggesting he did,' Logan assured her. 'But until we have more information, it's important we don't speculate.'

He gestured to a chair across from the couch. It was another Ikea contraption, with a bendy wooden frame and a folded padded cushion making up the seat and back. 'May I?'

Hannah nodded absently, and Logan carefully lowered himself onto the seat. It started to tip forward as soon as his weight was on it, and he was forced to slide back to counteract the imbalance.

On reflection, he thought, he probably should've stayed on his feet. Still, too late now.

'Like I was saying, it's important we don't get ahead of ourselves. It's possible Brodie's death was entirely accidental. Did he go out walking often?'

'No. Never. He had no interest in any of that stuff,' Hannah said.

'Not for want of me trying, eh, sweetheart?' Fulton offered, trying to lighten the mood a little, but failing miserably.

'He was supposed to be away at work. Offshore. Just for a few days this time,' Hannah said. Her bottom lip wobbled, making her look even younger than she already did. 'He was supposed to get back last night. We were going to have a chippy.'

'Had you heard anything from his employers about him failing to turn up?' Logan asked.

Hannah sniffed and shook her head. 'No.'

'No phone calls?'

'No. Nothing.'

Logan reached into his coat pocket and took out his notebook. He then spent several seconds fishing around in the other pockets trying to find a pen, until eventually Fulton took one from inside his jacket and handed it over.

'Here.'

'Thank you. Always losing them,' Logan said. The pen was cheap plastic, and had the name of some climbing guide company emblazoned across the side. Clicking the button on the end, the DCI held it above the pad, ready to write. 'Do you have the details of Brodie's employer? We can inform them.'

Hannah shook her head. 'It's fine. I'll do it.'

'Of course,' said Logan. 'I understand. But, we'd also like to talk to them. They may be able to provide some information.'

Hannah squeezed the bridge of her nose between finger and thumb. 'It's... I can't remember. It's on the bank statements. "Orwatt", or something. I can get it for you. They're Dutch. They gave us that thing.'

She nodded in the direction of the cuckoo clock. A Swiss clock seemed like an odd gift from a Dutch company, but he decided not to question it.

'That would be very useful if you could get us their name, thank you,' Logan said.

Fulton patted his daughter's hand and looked over at Logan. 'I'll dig it out for you later. I can drop it off.'

Logan fished in another couple of pockets until he found a business card, which he set on the coffee table between them. 'Here. Keep this. You can call me any time. Either of you. Night or day. We'll also have a liaison officer appointed. These are specially trained officers who can—'

'It's fine. No,' Hannah said.

Logan glossed over the interruption. 'They're very experienced in helping families who—'

'I said no,' Hannah barked at him, her eyes blazing with that same anger as before. 'I'm not having someone in here scaring Carrie. It'll freak her out. She's used to her dad being away. She'll be fine for a while, but if someone's in here with...'

The words stuttered to a stop and the tears came. Big, gulping, silent sobs that formed balloons in her throat, cutting off her air. Fulton slid over on the couch, put an arm around her shoulder and pulled her in closer. She buried her head against him, her tears sliding off his waterproof jacket and down onto the couch between them.

'God, what about Margaret?' she managed, the effort of speaking further crumpling the lines of her face.

'Brodie's mum. She lives in Fife,' Fulton explained. 'Does she know?'

'I don't believe so, no,' Logan said. 'If you have a number or an address, we can get someone round to her.'

Hannah shook her head and loudly cleared her throat. It took a few attempts. 'I'll do it,' she said. 'It should be me.'

'I'm not sure that's such—'

'I'll do it,' Hannah insisted. 'I know her. She should hear it from me.'

Against his better instincts, Logan relented. 'Right. OK, then. But, we'll still need to send someone round to talk to her, so if you can give us the address, that would be useful.'

'Oh God. Margaret,' Hannah said, her voice descending into sobs again. 'What am I going to say?'

Logan leaned forward in the chair, being careful not to tip it off-balance. 'Like I say, Miss Randall. We can do it. We have trained officers who specialise in just this sort of thing.'

If anything, this made the second shake of Hannah's head even more emphatic. 'No. It shouldn't be a 'specialist' she hears it from, it should be family. I just... I mean...'

Her face crumpled, her eyes screwing tightly shut as she sunk her weight in against her dad. Fulton kissed her on the top of the head and gave her back a rub, then turned to Logan and spoke in a soft whisper.

'Can we continue this later? I can get you all the information.'

Logan closed over his notebook. 'Aye. Of course,' he said, offering the pen back.

'Keep it. It's promotional. I've got hundreds,' Fulton said.

Logan glanced at the text printed on the side of the pen again—*Nevis Walking and Climbing: Guided Walk's and Climb's Across Lochaber*—and tried not to wince at the apostrophe usage.

'Thanks,' he said, tucking it into the same pocket as the notebook. 'Much appreciated.'

He stood up, a process that involved rocking himself forward in the chair, pressing both hands on the armrests, and launching himself to his feet, while simultaneously ruing the day that Ikea ever opened its doors in Scotland.

'Once again, Miss Randall, I'm sorry for your loss,' he said. 'I'll be in touch as soon as I have more information, and if you change your mind about the liaison—'

'I won't,' Hannah said. She pulled her sleeve up over her wrist and wiped her nose on it. 'But thanks.'

'She's going to come stay with us for a few days,' Fulton said, although the slight downward turn of Hannah's mouth suggested it was the first she'd heard about it. 'Best for everyone. So Mum tells me, anyway. You've got my number.'

'I'm not sure. Did someone take a note of it?'

'It's on the pen,' Fulton said. 'Mobile and landline.'

Logan patted his pocket. 'Right. Very good. We'll be in touch.'

He was at the living room door when Hannah spoke.

'Do you think he was murdered?'

Logan stopped and turned.

'Like I said, Miss Randall, we really don't know at this stage.'

'I'm not asking what you know. I'm asking what you think,' Hannah said. She seemed to have shrunk, so her freckles took up more of her face than before. 'Do you think someone killed Brodie?'

Logan stood with one hand on the door handle. On the wall beside him, the clock continued its steady tick-tick-tick.

'I think we need to prepare ourselves for that possibility,' he told her.

And with that, he left her to her sorrow.

# Chapter 8

'Excuse me, mate. You local?'

The man in the crumpled tan jacket turned slowly, in no apparent rush to find out who had spoken to him. Down at his side, a small but mean-looking dog growled and strained on the end of a chain-link lead. DC Neish eyed it warily, then relaxed when he saw the muzzle fastened across its snout.

'Who's asking?' the man grunted. The accent was definitely local. If not specific to this area, then somewhere not too far away.

He was taller than Tyler, but not by much. There was a scar across one cheek, and he had the sort of crooked, wandering nose that suggested very few of his years on this Earth had been easy. His baseball cap was a faded red, almost a dark pink, and cast a shadow across his eyes that made them hard to see in much detail.

Fully dressed, it was hard to tell if his bulk had been caused by too much working out, or not nearly enough, but his angular chin and telegraph pole neck suggested he was a regular gym-goer, steroid abuser, or both.

Tyler produced his warrant card, deciding he was marginally less likely to be beaten to death by the guy if he knew he was polis. 'Detective Constable Tyler Neish. We've had reports of someone acting suspiciously in this area who matches your description.'

'From who?'

Tyler blinked. 'What?'

'Who's reported someone acting suspiciously in the area who matches my description?'

'Just… it's…' Tyler waved a hand vaguely. 'I can't give you that information. What's your name?'

'That's none of your business, Detective Constable Tyler Neish,' the man told him. Down at his heel, his dog snarled its agreement. 'I don't have to give you my name.'

'Well, yes, you do.'

'I don't. Not without good reason,' he countered. 'What grounds have you got for asking for my details?'

'Like I say, we've had reports of someone acting suspiciously who—'

'You haven't, though, have you? If someone had reported that, they wouldn't go sending out CID, or whatever you are. And anyway, I'm not acting suspiciously, am I? I'm walking my dog.'

'Didn't look like you were walking,' Tyler argued.

'He was having a piss,' the man said. 'No crime in that, is there? A dog having a piss?'

Tyler could feel himself losing control of the conversation. If he'd even been in control of it in the first place. The guy was right, he had no real grounds to do a stop and search. Nothing that would stand up to any scrutiny, anyway, and the man in the baseball cap seemed well-versed in what his rights were.

'Right, well, fun as this has been, I'm going to shoot off,' the man said. He gave the dog's lead a jerk, and the dog stopped growling at Tyler long enough to let out a little yelp of surprise. 'Nice to meet you, Detective Constable Tyler Neish.'

'I'm sure I'll see you around,' Tyler told him.

The man snorted out a half-laugh, looked the DC up and down, then shrugged. 'Aye. Maybe you will at that,' he said, and then with another jerk on the lead, he set off down the road in the direction of the school, whistling loudly and tunelessly as he went.

—

Logan and Tyler reached the Volvo at almost exactly the same time. Tyler opened his mouth to speak, but Logan gestured inside the car, then clambered in without saying a word.

When they were both inside with the doors closed, it was Logan who spoke first. 'Well? You find the guy I told you about?'

'Eh, aye. Aye, boss. Found him. Think it was him, anyway. Dressed in black. Built like a brick shithouse. Horrible angry wee dog with him.'

'I didn't see a dog,' Logan said. 'But sounds like him. Who is he?'

Tyler filled a moment by fastening his seatbelt. 'I, uh, I didn't get a name, boss.'

Logan turned slowly in his seat. 'Eh?'

'He didn't want to give me his name,' Tyler said. 'Said I had no grounds to ask for his details. Seemed pretty clued up.'

Logan swore below his breath. There were few things more annoying than a suspect who knew their rights. He sighed. 'I mind the days when "looking like a right shifty bastard" was justification enough,' he bemoaned. 'What was your impression of him?'

'A right shifty bastard,' Tyler said. 'He said he was just walking his dog, but it was definitely more of a lurk than

53

a walk from where I was standing. Looked like he was watching the house.'

Logan stole a glance in the Volvo's mirrors, but saw no sign of the mystery man in the hat. 'We can ask around later. See if anyone knows him.'

'How did you get on with the girlfriend?' Tyler asked, nodding in the direction of Hannah Randall's front door. 'Anything interesting come up?'

'Not really. He worked offshore. Was away a lot. She thought he was working this week, and was due home last night.'

'Explains why she didn't report him missing,' Tyler said.

Logan drummed his fingers on the steering wheel. 'Aye. Suppose.'

DC Neish looked from Logan to the house and back again. 'Something you're not telling me, boss?'

'Hmm?' Logan blinked as if coming out of a trance. 'No. Probably not. It's just his work. They didn't phone.'

'Phone who?'

'The house. They didn't phone when he didn't show up. I saw the body. It's been there a week, easy. He didn't make it to work, but nobody phoned to check up.'

'Maybe they called his mobile?' Tyler suggested.

That was certainly a possibility, Logan admitted. Or, maybe Brodie had called them to tell them he wasn't coming in. There were a variety of very good reasons why the company wouldn't call the house.

And yet, it niggled at him, and he could never resist a niggle.

'The girl's father is going to get us the employer's details. I want you to follow up on it when we get them,' Logan said. 'Find out if he made it in or, if not, whether he gave them warning that he wasn't coming.'

'Right, boss,' Tyler said.

He tapped the button that kicked the engine into life and glanced at the time on the display. 'Shite. I told the crime scene lot we'd be there ten minutes ago.'

Logan's belt gave a definitive click as he slotted it into place. He shot DC Neish a smile that was perfectly balanced between 'apologetic' and 'amused.'

'Looks like I'll have to put the foot down.'

Tyler swallowed, his mouth already filling with saliva in anticipation of the long and winding road ahead.

'Aw,' he groaned. 'Great.'

# Chapter 9

Geoff Palmer, the head of the Scene of Crime team, stood with Logan by the narrow footbridge, listening to the distant retching of DC Neish.

Tyler had exited the Volvo before it had fully stopped, then gone tearing across the car park, one hand clamped over his mouth, his eyes practically bulging out of his head.

He had made it as far from the investigation site as he possibly could before erupting in quite spectacular fashion near the side of the road.

For the past few minutes, he had been alternately standing, crouching, and squatting there, emptying his guts over the bracken and heather, and receiving the occasional derisory horn-blast from passing articulated lorries.

'Christ. How much has he eaten?' Palmer wondered, as another 'hurrrp' went echoing off the hillsides.

'Long as he gets it all up here and not in my car, I don't care,' Logan grunted.

He wasn't Geoff Palmer's biggest fan. In fact, he wasn't even ambivalent about the man. He actively disliked pretty much everything about him, from his sneering, bulbous face, to the condescending way he spoke to everyone around him. He was good enough at his job, but seemed almost begrudging of that fact, like he'd had dreams of being something glamorous, and was now stuck dealing with crime scenes and corpses instead.

Every call out seemed like a personal affront to him. Every time he arrived on a scene, he acted like he was doing the world a favour, rather than simply doing the job he was being paid for.

Granted, he probably wasn't being paid enough—none of them were, when you got down to it—but that was the job, take it or leave it.

'Dramamine,' Palmer said.

Logan raised an eyebrow. 'What?'

'Dramamine. Travel sickness tablets. That's what he needs.'

Across the car park, Tyler loudly threw up again.

'Drama *queen*, more like,' Logan remarked, then he turned and gestured to the tent on the other side of the bridge. 'So, you done?'

Palmer pushed back the hood of the paper suit he wore, revealing a hairline that seemed desperate to put as much distance between itself and the face below it as possible. 'We're done,' he confirmed. 'We were done half an hour ago, but had to hang around for you to finally show up. The body's already halfway to Inverness, just like I should be.'

'I told you to hang on to it until we arrived,' Logan said.

'Aye, well, I didn't know when you were going to bother to show up, so I made an executive decision,' Palmer replied. 'Would you rather I'd let the body deteriorate further and risk compromising the evidence?'

Logan didn't rise to it. Now wasn't the time or place.

'No. Obviously,' he said. 'Fine. So, what have we got?'

'Shoes, mostly,' Palmer said. 'Come and see for yourself.'

The bridge was solid, but he picked his way tentatively across it like he was terrified it would collapse at any moment. Logan took great pleasure in stomping onto it behind him and crossing it with a series of bouncing steps that made the whole thing shake.

'Can you not do that?' Palmer asked, shooting a look back over his shoulder.

'Do what?' asked Logan, feigning innocence.

Palmer tutted, then scurried the last few steps onto solid ground. Logan smiled at him as he reached the end of the bridge. It was petty, aye, but it was probably the highlight of his day so far. The way things had been going lately, it might well turn out to be the highlight of his week, so he was going to savour it while he could.

'Very funny. We'd see who was laughing if it had collapsed,' Palmer whined.

'I don't know what you're talking about,' Logan insisted, but he was already addressing the back of the other man's head.

'Let's just get through this quick,' Palmer said. 'Some of us have homes to go to.'

As the SOC investigator had suggested, 'shoes,' was definitely the headline. One pair, size eight, had been active around the burial site in the past few days. Rain had washed most of the prints away, but a few had survived well enough for them to take casts.

'And they were definitely shoes?' Logan asked. 'Not boots?'

'Not hiking boots, certainly,' Palmer said. 'Nothing that would really be suitable for taking to the hills with. Very little tread.'

He gestured to the mountain rising up behind them. 'You wouldn't get very far up that thing, put it that way.'

'Right. And what do they tell you?'

'We don't know the make yet, and the weather means this isn't an exact science, but I'd say the wearer was pretty heavy, judging by the depth. Quite how heavy, I can't tell you, but no lightweight. From the size of feet, I'd say male,' Palmer explained. 'We found a couple of partial prints that were deeper, suggesting whoever it was, they were carrying something heavy.'

'The body,' said Logan.

Palmer shot the DCI a patronising look, but stopped just short of going, 'Duh!'

'Speaking of which. You know the teeth were smashed in?' Palmer said. 'There's something else, too.'

'Fingers?' Logan guessed.

A flash of irritation crossed Palmer's face, his big moment spoiled. 'Yes. Fingers. All removed. We didn't find them, but then leaving them nearby would sort of defeat the killer's point.'

'Anything on the body?' Logan asked.

'No identification, if that's what you're hoping for.'

Logan shook his head. 'We know who he is. A family member was with the search team that found him.'

Palmer looked into the tent at the hole in the ground. 'They were looking for him?'

'No, they were looking for someone else. They found him by accident.'

'Oh. Right. Well, that's lucky. Looks like the killers wasted their time trying to conceal his identity.'

'What else have you got for me?'

Palmer glanced pointedly at his watch, then tutted, before continuing. 'It'll all be in the report. He wasn't dressed for the outdoors. Jeans, t-shirt. Trainers. Size seven, before you ask, we've discounted them from the prints. There was no sign of his footprints anywhere in the area, in fact, although that's hardly surprising, given the time that's passed. We were lucky to get any casts at all.'

'You discounted the prints the mountain rescue lads would've left? There were two of them,' Logan began, but the chastising scowl on Palmer's face stopped him going any further.

'Of course we discounted them. Jesus.' He motioned across to the car park, where the rest of the team were loading up a van. 'We *have* been doing this a while, you know? We *do* know what we're doing. We also discounted the two idiots who set up the tent and trampled all over the place, and a certain Detective Chief Inspector who should've bloody well known better. I mean, seriously, what were you thinking?'

'I was trying to stop the scene becoming compromised,' Logan protested.

Palmer gave a snort. 'Next time, maybe just go the whole hog and invite the Orange Walk to march through. It couldn't make things much worse. You lot are all members, aren't you? Funny handshakes, and all that?'

'Only thing I'm a member of is the AA,' Logan said, although he stopped short of specifying which one he was referring to.

'He wasn't killed at the scene,' Palmer said. 'Not enough blood in the surrounding soil. Killed elsewhere, carried here, then buried. I'd say, two, maybe three days ago.'

Logan frowned. 'Two or three days? Body looked older.'

'Aye, well, the elements, maybe. Who knows? That's my estimate of when he was buried, anyway,' Palmer said, visibly annoyed by the question. 'If you can call it buried. They barely broke the surface. Going by the size, shape, and angle of some of the cuts in the soil, I'd say a large trowel or a small folding spade was used.'

'No wonder they didn't go deep, if that was all they were using,' Logan remarked. 'Seems like poor planning, though. If you're taking someone out into the wilderness to bury them, you'd bring a shovel. Wouldn't you?'

'I'll just stick to giving you the facts, if it's all the same with you,' Palmer said, practically lifting his nose in the air, 'and leave the wild speculation to your lot.'

Logan bit his tongue to stop himself saying anything he'd enjoy in the moment, but might later regret. He waited for the urge to pass, then got back to business. 'Any thoughts on cause of death?'

'Again, not my department, so not really for me to say,' Palmer sniffed. 'But I'd say the big slit in his stomach probably did him no favours. Dr Maguire will be able to tell you more, I'm sure. She's waiting to receive the corpse.'

He turned away from Logan and regarded the inside of the tent again. 'She's very good, isn't she? Very thorough. Really knows her way around a body.'

Something about the way he said it made the fine hairs on the back of Logan's neck stand up and the blood go swooshing through his veins. 'Aye. She's an excellent pathologist,' he said, choosing his words carefully.

'Oh. Yes,' said Palmer. He glanced back at Logan, and there was a smile on his face that made the DCI's fingers twitch briefly into fists. 'She's that, too.'

'Is there something you're trying to imply, Geoff?'

Palmer shook his head. It was his turn to feign innocence. 'Me? Imply something? What makes you say that?'

Logan stepped in closer so he loomed over the much smaller man. Whatever bravado had been puffing Palmer up escaped as a low squeak of fear.

'See me, Geoff? I don't imply. I'm not one for beating around the bush. Call a spade a spade, and a jumped-up wee bawbag a jumped-up wee... well, you get my point,' Logan told him. 'So, I'll say this as plainly as I possibly can. Back in the lab, you might act the big man. Maybe you throw your weight around, trying to impress the new folk who haven't yet figured out quite what a wholly unappealing wee prick you are. But here?'

Logan pointed to the ground at their feet. 'Out here, on one of *my* crime scenes, you do what I tell you. All right? And you do not *imply* things about our mutual colleagues. In fact, you don't imply things about anyone. Like you said, you give us the data. That's it. We'll take care of the thinking bit. Is that clear?'

Palmer had a stab at standing his ground, but he crumbled immediately when Logan leaned forward a little, bringing his scowl closer.

'Fine. Yes. I was just... it was a joke, that's all,' Palmer protested.

'Next time you try a joke, maybe have a bash at making it funny, eh? Or, better yet, don't bother. Stick to the day job, Geoff,' Logan told him. He indicated the van with a jab of his thumb. 'Now, fuck off and get me that report.'

Palmer didn't say a word as he gathered up a couple of bags from outside the tent and went trudging off over the bridge. He shot Tyler the briefest of sideways glances as they passed on the other side, and then looked back once more just before he reached the van and the rest of his team. From the way their body language changed as he approached, Logan was satisfied that they'd all formed the correct impression of him a long time ago.

'I can't stand that man,' Logan remarked.

'Who? Sex Pest Palmer?' Tyler asked. 'Can't think why that might be, boss.'

Logan raised a quizzical eyebrow.

'Nothing we could actually charge him for, even if we wanted to. Just stories. Cracking on to women half his age. That sort of thing,' Tyler said. 'He wrote a big rant on Facebook recently about some twenty-year-olds calling him out for being a creepy bastard after he tried chatting them up in a restaurant. Went a bit viral until he took it down.'

'What do you mean it went viral? In what way?' Logan asked.

'Oh. People ripping the pish, mostly. Calling him out. Brutal they were,' Tyler said. 'He had to shut his account down in the end.'

Logan gave a little grunt of satisfaction. Sometimes, justice came swiftly of its own accord.

While the Scene of Crime lot finished loading up their van, Tyler turned and stood, hands on hips, looking up at the mountains. 'So. This is Glen Coe.' He wrinkled his nose. 'Just a big hill really, isn't it?'

'Mountain,' Logan corrected. 'And no. I mean, aye, that bit is, but it goes on for miles. It's actually pretty impressive. And I'm not an easy man to impress.'

'Aren't you? You hide that well, boss,' Tyler said. He looked around them again, taking in what he could see of their surroundings. The low clouds didn't help make the place seem all that remarkable, cutting off the mountain-tops the way they did. 'Didn't Jimmy Savile have a house up this way?' Tyler asked.

'Aye. It's back there,' Logan said, indicating the road to the south. 'You'll know it as soon as you see it. It's got "Paedo" written all over it.'

'Really? What, you mean like a vibe it gives off?'

'No, I mean it literally has the word "Paedo" written all over it. In spray paint. Every time it gets cleaned off, someone writes it on again. And worse, too,' Logan remarked. 'Some of the spelling they use is really quite creative.'

A chill wind swirled along the glen, rustling the tent and cutting both men to the bone. Shoving his hands in his coat pockets, Logan took one last look inside the tent, then back up at the mountain.

Finally, he set off for the bridge, beckoning the detective constable with a tilt of his head. 'Right, then. Let's get back and get the kettle on,' he said. 'And if you could avoid heaving your guts up in my car, I'd very much appreciate it.'

# Chapter 10

'Jack? Pop in here a sec, would you?'

Logan and Tyler had barely set foot in the station when the door to Chief Inspector Pickering's office opened and Hugh Pickering himself leaned out. The startling resemblance he'd once had to Velma from *Scooby Doo* that had earned him the nickname 'Jinkies' had faded over the years, and now it was a passing one, at best. Still, once a nickname was established in the polis, there was no shifting it, so Jinkies he forever would be.

Logan gave Tyler a nudge on the arm with his elbow. 'Go fill the rest of them in. Get a door to door organised. I want to know who the guy with the dog is.'

'On it, boss,' Tyler said, continuing ahead towards the Incident Room.

'And stick the kettle on,' Logan added. He looked very deliberately at the man in the office doorway. 'This'll only take a minute.'

Jinkies flashed an insincere smile, then stepped aside to allow Logan into the office. He was about to close it, when he had second thoughts, and leaned back out into the corridor, instead.

'Moira, no interruptions for the next twenty minutes,' he said.

Logan let out a quiet snort. Twenty minutes. Aye, like that would be happening.

There was silence from out in the corridor. Jinkies ran his tongue across his lips, gave it a few more seconds, then shouted again. 'Moi—'

'What?' Moira snapped, appearing around the corner at the end of the corridor.

'Ah. There you are. Did you hear me?'

'What, shouting my name?'

'No, the other bit. About not wanting any interruptions for the next twenty minutes?'

'No,' came the reply. 'I didn't hear that bit.'

There was the slightest hint of desperation in Jinkies' voice when he spoke again. What was meant to be a demonstration of his authority was rapidly turning into a demonstration of something altogether less impressive.

'Well… no interruptions for the next twenty minutes,' he said.

Silence.

'Moira.'

'Yes! I heard. No interruptions.'

'Right. Yes.' Jinkies began to close the door.

'What if it's important?' Moira asked from along the corridor.

Jinkies opened the door again. 'Well, obviously, if it's important, then that's… right.'

He closed the door, waited for a moment in case the receptionist was going to add anything else, then turned to find Logan sitting behind his desk. Jinkies opened his mouth to protest, before he ultimately decided that it wasn't worth the effort.

'Good to see you, Jack,' he said, and he was almost convincing. 'Although, I admit, I didn't think you'd be on my patch again quite so soon.'

'Aye, well. Needs must,' Logan said.

'The Highlands treating you well?'

'Certainly keeping me busy. Starting to think there's something in the water up here. The rate you're all killing each other off, there'll soon be no bugger left.'

'Ha,' said Jinkies, mirthlessly. 'Quite. Terrible business up in Inverness recently. Good work on that.'

Logan was fast approaching his maximum small talk threshold and steered the conversation on to more pressing matters.

'What was it you wanted?'

'Oh, just a catch-up, really. To let you know that our resources are at your disposal,' Jinkies said, adding, 'Within reason,' after a suitable pause. 'CID is close to a break-through in a local drugs case. Big business. They're pretty much flat out on that, so their assistance will be limited.'

'Flat out? Aren't they off on some training course?'

'*Pretty much* flat out,' Jinkies reiterated. 'Important to keep up to date with all the current best practice, too.'

Logan had only ever given the occasional passing nod to 'best practice,' and reckoned his idea of what that meant was likely very different to the Chief Inspector's. There were laws, there were rules, and then there was best practice. As far as he was concerned, one of those things could be safely bent, one broken, and the other ignored in its entirety.

'I'd ask you to respect that investigation,' Jinkies continued. 'And to be aware that any resource I do allocate you may have to be withdrawn at short notice.'

'We're dealing with a murder here, Hugh,' Logan said.

'Are we? Has that been confirmed?'

'As good as.'

Jinkies rocked back on his heels. 'So, that's a no, then,' he said. He held up a hand before Logan could reply.

'Of course, it's important. I'm not disputing that. But he's dead, and he's unlikely to get any deader. We have the opportunity here to shut down a big player in the local drugs trade. A big link in the chain. Huge.'

Logan grunted. 'Sounds like the kind of collar that could really make someone's career,' he remarked.

Jinkies tried to look nonchalant, but the thick lenses of his glasses magnified the flicker of excitement in his eyes. 'Well, I wouldn't know about that. I just want these people off the streets, Jack. We're just trying to make a difference, as always.'

*Aye, a difference to your pay packet*, Logan thought, but he kept it to himself.

He stood up, making the unilateral decision that the conversation was now over. 'Aye, well, we'll do our best not to tread on any toes.'

'Good man. And, of course, my door is always open,' Jinkies said. 'Drop by any time.'

Logan loomed over him. 'Thanks. If you want to speak to me again, though, do me a favour and make an appointment,' he said. He let the sentence hang in the air between them. 'I'm a very busy man.'

–

Logan was halfway along the corridor when his phone rang. He stopped, hunted his pockets, then glanced at the screen. *Unknown Caller.*

'Hello?' he said, and was not particularly surprised when no reply came. 'Hello?'

From the other end of the line, there came a squeaking sound. It reminded Logan of two balloons being rubbed together over and over. It was possibly interference, but—he checked the signal, and saw a full triangle of bars—more likely someone playing silly buggers.

'Who is this?' he demanded. 'Is that you, Petrie? If it is, then—'

There was a laugh, not quite a snigger, and not quite a giggle, but somewhere in between. Male, he thought, but he couldn't be sure, and it lasted only a second before the line went dead.

Logan checked the screen, then checked his watch. He had just started to move when the phone rang again. A Glen Coe prefix this time. Local.

'Hello?'

Fulton Randall spoke in hushed tones at the other end of the line. He explained that he was still with his daughter, but had stepped away to call in with the information the DCI had asked for. Logan asked him to hold on and went marching into the Incident Room, miming for someone to give him something to write with.

Hamza gestured to the open notebook on his desk and handed Logan a pen. As Fulton spoke, Logan scribbled.

The company Brodie had worked for was called 'Oswatt,' according to his bank statement. Fulton apologised that they didn't have a contact number, but Logan assured him it wasn't a problem, and that they'd find it.

The address and phone number of Brodie's mother was recited and repeated back, and then, after a brief enquiry as to how Hannah was holding up—not great, but that was only to be expected—Logan ended the call.

'Who was that?' Ben asked, handing over a cup of tea.

'Fulton Randall. Victim's partner's father.' He looked down at the pad, already struggling to decipher his own handwriting. 'You heard of Oswatt? Offshore company, I think.'

Ben shook his head and took a sip from his own mug. 'No. Don't think so. Why?'

'Victim worked for them. He was meant to be there this week. They didn't follow up on his whereabouts.'

'Want me to give them a ring, sir?' asked Caitlyn.

Her offering to take on responsibility was not new by any means. She was driven and ambitious, and a damn good copper. What did take Logan by surprise was the way she said it—bright and upbeat, with the unmistakable suggestion of a smile.

'Eh, aye. Please,' Logan said, after a pause. 'Find out what you can. Did he turn up? If so, when did he leave? If not, why no phone call? When did they last see him?' He remembered who he was speaking to. 'You know what we need.'

'Aye. I'm sure I can figure it out,' Caitlyn confirmed, then she turned to her computer and her fingers danced cheerfully across the keys.

Logan watched her for a few seconds, then shook his head and pressed on.

'We've got the address of Brodie's mother. She's in Fife. Hamza, can you get on to the local boys and get someone round there to talk to her?' Logan turned to Ben. 'Who do we know over that way?'

'Fife? Hmm.' Ben took another gulp of tea. 'Duncan Donuts. He's over there, isn't he? Superintendent, I think, unless he's got himself demoted.'

'Perfect,' said Logan. He turned back to Hamza. 'Get on to him. Use my name. Ask him to send someone decent. CID, not Uniform. The mother will already have heard the news from Hannah, but we need to know if she can tell us anything. Did she speak to him in the last week? Did anything seem amiss?'

Hamza glanced between the two senior officers. 'Right, sir. Aye. But... Duncan Donuts?'

'Duncan Mitchell,' Ben clarified. 'Superintendent Duncan Mitchell. We call him Donuts.'

'Right. Does he eat a lot of them?'

'What?'

'Donuts.'

Ben frowned and shook his head. 'Oh. No. God, no.'

Hamza hesitated. His eyes narrowed briefly and his lips parted like he was about to ask a question, but then he shook his head. 'Right. Fair enough. Superintendent Duncan Mitchell. Got it.'

Logan clicked his fingers a couple of times and pointed to the phone. 'Get on to him. I want someone speaking to her within the hour. She might try to come over this way. Tell him to dissuade her, if he can. For a few days, at least. Don't need a grieving mother under our feet until we've made a bit of progress.'

'Right, sir,' Hamza said. He tore the top sheet off his notepad, studiously copied down the address details onto a new page in more legible handwriting, then reached for the phone.

'Tyler, what have you got on our man?' Logan asked, wheeling around to face the other detective constable. Tyler had a phone handset cradled between his cheek and his shoulder, and was tapping at the screen of his mobile.

'Nothing yet, boss. I tried calling the Kinlochleven station, but apparently it's been a Bed and Breakfast for years. Who knew? Closest station is in Glen Coe. It's not manned all the time, so we'll have to get some of the guys from here to head down that way.' He pointed to the phone handset. 'Just getting it authorised.'

'What man's this you're talking about?' Ben asked.

'Shifty bastard. Seemed to be snooping around near the victim's house. Wouldn't give his name.' The rest of the sentence came out through gritted teeth. 'Knew his rights, apparently.'

'Christ. One of them,' Ben remarked. 'Not like the old days. Eh, Jack?'

'No. Not like the old days,' Logan agreed.

'I actually think it's quite good, sir,' Hamza volunteered. He had the phone in one hand and a finger poised over the buttons, and eyed both men warily. 'That folk know their rights, I mean. Rights are important. You know, like... checks and balances, and all that?'

Ben opened his mouth to reply, but Logan held up a finger to stop him. 'That's a really good attitude to have, Detective Constable,' he said, to the surprise of pretty much everyone in the room. 'And I agree that rights are important. Vital, even. I have no problem whatsoever with people *having* rights. I just don't like it when they know what those rights are. It makes our job a hell of a lot more difficult.'

He pointed to the handset. 'Now, have you made that phone call? If not, would you mind getting down from your high horse for five minutes and doing it?'

Hamza turned his attention back to the task at hand. 'On it now, sir.'

Across at her desk, Caitlyn made a sound that could best be described as 'quizzical'. Her forehead furrowed despite the best efforts of her tightly-scraped-back ponytail, and all eyes went to her as she turned in her chair.

'Problems?' asked Ben.

'Uh, yeah. Maybe,' she said. She gave a click of her mouse, waited for the next page of search results to load, then shrugged. 'I can't find it. Oswatt. The company the

72

victim worked for. I can't find any reference of it. Not as a business, I mean.'

She gestured to the screen. 'It's a surname, and possibly the name of a Pokemon—although, I didn't go too far down that particular rabbit hole—but I'm not seeing it as a business. Definitely nothing in the offshore sector.'

Logan lowered himself onto the edge of Hamza's desk and crossed his arms. 'You sure?'

'Positive, sir,' Caitlyn confirmed. 'I've Googled it, checked Companies House, Facebook, LinkedIn, Twitter. Nothing.'

DI Forde rolled the question around inside his mouth a few times, before spitting it out.

'So, if there's no Oswatt, who the hell has been paying Brodie Welsh's salary every month?'

'And, more importantly,' Logan added. 'Where has he been going?'

# Chapter 11

Logan sat in the small office at the back of the Incident Room, tentatively jabbing buttons on his keyboard while the woman on the screen mouthed silently at him, equal parts amused and exasperated.

'Now? What about now? Hello? Can you hear me now?'

On the monitor, the pathologist, Dr Shona Maguire, gave a double thumbs-up, pointed to her camera, then pointed to her ears.

'You can hear...? No. Me? No. I still can't hear...' He muttered a selection of obscenities under his breath, then raised his voice in the direction of the door. 'Hamza! This stupid thing's not working. I can't hear a thing.'

There was a moment of hesitation, while Hamza had a stab at diagnosing the problem.

'Are you wearing the headphones, sir?'

'Headphones? What bloody—'

He spotted the headphones hanging over the edge of the monitor, made a general sort of grumbling noise, then pulled them on.

'Hello?' Shona Maguire's Irish lilt was suddenly right there in his ears, like she was standing just a few inches away. 'Can you hear me?'

'Aye. Got you. Can you hear me?' Logan asked.

'I've been able to hear you the whole time,' the pathologist replied. 'I was quite impressed by some of the language you were using at one point. I learned, like, four new swear words in the space of about eight seconds. That must surely be some kind of record.'

Logan shifted awkwardly in his seat. 'Aye. Well. I'm not really a big one for technology. All too complicated, for my liking.'

'I know what you mean. Luckily, I've got a PhD, or I'd never have figured out how to put these in.' She pointed to the Bluetooth earphones tucked into her ears, and smirked down the camera lens.

'Good one,' Logan told her.

'Thanks,' Shona said, her smile widening. 'So, you cracked the case yet?'

'Oh, aye. All figured out,' Logan said. 'Piece of cake. I'm just calling you so you don't feel left out.'

'Very generous of you,' Shona said. 'I'm putting the report together, and I'll fire it over shortly, but you want the top stories?'

Logan picked up a pen, clicked the button on the end, then held it ready above his notepad. 'Go for it.'

'Hang on, I'll pick you up,' Shona said, and the image on screen lurched as she reached forward. There was a loud crack, and a panicky, 'Oh, shit,' and then the pathologist's face appeared again, this time viewed from below. It wasn't the greatest angle, but it also wasn't the worst. 'Hello? Still there?'

'I'm still here,' Logan confirmed.

Shona let out a sigh of relief. 'Dropped the phone,' she explained.

'I guessed.'

Shona must've caught sight of herself in the little inset picture, because she quickly moved the phone so it wasn't capturing her from quite such an unflattering angle. As she moved it, Logan caught a glimpse of the corpse on the table behind her, a sheet covering its modesty.

'Right. OK, here goes, then,' she began, turning the phone so the body filled most of the screen. 'Male victim, obviously. Mid-twenties, but you know that. Teeth removed, fingers cut off from around the first interphalangeal joint.'

Logan raised a hand and pointed to the middle knuckle of his index finger.

'Precisely. Well done. That was a test, and you passed. You know your knuckles,' Shona told him. She focused in on one of the victim's hands. Her shaky camera work didn't make it easy, but Logan was able to see the blackened stumps of his fingers. 'As you might be able to see, it wasn't a neat job. The fingers weren't removed individually, but in a couple of strikes with something like an axe. Machete, maybe. Once across the fingers, then across the thumb. Same on both hands.'

'Pre- or post-mortem?' Logan asked.

'After. I'd expect to see a lot of blood staining on his hands if he'd been alive, and the clotting situation would be very different. He wasn't bleeding when his fingers were cut off. Same with the teeth. Done after he was dead. Blunt instrument. Bad aim, too. Nose took a few cracks. One of the cheeks, too. You ask me, either the face was covered, or whoever did the smashing didn't want to look too closely at what he was doing.'

Without warning, Shona angled the phone's camera to give a clear view of Brodie's face. Logan had only seen half of it when the body was face down on the ground, and the damage was substantially worse than he'd first thought.

'Want a look?' the pathologist asked. Somewhat late, Logan thought.

'I'm looking,' the DCI told her. 'Christ. He'll no' be winning any beauty contests, will he?'

'Depends on who he's up against, I suppose,' Shona remarked from behind the camera. 'Someone didn't want him identified.'

'Well, luckily, we got a break there,' Logan told her. 'What about the stomach? Palmer said something about a slit?'

'Bit of an understatement,' Shona said. The image on screen moved down past the victim's chest, to an open wound in his stomach that caught Logan off-guard.

'Jesus.'

'Sorry, should've warned you. Yeah, it's a bad one,' Shona said. 'Bad two, actually. The initial cut went through the muscle and sliced open the stomach wall. There was then a secondary cut into the bowel. Neither were done particularly delicately. From what I can tell, both were done while he was still alive. There's also a stab wound to the chest. Close to the heart, but missed.'

Logan wasn't particularly enjoying the view of the victim's insides, but leaned in for a closer look, anyway. 'But the knife wounds were the cause of death?'

'Actually, no,' Shona said. 'I found sand and grit in his lungs. Breathed in. It's a close-run thing, but I'd say he suffocated before he bled to death.'

'Buried alive,' Logan remarked. His eyes narrowed. 'Wait. Sand?'

'Yeah. And grit. Like… fine gravel, I suppose. I've sent it off for testing.'

'Not soil?'

'No. Plenty of soil on the outside and in the wounds, but nothing in his lungs. I take it that doesn't match the scene?'

'It doesn't, no.'

Logan scribbled a few notes in his pad. 'When did he die?'

'Based on deterioration, conditions…' Shona said mulling it over. 'Six days. Ish. I should be able to be a bit more accurate once some results come back.'

'Palmer reckons the burial site was only a couple of days old,' Logan told her.

'Geoff would know more about that than me, I'm sure,' Shona said. 'He knows his stuff.'

Logan couldn't argue, but it annoyed him immensely to hear the pathologist praising that creepy bastard, particularly after what he'd said about her back at the burial site.

The image on screen changed to show Shona's face. 'Body's definitely older, though. No way he was killed in the last seventy-two hours. Not possible.'

Logan nodded, the suspicion that had formed while speaking to Palmer at Glen Coe now confirmed. 'He was moved, then. Killed somewhere, left a few days, then relocated and buried.'

Shona glanced down at the body which was now, mercifully, off-screen. 'Maybe they were worried he'd be found?'

Logan sat back in his chair. 'I don't think it's that,' he said, although he didn't elaborate further.

'One other thing worth mentioning, his rectum was partially distended, and there was some damage around the anus. Not major, but worthy of note. I don't think it's particularly recent, either. Historical.'

'A sex thing?' Logan wondered.

'I couldn't rule that out,' Shona said. 'But not necessarily.'

'Right. Thanks,' Logan said. He was still thinking about the body being moved, trying to figure out why. He folded his notepad closed, and drummed his fingers on the cover, lost in theories and 'what ifs'.

'Like I say, I'll get the report to you shortly,' Shona said, interrupting his train of thought.

Logan blinked, then nodded. 'Good. Thanks. I'll keep an eye out.'

'Right. OK, then,' Shona replied. Her tone changed, becoming more conversational. 'How did your trip go, by the way?'

The DCI frowned. 'Trip?'

'Glasgow. The hospital. I mean… *Carstairs*,' she said, dancing around the hospital's name like it might be booby-trapped. 'Did you get what you needed?'

Logan puffed out his cheeks and looked away, as if contemplating this fully for the first time. 'No,' he said. 'Not really.'

'Oh. Right. Well, sorry to hear that,' Shona said. She raised the phone a little, so it was looking at her from a slightly higher angle. 'Maybe, when you're back… if you want, like. Maybe we could have a chat about it? Problem shared, and all that. I'm sure one of us still owes the other one lunch, or dinner, or breakfast, or whatever it is.' She smiled. 'I've lost track.'

Logan had just started to return the smile when there was a knock at the door, and DC Neish's head appeared around the door frame.

'Sorry, boss. Thought you'd want to know. The guy in the baseball cap? I think we've got a hit.'

'Anyone of interest?' Logan asked.

Tyler made a weighing motion. 'Aye. Worth a look, anyway.'

'I'll be right there,' Logan told him. He turned back to the screen. 'Listen, I—'

'I heard. Go. We'll talk later,' Shona said, then her eyes widened and she quickly garbled out a, 'Wait!'

There was no real need for the urgency. Logan had no idea how to hang up the video call, and had been relying on the pathologist doing it from her end.

'What's up?' he asked.

'Forgot to say, got some very early toxicology reports. Basic stuff, but it might be something,' she said. 'Looks like he was a cannabis user. Regular, and long-term. Not sure if that's worth noting.'

'I'm sure it is,' Logan told her. 'Thank you. Keep in touch.'

'Will do,' Shona said.

There was a hollow silence as they both sat there for a few moments, saying nothing.

'You'll have to hang up,' Logan told her.

On the screen, Shona looked amused. 'Is that the game we're playing, is it? No, *you* hang up.'

Logan quietly cleared his throat. 'No, I mean it. I don't know the buttons.'

Shona's smile quickly fell. Her cheeks blushed red. 'Oh. Right. Gotcha. Sorry. Bye!' she said, and then the tip of one of her fingers filled the screen, and the call was terminated.

'Well,' said Tyler, and Logan winced when he realised the DC was still standing in the doorway. 'That was all a bit awkward, wasn't it?'

## Chapter 12

There was an ugly bastard on the Big Board when Logan emerged from the office.

Usually, he tried not to judge people on their appearance, but it was difficult in this case. That was because it wasn't his appearance that was the problem. Not really. The ugliness Logan could see was all there on the inside.

You got to know it, eventually. You could see it in the eyes and in the lines of the face. A coldness, but something more, too. Something deeper. Something worse.

Sure, with his crooked nose, caterpillar eyebrows, and sunken, piggy-little eyes, the guy was certainly no oil painting on the outside, either, but the real ugliness lurked within, and Logan could see it as clear as day.

'That our man?' he asked, taking a seat on the edge of a desk.

'Aye, that's him, boss,' Tyler confirmed. 'We got a hit pretty much straight away from one of the neighbours. Old boy. He was the only one who pointed the finger, although Uniform reckons there were others who knew, but didn't want to say.'

'And this is the man you spoke to?' Logan asked.

'Reckon so, boss, yeah,' Tyler confirmed. 'He's bulked up a bit since the mugshot was taken, and sorted out them eyebrows, but that's him.'

'Sandy Gillespie,' DI Forde said, reading from a prin-tout. 'Part of a local family of toerags. Youngest of three siblings, all of them with a record. Fighting, in his case, on the High Street, mostly. One charge of B&E a few years back, but it was dropped. Nothing major, just a recurring pain in the arse.'

'Any connection to Brodie Welsh or Hannah Randall?' Logan asked.

'Only a disappointing one,' Ben said. 'Neighbours. He lives just around the corner.'

'Regularly walks his dog up that street,' Tyler added. 'According to the neighbour who ID'd him, anyway. The old boy had plenty to say about him. No love lost there. But, he did back-up the dog-walking story.'

Logan tutted. 'Bollocks.' He ran his tongue across the roof of his mouth, eyeballing the photograph. Ugly bastard. No doubt. 'Worth bringing him in on some-thing?'

'On a charge?' asked Ben. 'Because I can't see him volunteering to pop in for a chat.'

'Anything we can get him on?' Logan asked, looking around for suggestions.

Ben and the others exchanged blank looks.

'Come on. Get creative,' Logan urged. He pointed to the mugshot pinned to the board. 'My gut tells me that bastard was up to something, but he'll be only too aware that we can't bring him in on that. So, what can we bring him in on?'

The silence that followed was eventually broken by an, 'Oh!' from DC Neish. All eyes went to him.

'Tyler?'

'Dog shit, boss!' the DC announced. Quite proudly, too.

Logan's face remained impassive. 'Dog shit?'

'Aye. That's one of the things the neighbour said. Here...' Tyler picked up his notepad and rifled through the pages. 'Got it. Apparently, the dog shites on the pavement and Gillespie never bothers to pick it up. The old boy confronted him about it a few times, but he just laughs it off. So, he took photos. The neighbour, I mean. He took photos on his phone. Showed the lassie from Uniform. Dozens of pictures of dog shit, and a couple of Gillespie's dog in the act. He went through them all with her.'

'Bet she was delighted,' Hamza remarked.

DS McQuarrie tapped a pen against her desk. 'Fixed Penalty though, isn't it?'

'Aye.' Ben looked doubtful. 'Can we bring him in on dog shit?'

'I've brought people in on less,' Logan told him, and Ben could only concede that point with a shrug.

'But, how's that conversation going to go?' Hamza wondered. ' "We know we brought you in about the dog shit, but while you're here, did you happen to murder anyone recently?" '

DS McQuarrie nodded her agreement. 'If he's clued-up, like Tyler says, he's going to see right through it.'

Logan shrugged off her concern. 'He might know his stop and search rights, but that doesn't mean he knows his rights under the dog shite... Whatever.'

'Dog Fouling Scotland Act, 2003,' Caitlyn recited.

'Aye. That. Thank you,' Logan said.

'Suppose, sir. But, if he gets a solicitor and puts in a complaint...' the DS continued.

'We'll cross that bridge when we come to it,' Logan said. He rubbed his chin, his fingers rasping across the

83

stubble. 'Aye. Let's do it,' he decided, giving Tyler the nod. 'Let's go with the dog shit.'

–

Sandy Gillespie was hurling abuse at a ten-year-old when the knock at the door came. He ignored it at first, his thumbs tapping on the X-button of his PlayStation controller, as he slide-tackled the legs out from under his online opponent, and cackled at the squeals of complaint in his headset.

'Fucking grow up, you wee Yank prick,' Sandy sneered. 'Away and greet to *Mommy*. You lot don't even fucking play football, so I don't know what you're even—'

The knocking came again. Louder and more insistent. Sandy recognised it, then. Not the specific knock, but the specific type. Polis. Fucking polis.

He dropped out of the game with a couple of button taps, swore a handful of times at the random kid he'd been paired up against, then rolled off his beanbag and onto the dirty carpet.

Snatching up the joint he'd left sitting in the ashtray, he stuffed it, his lighter, and a thumb-sized block of hash into a tin. Then, he shoved the tin into the little flap he'd created in the base of the couch, fastened it shut with the Velcro, and cracked open a window.

He'd just turned in the direction of the hallway when the hammering came again, shaking the front door in its frame.

'Mr Gillespie? We know you're in there,' said a male voice. One of the local plods. Sandy couldn't remember the name, but he could picture his face.

'All right, all right, I'm coming,' he said. It was only when he shuffled past the kitchen door that the barking

84

started on the other side. Sandy thudded a fist against it on the way past. 'Shut the fuck up,' he ordered, but this only egged the animal on, and the barking became ever-more furious.

'What?' Sandy asked, spitting the word out before the door was open. Not that it opened far. He'd left the security chain across it, so there was only a six-inch gap through which anyone could see in or out.

Two uniformed officers stood in the garden. The first was the guy he'd been expecting. Two or three years older than Sandy himself. Moved to the area a couple of years back. Thought he was the Big I-Am.

He stood up front on the step, chest all puffed up beneath the high-vis jacket. His fist was raised like he had been getting ready to knock again. It lowered to his side when Sandy squinted out at them through the gap.

Behind the first officer was a woman. Short. Squat. Unsure of herself. New, probably.

'Mr Gillespie?' the male officer asked. 'Mr Sandy Gillespie.'

'Aye. You know fine fucking well,' Sandy said. He looked the man on the step up and down. 'What's your name again? Farmer, or something, wasn't it?'

The officer opened his mouth to reply, but Sandy clicked his fingers and pointed. 'Farler. James Farler. Jamie-Boy. That's right, isn't it?'

'Police Constable James Farler, yes,' he confirmed. 'Now, Mr—'

'Your kids go to the school, don't they?' Sandy continued. 'Boy and a girl, isn't it? I see them go past.'

PC Farler quietly cleared his throat. His shoes creaked as he shifted his weight on them. 'That's not any of your business.'

Sandy snorted, draining his sinuses, then swallowed it down. 'Everything round here's my business, Jambo,' he said. He turned his head back in the direction of the kitchen, bellowed, 'Fucking shut up!' at the barking dog, then faced front again, flashing a smile that showed off his yellowing teeth. 'Now, what can I do for you, orifice? Sorry, *officer.*'

He looked past Farler to the female officer standing behind him. 'I'm always making that mistake.'

'Well, Mr Gillespie,' she said, holding his gaze with a calm composure that disappointed him no end. 'It's about your dog...'

# Chapter 13

Ben and Logan stood in half-darkness, peering into the brightly-lit room on the other side of the glass, where Sandy Gillespie slouched in a chair that had been carefully hand-selected for its uncomfortable back and complete lack of padding.

He hadn't asked for a solicitor. He'd seemed amused by the charge, by all accounts. He'd been cracking jokes when Uniform had checked him in, then had sung to himself as he was led along the corridor and into the interview room.

He still looked amused now, although boredom was starting to creep in. Logan and Ben both watched as he picked his nose, studied the findings, then flicked it in the direction of the glass.

'Can we hurry this up?' he asked, his voice stabbing at them through the speakers. 'I haven't got all fucking day.'

'Charming lad,' Ben remarked. 'Be nice if he did it, and we could wrap it all up before home time.'

'Aye,' Logan agreed. 'That'd be handy.'

On the other side of the soundproof glass, Gillespie started to chant. 'Why are we waiiitiiing? Why are we waiiitiiing?'

'God. What a horrible little bastard,' Ben said, his already low opinion of the man worsening by the second.

He shot Logan a warning look. 'You watch yourself in there. Don't go letting him under your skin.'

'What, this wee dick? Come on, Benjamin. You know me better than that,' Logan said. 'How many times have we dealt with arseholes like him before?'

Ben nodded, but it was hesitant. 'True. But, there's something about this one, Jack. He's got my guts churning.'

'Sure that's no' Alice's cooking?' Logan asked, and both men shared a grim smile. 'I'll be fine,' Logan said. 'Besides, I'm letting Tyler take the lead.'

'Why are we waiiitiiiing? Why-aye are we waiiitiii—'

Ben tutted and turned the dial that lowered the volume from the speakers. Silence filled the viewing room.

'Tyler?' he asked, almost spluttering the word out. 'I mean, he's coming along, but... taking the lead? Are you sure that's a good idea?'

'He wants another crack at him,' Logan said. 'After what happened down the road.'

'What, you mean when he failed to even get so much as a name from the bastard?'

Logan nodded. 'I'll be in there with him. I can jump in, if needs be, but it'll be good to observe Gillespie's reactions. I want you and Caitlyn through here. Leave Hamza digging into the employer thing. Oswatt.'

Reaching into his pocket, Logan took out the promotional pen and handed it over. 'Tell him to check in with Fulton Randall. See if Hannah will give him a copy of the bank statement. We might get an account number for them off there, or be able to check with the bank where the transactions have been coming from.'

Ben took the pen, shook his head disapprovingly at the apostrophe usage, then tucked it into his shirt pocket.

'Hamza might need to go down there and talk to her himself. See what she knows about the company, if anything. When did Brodie start there? Does she have payslips? Has she ever spoken to his boss or colleagues? That sort of thing.'

'Right. I'll get him on it,' Ben said. He glanced at his watch. It was just after eight, and darkness had come creeping in a few hours ago. 'Getting late, though. Maybe best leaving the visit until tomorrow?'

Logan conceded the point with a sigh. 'Aye. But have him phone Fulton tonight. We can make a start there, at least, then follow up in the morning.'

Ben tapped the breast pocket, and the pen it contained. 'I'll go get him on it, and bring Caitlyn in. You going to give Tyler a pep talk?'

'Aye,' Logan said. He put a hand on the back of his neck, kneading the muscle. 'Something like that.'

-

'Do *not* fuck this up. Is that understood?'

Tyler briefly regarded the finger jabbing in his face and gave a quick shake of his head. 'I won't, boss. I've got this.'

The finger dropped. Logan ran the other hand down his face, mumbled quietly, then pulled together something that could almost, under the right lighting conditions, be passed off as a smile.

'Aye. You've got this,' he agreed. 'But if at any point you feel you haven't got it, you let me know, all right?'

'Will do, boss.'

'And, if I think you're struggling, then I'll jump in, and that's your cue to shut your mouth. We're only going to get one crack at this bastard. We cannot blow it.'

'Got it. No bother, boss,' Tyler said. He grinned. 'But relax. I've got this. Honest.'

Logan approached the door to the interview room, checked the code on the slip of paper he'd been given, then keyed it into the pad. The door buzzed.

Tyler took a deep breath. 'Well, here goes nothing,' he said.

Logan grunted. 'That doesn't exactly fill me with confidence,' he muttered.

And with that, he pulled open the door.

–

Fulton Randall sat in his armchair, his granddaughter, Carrie, snuggled in at his side, a picture book spread across their legs. Realistically, the armchair was too big for the room, and it made the place look cramped and untidy. But Fulton had settled on it for just this very purpose. For moments just like this one, with Carrie coorying in beside him, one leg hooked over his, her wee body tucked in against his arm.

She should've been in bed by now. Should've been tucked up, fast asleep, oblivious to the fact her life had been irrevocably changed. But, she'd wanted to read the book again. 'Again-*again*,' in fact. She'd insisted on that, and he didn't have the heart to say no.

Hannah had refused to come and stay over. Point blank. Even when Fulton's wife, Sandra, had insisted, Hannah had stood her ground. She wanted to be home. She wanted to be in their room, her and Brodie's, in the bed they'd shared for the past few years. She wanted to be close to him.

Fulton and Sandra had offered to stay over with her. She'd refused that, too, but had accepted their offer to watch Carrie for another night. Hannah didn't want the girl to see her crying, she'd said. It would come. It was bound to come. But not now. Not yet. Not tonight.

'Look at the tutu. Is that funny?' Fulton asked, pointing to one of the pictures in the book. A cow was strutting around in a ballerina dress, and it was always one of Carrie's favourite pictures.

'Yeah!' she said, the word coming out as a giggle.

'Have you ever seen a cow wearing a tutu?' Fulton asked her, looking down. She grinned up at him and nodded enthusiastically. 'You have?'

'Yeah! Two times.'

'*Two* times? Wow!' Fulton said. 'Lucky you. I don't think I've ever—'

His phone buzzed on the table. Normally, he'd have let it go to voicemail, but given everything going on, he knew he had to answer it.

His initial reaction was that it might have been Hannah, but the number wasn't one he recognised. Local one, though. He turned the page, pointed at another cow in fancy dress, then tapped the 'answer' icon.

'Hello?'

The voice on the other end was broad Aberdonian. It took Fulton's ear a moment to adjust.

'Mr Randall? This is DC Hamza Khaled. You spoke to one of my colleagues earlier. DCI Logan.'

'Yes.' Fulton sat forward, leaving Carrie looking at the book. 'Is everything all right? Have you got news?'

'Sorry, nothing to report yet, Mr Randall. But we're pursuing multiple lines of inquiry, and working on getting a result as soon as we possibly can,' Hamza said. 'We were just hoping you might be able to help us with something.'

Carrie tugged on Fulton's arm. He smiled, held up an index finger to indicate he'd only be a second, then returned to the call. 'Of course. Anything. What do you need?'

'It's Brodie's employer. Oswatt. We're having difficulty tracking them down.'

Fulton frowned. 'Really? I think he said they're a Dutch company. Based in the Netherlands. Oil. Or… I assume oil. He never really specified, but he works offshore a lot.'

He glanced sadly back at Carrie, then quietly corrected himself. 'Worked offshore.'

'I'm sorry for your loss, sir,' Hamza said.

'Not my loss. Not really,' Fulton said, giving his grand-daughter's leg a squeeze. She beamed at him, then tapped a fist on the book impatiently. He made the same 'one-second' gesture with a finger again, then turned it into a tickle that made her squeal with delight.

'We were hoping there might be something on the bank statement that would help us identify the company,' Hamza continued. 'Do you have a copy?'

'No. I mean, yes. Hannah wasn't in much of a mood for going through the paperwork stuff, so I just took a photo on my phone so I could give you the details. I can email it to you, if you like?'

'That would be perfect, Mr Randall,' Hamza told him. 'I'll text you through my email address now. Easier than spelling it out.'

'Right. Yes. No problem,' Fulton said, then they said their brief goodbyes. He sat back, the phone in one hand, Carrie snuggling in against him again on the other side.

The text came through almost immediately. Fulton tapped it, attached the photo of the bank statement to the email window that popped up, and sent it off.

Returning to the phone's home screen, he selected the search box, then read a few lines of the book's next page while tapping his thumb across the phone's on-screen keyboard.

O-S-W-A-T-T.

A page of search results was returned. None of them relevant.

Glancing down, Fulton read off the next few lines of the story, then added the words 'oil' and 'Dutch' to the phone search. The screen refreshed. He swiped up, scanning the results. They were mostly links to sites selling Danish Oil for treating wood. In fact, not *mostly*. Exclusively. No offshore companies. No Dutch energy firms.

No Oswatt.

'Grandpa.'

Fulton tore his eyes from his phone. Carrie pointed to the words at the bottom of the page and stared expectantly up at him.

'Sorry, sweetheart,' he said, then he set the phone down, shuffled lower in his seat, and got back to reading.

# *Chapter 14*

On Logan's nod, Tyler pressed the button between them on the table. It illuminated red. On the other side of the room's large mirror, the display on a digital recorder began to count upwards.

'Interview begins at...' Tyler checked his watch. 'Nine-sixteen PM. Present in the room is, um, me. Detective Constable Tyler Neish.'

'Detective Chief Inspector Jack Logan.'

Tyler looked across the table at the third man and waited.

'State your name for the recording,' he urged.

'Sandy Gillespie,' the other man said, after a few moments of unflinching eye contact with the DC.

'Thank you. We should note for the recording that Mr Gillespie has declined his right to a solicitor. Can you confirm that for us?'

'Aye. Whatever. Can we just get a fucking move on?' Gillespie asked.

He was slouching back in his chair, his arms draping down almost all the way to the floor. There was an air of a petulant teenager about him, despite him being old enough to know better. One of his legs was bouncing, so that the knee bumped softly against the underside of the table, shaking it.

At first, Logan had thought the movement was unconscious, a sign of nervousness, but he had quickly come to suspect Gillespie was doing it on purpose just to be annoying.

He was succeeding, too.

'Mr Gillespie. Sandy. Can I call you Sandy?' Tyler asked.

'Call me what you like.'

'Sandy. Do you know why you're here?'

'Aye, but I want you to tell me,' Gillespie said. 'I want to hear you say it.'

Logan sat in silence, eyeballing the man across the table, a look of mild irritation fixed on his face. It was a look he had honed carefully over the years. The 'mild' part was important, as he didn't want to come across as too aggressive from the off, but it was vital that the look implied that his irritation levels could become substantially less mild at any given moment.

'You're here because we've had reports of multiple offences you've committed that contravene the Dog Fouling Scotland Act of 2003,' Tyler explained, briefly glancing at Caitlyn's notes to ensure he got the wording right.

'Bullshit,' Gillespie spat.

Tyler flipped open a folder on the desk in front of him. 'Dog shit, actually. And lots of it. We had some printouts done of the photos. Do you want to see?'

Gillespie ignored the ten-by-twelve glossy pictures that were pushed to his side of the table. 'I mean bullshit, that's not what I'm here for.' He jabbed a finger down on one of the photos. It showed a particularly impressive evacuation. 'This is Fixed Penalty stuff. Forty quid. This is fucking council work, not you lot.'

He flicked his gaze across to Logan. It was only the second or third time he'd so much as glanced in the DCI's direction since the detectives had entered the room. There was a flash of uncertainty there, but it was quickly pushed down.

'What's up with your face? You fucking constipated or something?'

Logan said nothing. He didn't even ramp his irritation levels up a notch. He just sat there, silent and staring, and let Tyler do the talking.

'What else would we have brought you in for, Sandy? What other reason would we have had to drag you all the way up here at this time of night?'

'You tell me.'

Tyler clasped his hands in front of himself. Logan didn't like it. It didn't seem natural, like something the DC had seen on a training course, or an episode of *Prime Suspect*.

'We brought you in here to discuss the dog fouling, as I think we've made clear,' Tyler said. 'But, we're particularly interested in earlier today. Where you and I had our little chat. See, I've had a couple of officers go and check that area, Sandy, and they found not one, not two, but three dog turds all around the same spot. Three. That's a lot of shit for a wee dug.'

He side-eyed Logan. 'You think, boss?'

Logan nodded, just once, never breaking eye contact with the scrote across the table.

'All looked much the same. Similar size, shape, consistency. I had them check. They weren't happy about it, but I can't really blame them. Not a nice job,' Tyler said. He stuck out his tongue, pulled a disgusted face, then shook his head. 'The point is, though. They reckon it was the same dog. They took samples, in case we wanted to test it, but I don't think that'll be necessary.'

'What's he fucking on about?' Gillespie asked Logan. Predictably, he got no response.

'Is your dog fit and well, Sandy? No problems with the plumbing?'

'No.'

'Good. That's great. Because going three times like that would either suggest he's got a dicky tummy, or that you and he were hanging around there for a good wee while. In that same spot. Why would that be, Sandy?'

'No crime in standing on the street,' Gillespie said.

Tyler shrugged. 'There is if you let your dog repeatedly shite on it,' he pointed out. 'Why that spot, in particular? There are fields not far away. Nice walks through the woods. Why stand at that particular spot, outside those particular houses, long enough for your dog to empty its guts three times? That's what we're struggling to understand, Sandy. That's what we're hoping you can help us with. Why were you standing *there*? What were you doing there for that length of time?'

Gillespie glanced at the empty chair beside him. It had been set out for the solicitor he had chosen not to bring in, and for a moment he looked like he might be regretting that decision.

But then, the petulant teenager returned and he sat back, plastering a sneer across his weaselly little face. 'I just like that spot.'

'Certainly seems like it,' Tyler agreed. 'We checked, and the school has CCTV. You know? The one at the end of the road? It's not all that clear, but if you squint, you can see you walking up the street earlier today. Want to hazard a guess what time?'

'Not really.'

'Quarter past eleven. Thereabouts. Eleven seventeen. May as well be exact about it. Eleven seventeen this morning. That's a good, what, three or four hours before I bumped into you? Something like that. We can check the school CCTV to get the exact time. I'm on there, too, wandering about. Looking for anything that might be considered suspicious.'

Tyler gave that a moment to bed in. 'Like, for example, someone standing in the same spot for four hours, letting their dog shite the place up. Some would consider that suspicious, Sandy. Especially given what's happened.'

'There you go! Here it comes,' Gillespie said. 'Wondered when you'd get around to it. This is about Brodie Welsh, isn't it? You're trying to pin that on me.'

Tyler looked surprised. Even Logan couldn't tell if he was feigning it, or if it was genuine. 'Pin what on you, Sandy?' he asked. 'What is it you're referring to?'

Another voice spoke before Gillespie could respond. It was amplified by the speakers on the wall, the tone clipped and authoritative.

'DCI Logan.'

Logan recognised the voice as Jinkies'. What the hell was he doing here at this time of night? Not like him to show face outwith normal office hours.

'I'd like a word, please,' Jinkies told him. 'Urgently.'

Gillespie drew in a breath and grinned, showing his scum-coated teeth. 'Oops. Someone's in trouble.'

Logan continued to stare Gillespie down as DC Neish hovered a finger over the recording button.

'Interview suspended at nine-thirty-four PM. DCI Logan leaving the room,' Tyler said, and then he pushed down on the button and the recording stopped with a click.

'Bring us a coffee when you come back, will you?' Gillespie asked. 'Milk and two. And not that shit from the machine.'

Logan stopped at the door but didn't look back. 'Coffee. Right,' he said. 'I'll see what I can do.'

And then, he left the interview room and let the door swing closed behind him.

## Chapter 15

Jinkies was installed behind his desk, staking his rightful claim to the seat, when Logan entered. The Chief Inspector was tapping a pen against a pile of paperwork, and his teeth were digging into his bottom lip hard enough to leave a temporary mark in the flesh.

'You wanted to see me, Hugh?' Logan said, delivering the question almost like an accusation. He indicated the corridor with a tilt of his head. 'Not sure if you noticed, but I was kind of in the middle of something back there.'

'I noticed. Oh, I noticed. Close the door,' the Chief Inspector said. He waited until the door clicked into place before ejecting a furious, 'What the hell do you think you're playing at?'

Logan's shoulders stiffened and went back. He felt his chest expanding, but while the body was able, the mind was not willing. It had been a long day. He was in no mood for a fight.

'Interviewing a suspect, Hugh,' he said, keeping his tone level. 'I know it's probably been a while, but I thought you'd still be able to recognise it if you saw it.'

'And he's a suspect, is he? Sandy Gillespie? You've got evidence that ties him to your investigation, have you?'

'He was outside the victim's house for several hours the day his body was discovered,' Logan said. It was wafer-thin, but he said it confidently, like it was beyond questioning.

Jinkies, unfortunately, saw it very differently.

'You were asking him about dog shit, Jack!' he said. 'You brought him in on a jumped-up charge that should've been a spot fine. It's ridiculous. Unacceptable. Completely unacceptable.'

Logan shrugged. 'Well, that depends on your point of view,' he said. His gaze gave the Chief Inspector a quick once over. Jinkies was dressed in his civvies. Scruffy ones, at that. He'd come in for this, specially. He'd rushed in to pull Logan out of that interview and to put a stop to it. 'You seem very invested in Mr Gillespie's situation, Hugh. Friend of yours, is he?'

Jinkies sneered. 'No, he is not. What he is, *Jack*, is a major suspect in an ongoing CID investigation. An investigation which your little dog shit stunt is at risk of jeopardising.'

Logan groaned inwardly but remained impassive on the outside. 'The drugs thing?'

'Yes, Jack. As you so rightly say, "the drugs thing",' Jinkies retorted. 'We've got a net around the whole Gillespie family right now, and it has taken us a long time to manoeuvre it into position. That net is going to close on them in the very near future. Our dominoes are all in a row, but if they get a clue—a snifter—that we're after them, then those dominoes fall over, and we're down the snake all the way back to square one.'

'Pretty sure that's no' how dominoes works,' Logan remarked. 'I mean, it's been a long time since I've played, but—'

'You think this is funny, Jack?' Jinkies demanded, leaning forward in his chair. He prodded the desk with a fingertip. 'Thousands of hours have gone into building this case. Resources brought in from all over the country. We're trying to bring down one of the key suppliers of illicit substances to the whole of the Highlands here. To the whole of the north of Scotland, in fact. One of the big boys. And you're going to blow it all over... over some *dog shit*?'

'You know as well as I do that he's not here about the shite, Hugh,' Logan said, still managing to keep his voice steady. He didn't want to give the other man the satisfaction of seeing him annoyed. Especially when, Logan hated to admit, Jinkies was in the right. 'He's here about the murder of a young man. A father.'

'A murder you can't remotely connect him to!'

Logan puffed out his cheeks and gave a grunt of acknowledgement. 'Look. I didn't know. About the investigation. We didn't see anything about it.'

It wasn't an apology, but it was as close to one as he could muster.

'The Gillespies have a lot of influence locally. We're keeping it low-key, for fear it gets out and gets back to them,' Jinkies said. 'Which is why I told you—'

'You've got a leak?' Logan asked. The Chief Inspector ignored him.

'Which is why I told you, way back when you first came here for the missing boy case, that you need to go through me. You can't just go running around like you own the place like... like...'

He waved a hand, trying to conjure up a name.

'Like *Magnum, P.I.* There are procedures, Jack. There's a pecking order, and I'm at the top.'

Jinkies raised the same hand and indicated a range of different heights. 'There's me, bit down, you, bit down, everyone else. Stick to that. Keep that in mind at all times, and it'll prevent this sort of situation from happening again, won't it?'

The Chief Inspector sat back and smiled. It was a smile so intensely patronising that Logan had to physically plant his feet to stop himself lunging for the bastard.

'Next time you're going to do something like this, think, "What would Hugh do?" And, if you don't know the answer to that question, by all means, just go right ahead and ask. Like I say, my door is always open.'

–

The door to the interview room buzzed, then was thrown open. Logan entered, carefully carrying two cups of coffee, each with a chocolate digestive balanced on the saucer.

Gillespie smacked his lips together and grinned. 'About time,' he said, then his smile fell away as Logan set the cups down, one in front of Tyler, the other in front of his own empty chair.

The chair legs scraped on the floor as he pulled it out and sat down. He went back to holding Gillespie's gaze as he took a wee bite of the digestive, then slurped a glug of coffee to wash it down.

'Cheers, boss,' Tyler said, raising his own cup in toast.

'No bother, son. I got us the good stuff,' Logan replied. 'No' that shite from the machine.'

Tyler's finger moved over to the button that would start the recording, but Logan blocked it. 'We've decided to let you go, Mr Gillespie.'

Across the table, Sandy snorted. 'Oh. *Decided*, did you? Were fucking told to, more like. What's the matter, someone higher-up give you a smack on the end of your cock?'

Logan and Tyler's eyes met. The DC shrugged. 'New one on me, boss.'

'I mean, I've heard of a slap on the wrist,' Logan remarked.

Gillespie scowled at them, then stabbed a finger in the direction of the door. 'So, I can go, then, yeah?'

'You can,' Logan confirmed. He waited until Gillespie had moved to stand before finishing the sentence. 'Once we issue you with your Fixed Penalties.'

Across the table, Gillespie's face darkened.

Tyler drew a breath in through his teeth. 'That's going to mount up.'

'We're not going to pursue all of the alleged instances, obviously,' Logan said, and a look of relief flitted across Gillespie's face. He took immense pleasure in stamping on it. 'Just the ones we have photograph evidence for.'

Logan turned to Tyler. 'How many is that, Detective Constable?'

'Oh, not sure, boss. I'll have to look through. Thirty-odd, maybe?'

The DCI winced. He wasn't subtle about it. 'Wow. You're right,' he said, shooting an almost apologetic look at the man on the other side of the table. 'That *is* going to mount up, isn't it?'

# Chapter 16

Hannah Randall was sitting on the end of the bed, gazing down at a pair of Brodie's dirty socks on the floor, when she heard the crack. It was low and muted, like something falling off a high shelf onto a linoleum floor. An unremarkable enough sound, but in the otherwise silent house, it made her breath catch somewhere at the back of her throat.

She listened, unmoving, her blood whooshing through her veins, her heart beating a staccato rhythm inside her ribcage. *Ba-dum. Ba-dum. Ba-dum.*

Twenty seconds passed. A minute. The house remained silent, and her breath emerged as a shaky gasp of fear, relief, and everything else between.

Getting up from the bed, she crossed to the window and peered outside, where the glow of the street lights did their best to push back against the gathering darkness. Everything looked normal enough. No cars she didn't recognise. Nobody hanging around. The same old street in the same old town, in a world that was never going to be the same again.

She turned back to the socks and, for a moment, considered picking them up like she'd done a hundred times before. Hannah thought about gathering his dirty washing, and putting away the stack of clean clothes he'd left balanced precariously on the edge of the chest of drawers.

That spot was where his clothes generally lived until either he'd worked his way through the pile, picking out what he was wearing that day, or Hannah had given up and put it all into drawers for him. They'd laugh about it sometimes, argue at others. She knew not to push it too far, though. He loved her—God, he loved her, and he never stopped telling her that—but his temper wasn't always easy to control.

That didn't matter now, though. Today, she wanted those clothes to perch there forever.

If she put them away—or worse, got rid of them—then it was over. If she put them away, he was gone.

One of his T-shirts was draped over the end of the bed, all creases and food stains. She picked it up, slowly and cautiously, like it was some rare and ancient artifact, then brought it to her face and sniffed. Smelled him. Breathed him in.

Grief hit her again then, a sucker-punch that made her slide down off the bed and onto the floor, still gripping the dirty T-shirt. What was she going to do? What would she say to Carrie? How would she explain to her daughter that her daddy was gone, and was never coming back?

She sat there for a while, alternating between sobbing and pulling herself together, going round and around in circles. After each teary outburst, she'd chastise herself, tell herself she had to get up, be strong, for Carrie's sake, as much as her own.

And then, the thought of her daughter and the days, weeks, months, and years that lay ahead would bring the tears again. She'd bury her face in the T-shirt then, and let the sobs take hold.

Hannah was on the fourth or fifth cycle of crying and self-recrimination when she heard the creak. The first sound she'd thought she'd heard had been downstairs. A concern, but a distant one.

This sound, though, had been closer. Upstairs, on the landing.

Right outside the bedroom door.

She checked her pockets for her phone, then remembered she'd left it downstairs after talking to her mum and dad. She could picture it on the windowsill in the living room, fully charged, but completely useless.

Leaning on the bed, Hannah quietly got to her feet. She had almost made it when the door flew open, and the room erupted into movement and noise. She saw a black balaclava, dark eyes glaring out through the holes, then the glow of the streetlights reflected off a knife blade.

Hannah tried to scream, but her chest had constricted and her throat had gone tight, and the sound that escaped was barely a gargle. A gloved hand clamped over her mouth and the world lurched until she was on the bed, the weight of her attacker pressing down on her, pinning her.

From downstairs, there came a series of loud bangs and crashes. She barely heard them. Didn't care. The hand on her face forced her harder against the mattress. The weight of the man's knee on her leg sent shockwaves of pain through her until they eventually escaped through her nose as a whimper.

The eyes blazed down at her through the balaclava. The man's voice, when it came, was raw with anger.

'What did he do with it?' he screamed at her, flecks of saliva hitting her face through the knitted material. He shook her violently, driving her harder against the bed. '*What did he do with our stuff?*'

# Chapter 17

'Right, there've been a few developments in the last...'
Logan glanced at his watch, then gave it a shake. '...Christ
knows. Wee while. It's important we're all up to speed
with the latest.'

He stood on one side of a desk, leaning forward, his big
hands gripping the edges like it was a lectern. Ben and the
rest of the team sat on the other side, at least one of them
doing his best to stifle a yawn.

'And yes, I'm aware it's late, Detective Constable,' he
remarked. 'I'll try not to keep us all too much longer.'

'Sorry, boss,' Tyler said, forcing his eyes wider and
sitting up straight in his chair. 'Go on.'

Logan motioned to DS McQuarrie, who handed
around a small stack of printouts. 'Caitlyn's got a summary
of the pathology report. The full report is in your email
inbox. What we have of it at the moment. Toxicology
is still to come, and we're waiting for DNA testing from
the lab bods, too. I want you to read the full thing before
tomorrow morning.'

Once they'd been given a copy, Tyler and Hamza
flicked the report open. Ben, who'd already been through
it, didn't bother.

'So, headline news is that he was murdered,' said Logan.
'He sustained two deep puncture wounds in the stomach
and bowel. They'd have killed him in a matter of minutes,

but it seems the actual cause of death was from asphyxiation. He was buried alive, during which he inhaled the gritty substance found in his lungs.'

'Page two,' Caitlyn told the detective constables, and they both turned the page in near-perfect unison.

Tyler winced at the photograph of Brodie's injuries. Hamza said nothing but instinctively moved a hand down to his own stomach.

'And we're sure that didn't kill him?' Hamza asked. 'Looks like a fatal injury to me.'

'Aye, well, it would've been, had he not suffocated before the injuries or blood loss could do the job. Although, as you say, it would've only been a matter of time.'

Ben cleared his throat. 'You probably don't need me to tell you what the wounds make me think of, Jack.'

Logan shook his head, his mouth becoming small and tight as his lips drew together. 'No.'

'The truck,' Ben said.

'Aye. I know.'

Tyler glanced around at the others. 'What truck?' His gaze tick-tocked between the two older men. 'Care to fill us in?'

'No' really,' Ben confessed. 'But aye. I suppose we should.'

And so, they did. Ben launched hesitantly into the explanation, but when he started to struggle to recall the details—either due to his advancing years or, more likely, through a sense of self-preservation—Logan took over.

They'd hunted the truck in question for days. It had come from the continent, delivering some unspecified cargo to a company in Glasgow. A random check had flagged it up before it left France, and while an initial search had turned up empty, it had niggled the powers-that-be enough that they'd put out a call for it to be pulled over once it reached the UK.

Somehow, they lost track of it. Somehow, despite all the manpower and technology at their disposal, they lost track of it.

The driver, they found. Eventually. It took the big boys two days to track him down. When he was eventually found in a Costa Coffee in East Kilbride, the then Detective Inspector Logan and DS Forde had found themselves with the job of questioning him, to try to find out what had happened to the truck.

'Did you find it?' Tyler asked. 'Did he talk?'

'Eventually,' said Ben, taking up the story again. 'We guilt-tripped him, basically. Got him to spill the location.'

'There was a false wall,' Logan said. 'Up the back. When the truck was fully loaded, it would've been impossible to see. Someone had emptied it by the time we turned up. Or, mostly emptied it, anyway.'

He chewed his bottom lip, thrust his hands into the pockets of his trousers, then looked down at the floor.

'There were people. In the hidden compartment. From Syria.'

'How many?' asked Hamza.

'Eight or nine,' Ben told him.

'Nine,' said Logan. 'Five men, three women, and one girl. Aged six. We think. We never found out for sure.'

'Dehydration?' Caitlyn guessed.

'No. No, not dehydration. Usually a good bet, but no,' Logan said. He was still looking down at the floor with his hands in his pockets, and did a little shuffle on the spot like he was physically unable to stand still. 'Someone cut them open. Toxicology reports showed one of the men had a lethally high dose of heroin in his system. Bag must've burst. He died a full day before any of the others.'

'Jesus,' Tyler muttered.

'The girl was the last to go,' said Ben. 'She watched what happened to the rest. They *made* her watch. 'Course, we didn't know that at the time.' He raised his head a fraction. His eyes met Ben's, just fleetingly. 'But we got it out of them. Eventually.'

'So, they were illegally bringing in immigrants loaded up with heroin?' Hamza asked. There was a flatness to his voice—a resigned acceptance that suggested he was saddened but not in the least bit shocked by the story. 'And then, once they had them in the country—'

'They cut it out of them. Aye,' Logan confirmed. 'Had the truck not been flagged, if the driver hadn't been questioned, the bastards behind it might've waited. Let nature take its course. But, with the heat on, they had to move fast. They had to get them out the quickest way possible.'

There was a hush as they all considered this. Tyler's eyes reluctantly returned to the photograph of Brodie Welsh's exposed innards.

'And what? We reckon that's what happened here, boss?'

Logan took his hands from his pockets, flexed his fingers, then shrugged. 'He travelled a lot. At present, we still don't know who his employer is, and his house was being watched earlier today by someone considered a prime suspect in an ongoing sizeable drugs investigation.'

'Likely, then,' Caitlyn remarked.

'We can't get a conviction on "likely". It's a solid line for us to look into,' Logan replied, not yet fully committing to the theory.

'Trips were a cover. He brought something back, swallowed it...'

'Or shoved it up his arse,' Tyler interjected.

'He's hardly going to shove it all the way up into his lower intestine, is he?' Hamza said. 'What did he use, a broom handle?'

'Well, no, but he did have bruising around the rectum,' Tyler pointed out. He grinned triumphantly. 'Top of page three. I skipped ahead.'

Hamza flicked the page, looked briefly irritated, then continued. 'Right. Well. So, if we assume he's a courier, and fails to drop off with the next man in the chain—'

'Or woman,' Tyler said. He glanced at Caitlyn and gave a disappointed shake of his head. 'Sexism.'

'You know what I mean,' Hamza said. 'The next link in the chain. Male, female, transgender, gender fluid. Whoever they are. He doesn't make the delivery, so they come looking for it.'

Caitlyn nodded. 'Take him out into the middle of nowhere, cut him open, but find nothing there, so they bury him.' She looked across the desk to where Logan stood. 'It's plausible, sir.'

'Last part's no' quite right,' said Logan. 'He was moved after death, but otherwise it isn't bad. Plausible, like you say.'

Tyler sat back, crossed his arms, and eyeballed the sneering mugshot pinned to the Big Board. 'Gillespie, you think?'

'Too early to say for sure,' Logan replied. 'But, if what CID are saying is right and he's as big a player as they reckon, then he's got to be worth a flutter.'

He flicked a look at the mugshot. 'Didn't strike me as the brightest, though.'

'He knew all the legal stuff, boss,' Tyler reminded him.

'Aye, but so do you,' Ben pointed out. 'That's no' exactly saying much.'

'Doesn't take a PhD to hack someone's guts open, sir,' Caitlyn said.

'True,' Logan conceded. He stole another glance at the mugshot, then shook his head and turned back to the rest of the team. 'Either way, Jinkies has made it very clear that he's off-limits for now.'

'Since when did you listen to Jinkies, boss?' Tyler asked.

Logan sighed. 'Generally speaking, I don't. But this is one of those rare occasions when he's right. We should've checked if he was under investigation. It's a big case, with the potential to take some right bad bastards off the streets. We don't bring Gillespie back in without good reason. Something more solid than dog shite.'

'No pun intended,' Tyler said. He grinned until the deadpan look from Logan wiped it clean off his face. 'Sorry, boss.'

Ben took a look at the clock, then it was his turn to fight back a yawn.

'Aye. That'll do us for tonight,' Logan said. 'We're not wrapping this up any time soon, so no point us all wandering about like half-shut knives. Did we get a hotel sorted?'

'Premier Inn, sir,' Hamza said, as he and the others got to their feet. 'We're all booked in. They're not doing breakfast, though. Restaurant's being refitted, so we'll have to eat somewhere else.'

'Fine. I think there's somewhere just up the road. By Farmfoods. Grab something there on the way in.'

Ben paused with his jacket half on. 'You're coming, Jack?'

Logan rasped a hand across the lower half of his face. 'I'm going to hang on here a bit.' He indicated the board with a look. 'See if inspiration strikes.'

Ben lifted the DCI's coat from the table it had been dropped onto earlier. 'Like you say, no point us wandering around like half-shut knives.' He held the coat out. 'Go and rest. You look like shite. More than usual, I mean.'

'Besides, the restaurant's shut, but the pub's open, boss,' Tyler said.

The awkward silence that followed made him realise his mistake. His grin became a flash of shock, then a clumsy series of aimless mouth movements that somehow managed to form words. 'I mean… I'm sure they do soft drinks… you know, if you don't…'

Logan took his coat from Ben. 'Aye. I'm sure they do, son,' he said, throwing the DC a lifeline. 'And for that, you're getting the first round.'

Tyler conceded that this was more than fair, and headed for the door with Hamza and Caitlyn.

'It's by the Morrison's,' Hamza said. 'There's a McDonald's next to it, too.'

'Maccy Ds!' Tyler cheered, and then they left the Incident Room and set off along the corridor.

In the silence that followed, Logan didn't even have to look at Ben to know what he was thinking.

'No. I'm not going to stand you up. I'll be there.'

Ben grunted. 'I've heard that before,' he said, pulling on his jacket and fixing the collar. 'If you're not there in twenty minutes, I'm sending Uniform to find you.'

'I'd be worried, if I thought that lot could find their arses with both hands,' Logan said. He gave his friend a nod. 'I'll be there. It'll be... you know...'

'Good?' Ben guessed.

A frown troubled Logan's brow. 'I wouldn't go that far. What's between "OK" and "bearable"? Is there a word for that?'

'Aye. "Marriage",' Ben said. He stopped by the door, took a look around the Incident Room, then fixed Logan with a stern glare. 'Twenty minutes. I mean it, Jack.'

'I'll be right out. Honest,' Logan said, making a show of putting an arm into a coat sleeve. 'See? I'm already on route. I'll just grab my phone and be right there.'

Ben nodded. 'What are you having?'

Logan blew out his cheeks. 'Morgans and Coke?'

'Right you are,' said Ben, opening the door. 'I'll get them to hold the Morgans.'

He was gone before Logan could argue. Not that he would have. Not that there would have been much point, even if he'd wanted to. Ben was more a guardian of Logan's sobriety than Logan himself could ever be. Much as he hated to admit it, he'd never have made it off the stuff without the older man's help.

Then again, without his influence, he might never have started. Not to the extent he did, anyway. Ben knew it, too. Probably why he'd been trying to make up for it ever since.

Logan had his coat on and was just taking what he told himself was a final quick look at the Big Board when a phone rang at one of the desks.

It took him a few moments to figure out which of the five phones in the Incident Room was responsible for the ringing, and it—predictably—cut off just as he reached it.

He prodded at a couple of the buttons on either side of the display, hoping to bring up the number that had been calling. Just as he hit on a menu option that looked promising, another phone rang behind him and two desks over.

Logan reached it more quickly. His fingers had touched the handset when it rang off. He brought it to his ear, anyway, to be sure.

'Hello?'

He heard the eager purr of a dial tone, ready and waiting to serve. He clicked the phone back into the receiver.

Brr-brr.

This one came from Ben's desk. Before Logan could even start to turn, it stopped, and was replaced almost immediately by the sound of Tyler's phone.

'What the hell is this now?'

Logan didn't bother grabbing for the phone. He stared it down, instead. It lasted three rings, then cut out halfway through the fourth and was replaced by an expectant hush, like the whole station was holding its breath, waiting to see what would happen next.

Another phone rang, further away this time. Logan had almost been expecting this one. It was muted by the door of the private office up at the back of the room. The office that was usually the domain of the person leading whatever investigation had set up shop in the Incident Room that week.

Logan's office.

It kept ringing as he approached the smaller room, grew louder when he opened the door.

He had time to read the single word that filled the display. *Unknown.*

The ringing continued right up until he lifted the handset from its cradle. He was on full alert when he spoke into the electronic void.

'Who is this?'

He said nothing more and just listened for a reply, the phone cradled between his shoulder and his ear as his hands grabbed for a pen and a notepad.

At first, the only response was the faint hissing of the open line. It was intriguing. Intoxicating, almost, tempting him to speak again.

He resisted.

He waited.

And then, there it was, the faintest suggestion of someone on the other end. Not a word. Not even a sound, really. Barely a breath. Barely anything.

But something.

Someone.

He resisted.

He waited.

The voice that emerged seemed amiable enough. Friendly, even.

'How's Vanessa, Jack?' it asked.

Logan's stomach knotted, processing the question before his brain could catch up. He had only just begun to form the first syllable of what would've been an extremely expletive-filled sentence when the line went dead.

He was out of the office in three big strides and storming out of the Incident Room in half a dozen more.

Out in the corridor, a uniformed sergeant jumped in fright at the sight of him. Logan recognised him as the one from the car park at Glen Coe. The sheep-lifter.

Great.

'Sorry, sir. Wasn't expecting to see you there,' he said, pulling the bottom of his jacket down and then smoothing the front. 'Thought you'd all gone home. I heard the phones ringing, so I thought I'd better check everything was—'

'I need to know who was calling those lines, Sergeant…' Logan clicked his fingers.

'Jaffray.'

'Jaffray. I need you to do a trace on that call.'

Sergeant Jaffray's smile remained fixed, but his eyes crept uncertainly in the direction of the Incident Room door. 'Er…'

'Not you personally, necessarily,' Logan told him. 'Call someone in, if you need to. Find out if it's possible to get a number.'

It wasn't. He knew that. Not unless the caller was very sloppy, or Logan's usual luck had miraculously changed for the better.

Neither of those things would be the case. He'd put money on it. But, still. Worth a try.

'Get them out of their bed, if you have to,' he instructed. 'I want to know by the morning who was calling, and heads will roll if I don't. Heads will be trundling up and down this corridor like fucking bowling balls. You won't be able to move for the bastards. Is that clear, Sergeant…?'

'Jaffray.'

'Is that clear, Sergeant Jaffray?'

'Yes, sir. No problem, sir. I'm sure…' The sergeant's eyes flicked from side to side as if searching for a name. '*Someone* will be able to figure it out.'

Logan shot the uniformed officer something that looked like a smile but was, in reality, a rather stark warning.

'Aye. Let's hope so, son,' he said. 'Let's hope so.'

And then, with a final glance in the direction of the Incident Room, he buried his hands in his coat pockets and headed out into the cold, dark Highland night.

# Chapter 18

The hotel bar was almost empty when Logan turned up, the arrival of the detectives having more than doubled the number of punters in the place.

Even if it had been busy, Logan reckoned it would've remained a pretty soulless affair. It was one of those generic bar/restaurants attached to the Premier Inn, and looked like an identikit version of every other one he'd ever been in.

It was fine in one way, in that you always knew what you were going to get. The problem was that what you were going to get was going to be a largely forgettable experience where the drinks were expensive, the craic was shite, and the air smelled faintly of disappointment.

There was a sharp whistle, followed by an 'Over here, boss!'

Logan muttered under his breath and proceeded across the bar to the only occupied table in the place, where Tyler was beckoning him over with a wave.

'Thanks for the heads-up there, Detective Constable,' Logan said. 'Almost didn't spot you in amongst all this...' He gestured around them. '...fuck all.'

'No bother, boss,' Tyler said, either missing the sarcasm or deliberately ignoring it. Logan wasn't sure which of these possibilities annoyed him more, so decided not to dwell on it.

A pint of a dark brown liquid was lifted from one side of the table and deposited in front of him with a clunk. 'Pint of Coke,' Ben told him. 'Well, it's Pepsi, but next best thing. And they only do diet, because of the sugar tax.'

Logan regarded the glass with something akin to contempt, then sat down at the empty chair that the drink had been placed in front of.

'Great. Thanks.'

'Oh, and the ice machine's broken, so it might not be very cold.'

'Jesus Christ,' Logan muttered. 'Anything else wrong with it? Did you all take turns gobbing in it, too?'

'No. But, missed opportunity there, right enough,' Ben replied. 'I'll bear it in mind for next time.'

Hamza and Caitlyn shuffled their own chairs aside a few inches, making room for the DCI to shrug off his coat. Hamza was drinking something that might have been alcoholic, but might equally have been just orange juice.

DC Khaled had once told Logan that he was a practising Muslim, but had admitted that he wasn't practising very hard. He'd demonstrated a vague preference for halal food in the past, but had also jumped on the odd bacon roll without stopping to ask questions, so Logan wasn't sure which direction the wind was blowing when it came to alcohol, and didn't really like to ask.

He had no such doubts about Caitlyn. She was sitting on his right, already a third of the way through a large glass of red, and had a look in her eye that suggested it would be the first of many.

Coppers drinking to forget, or to numb some unspoken pain was not unusual. Logan didn't think that's what was happening with Caitlyn, though. She swirled the drink around in her glass, half-smiling as if the red-purple liquid amused her in some way.

She'd been acting oddly, lately. She was different. Not in a way that made her any less excellent an officer, she was just... more animated, maybe. Less severe. He wasn't yet sure if he approved or disapproved. The jury was still out.

He looked along the table. Tyler, predictably, was on a pint. Stella, Logan assumed. Tennent's, maybe. Nothing too inventive, anyway. He raised it in the DCI's direction when he caught him looking. 'Cheers, boss.'

'Hold your horses, son, that's no' your job,' Ben said. He looked around at the assembly of polis. 'This, by my reckoning, is the first night out we've ever had. All of us together, I mean.'

'It's not exactly a night out,' Logan said.

'You know what I mean,' Ben said, dismissing the objection with a wave. He nodded down at Logan's glass. 'So. Toast.'

The others all took hold of their glasses. Tyler cupped one hand at the side of his mouth and bellowed, 'Speeeeech!' until the guy behind the bar shot the table a dirty look.

'All right, all right,' Logan sighed. He wrapped a finger and thumb around the top of the glass until they met at the other side, thought for a moment, then raised the Coke over the centre of the table. 'To the bad bastards and the mad bastards. Without whom, we'd all be out of work.'

The team echoed the toast back at him, then took a gulp of their drinks. All but Caitlyn smacked their lips together and made identical appreciative 'aaaah' noises, before setting the glasses down again.

'That was emotional stuff, sir,' Caitlyn said. 'Really touching.'

'Heartfelt,' Hamza agreed, grinning.

'You should be flattered,' Ben chimed in. 'Last toast I heard him give started with, 'You're a shower of useless bastards,' and ended with, 'Get back to bloody work,' so, compared to that, this one was practically a tearjerker.'

Logan took a gulp of his Coke, then flicked his gaze in the direction of the front door. 'You got a minute, Ben?'

Ben sipped at the amber liquid in his glass. His lips drew back over his gums as if recoiling from the stuff, then he nodded. 'Aye,' he said. Standing, he motioned towards the door. 'After you.'

—

'Vanessa?'

'Aye,' Logan confirmed.

'*Your* Vanessa?'

'Well, I mean, I don't know. He didn't specify, but I'm assuming so. I don't know any other Vanessa. Not that I can remember, anyway. Think there might have been one in my class in Primary Five, but I have my doubts he'll have been referring to her.'

'Have you phoned her?'

Logan looked out across the hotel car park, the road, train tracks, and buildings beyond, and up to where the dark outline of Ben Nevis was imprinted against the night sky. He couldn't see the mountain, exactly, but he could tell it was there by the way it subtly altered the texture of the darkness.

'No,' he said, with a shake of his head. 'Not yet.'

'*No?*' Ben spluttered. He gawped at the DCI in disbelief. 'You get a call like that, and you haven't rung her to let her know?'

The dog-end of an abandoned cigarette was smouldering on the path between them. Logan ground it out under a heel.

'I thought maybe—'

'I'm no' phoning her,' Ben interjected. 'You can get that idea right out of your head for a start.'

'It'll be easier coming from you,' Logan insisted.

'Aye, easier for you, not for me. Or her, for that matter,' Ben said. He caught Logan's dubious look. 'Aye, well. But still, no.'

'Maybe it's fine,' Logan sighed. 'Maybe I shouldn't even be worrying her about it.'

Ben glanced back into the pub and lowered his voice a fraction. 'If someone's playing silly buggers, Jack, she needs to know about it.'

'Not someone,' Logan said. He was still gazing up at the black-on-black outline of Ben Nevis, his hands thrust deep down in his pockets. 'Petrie.'

'Aye. Well. Whoever,' Ben said, quickly glossing over that particular detail. 'She needs to know, and she needs to hear it from you. If you think it's a serious threat, she might even need Uniform round there, keeping an eye on her.'

Logan snorted, picturing his ex-wife's reaction to being put under police protection. 'There wasn't a threat. Not really,' he said. 'She was just… mentioned. That was all. In passing. It's probably not even worth bothering her with, to be—'

The expression on Ben's face stopped him short. Logan might be the superior officer, but he knew this particular point wasn't up for debate. He had to phone her. Of course, he did. He should've done it as soon as her name had been mentioned on the call.

But it had been three years. Three years since the last conversation. Three years since the last argument. Three years since she'd told him she never wanted to see him again, and he'd assured her he was only too happy to oblige.

Three blissful, torturous years without her in his life.

Three years that would end the moment he dialled her number and heard her voice.

'Christ's sake,' Logan muttered. He reached into his pocket and slapped Ben with a look so sour it could've curdled milk. 'Has anyone ever told you what a smug-faced wee bastard you look when you're right?'

'Aye, you. Regularly. And the wife, of course,' Ben replied. 'Although, she assures me that I'm never right, so it's no' really an issue.'

He gave Logan a pat on the back and pulled open the bar's front door. The sound of Tyler swearing at the quiz machine rolled out from within.

'What? No way it was C! It was definitely D!'

'The wee cartoon quizmaster would beg to differ,' Hamza replied, then both voices were drowned out by a sad 'wah-wah-wah-waaaah' from the machine.

'Good luck, Jack,' Ben said. 'And assuming she lets you get a word in edgeways, say hello from me.'

With a final smile of encouragement, DI Forde headed inside, leaving Logan alone with his phone on the bar's front step.

# Chapter 19

The phone reception was pretty poor when Logan finally summoned the courage to make the call. The reception he received from his ex-wife wasn't exactly stellar, either.

Her voice had been light and airy when she'd first answered, like she'd just heard the punchline to a joke right before the phone had rung. For a moment, Logan had been reminded of better days and better times, back before everything had gone wrong between them. Back before the arguments and the divorce.

Back before Owen Petrie.

The levity had lasted right up until the point he'd opened his mouth.

'Hello. Vanessa?'

The tone had changed in an instant. The laughter had died in her throat, and the voice that came back to him down the line may as well have been accompanied by a blast of cold air.

'Yes. What? What's wrong?'

No small talk, then. Thank Christ.

'Yes. No. It's Jack,' Vanessa said, her voice muted as she turned away to speak to someone else in the room. 'Yes, *that* Jack. No. I won't be long.'

'Sorry, did I catch you at a bad time?'

'It was a great time, actually,' Vanessa said. 'And then you called.'

Logan chuckled mirthlessly. 'Right. Aye.'

'What is it, Jack? What do you want?'

'It's… I mean, it's probably nothing,' Logan said.

Down the line, Vanessa tutted. 'Then why the hell are you—'

'*Probably* nothing. But I thought it was worth calling to give you a heads up. Just in case it turns out to be, well, something.'

There was a silence. It wasn't lengthy, but it was full and heavy with expectation.

'Are you ill?' Vanessa asked. Her voice was still cold and unwelcoming, but there was a faint thawing around the edges of it that almost made Logan wish that he was.

'No. No, nothing like that,' he said. 'It's just… God. OK. Earlier tonight, I had a phone call. Your name was mentioned.'

Vanessa sighed irritably. 'And?'

'The call was…' Logan glanced back into the bar, then out into the darkness, searching for the right words. 'Well, it was threatening in nature.'

'Threatening? Threatening who? Threatening me?'

'Aye. No. I mean, not threatening, exactly. Not, you know, overtly. But it was implied.'

'How was it implied? Implied by who? What are you talking about, Jack?'

The door to the bar opened. A member of the kitchen staff emerged, barely old enough to shave. He drew a cigarette from his pack and was patting himself down looking for a lighter when Logan caught his eye.

'I'm in the middle of a conversation here,' the DCI said.

'That's fine. Doesn't bother me,' the lad replied. 'Do you have a light?'

'No, I don't. And it does bother me, so going to piss off somewhere else?'

He could hear murmuring down the line, as Vanessa spoke to whoever else was in the room. Whatever she was saying was too low for Logan to hear, and he resisted the urge to even try.

'I'm on my break,' the lad protested.

'Good. I'm delighted for you. But can you maybe be on your break over there?' Logan asked, pointing to the main hotel entrance further along the side of the building.

The lad looked Logan up and down, as if sizing up his chances. The door squeaked as he came to the conclusion that the odds were very much not in his favour.

'Need a lighter, anyway,' he said, in a valiant attempt to save face.

Logan waited until the door had closed, before returning his attention to the call. 'Sorry about—'

'Threatening how?' Vanessa demanded. 'What are you talking about, Jack? Fucking explain. Am I in danger?'

'No. No, you're fine. As far as I know.'

He pulled the phone from his ear as Vanessa's voice screeched out of the speaker. '*As far as you know*?'

Logan pinched the bridge of his nose, exhaled slowly, then just launched into it. 'I've been getting calls lately. Silence, mostly. Heavy breathing. Coming through on numbers that nobody should even have. Christ, numbers I don't even know. Tonight, he spoke. He mentioned you.'

'Mentioned me how? What did he say?'

'He said, "How's Vanessa?"'

There was a moment of expectant silence.

'What? That's it? "How's Vanessa?" That's all?'

There was a beeping from the handset. For a moment, Logan thought she'd hung up on him, but a quick glance at the screen told him the station was calling. He swiped the icon that he hoped would send it to voicemail.

'Jack?'

'Sorry, aye. That's all.'

'How is that threatening?' Vanessa asked.

Logan shifted uncomfortably. Here we go.

'It wasn't so much what was said as who said it,' he told her.

He should've continued then, but the knowledge of what would follow stopped him, and she was forced to drag it out of him.

'OK, then. So, who said it?'

The phone beeped again. He ignored it.

'It was... I mean, we're still looking into it, but I'm pretty sure... I'm almost certain...'

'Jesus. Spit it out, Jack. Who was it?'

'Petrie,' Logan said. 'It was... it was Owen Petrie.'

If her voice had been cold before, it became an Arctic Tundra now. She snorted, but there was no humour in it. It was a snort of derision. Of mockery. Of incredulous disbelief.

'Right. Yes. I mean, of course, it was,' Vanessa said. 'Who else could it have been?'

'I know what you're thinking,' Logan said. She jumped on it immediately.

'Do you, Jack? Do you really? Do you honestly believe you have the first fucking clue what I'm thinking right now?' she spat.

The voice in the room with her said something soothing, but she brushed it off. 'No, he needs to hear it,' she said, her voice momentarily muted again as she turned away, before returning more forceful than before. 'Maddie told me. Phoned me earlier. Told me you'd stood her up, then told me why. You want to know what she said?'

Logan didn't. She told him, anyway.

'She said, "I'm such an idiot, Mum. When am I going to learn?" That's what she said, Jack. That's what our daughter said. About you. She gave you a chance. I warned her. I warned her time and time again, but she gave you another chance, and you go and throw it back in her face. You keep hurting her, over and over, and she lets you. She lets you cause her pain.'

Logan shook his head. 'No. It wasn't like that. I didn't mean for... the traffic was—'

'Why are you telling me? Why am I sitting here listening to you trying to explain yourself? Again. I'm long past that, Jack. I'm years past that.'

The volume of her voice had been steadily rising for the last few seconds. She stopped, took a breath to compose herself, and then continued in a much more measured tone.

'If your mystery caller gets back to you and asks how I am again, tell him I'm fine, all right? Tell him I'm better than I've been in a long, long time.'

Logan winced at that one, although he knew her well enough to have seen it coming.

'Aye. Well. Just be careful, all right? If you see anyone acting strangely, or you don't feel safe, call—'

'Goodbye, Jack,' Vanessa said, cutting him short.

The line went dead. A moment later, the beeping of the 'call waiting' notification transitioned into a full-on ring. Logan's thumb stabbed down on the green button and brought the phone to his ear.

'DCI Logan. What is it?' he demanded.

He listened to the officer on the other end of the line, his eyes slowly widening.

'Right. Aye,' he said, once the message had been conveyed. He pushed open the door to the bar, and the ka-thunk-ka-thunk of the quiz machine spewing out pound coins emerged into the cool night air. 'Tell them I'm on my way.'

# Chapter 20

The lights of three squad cars and an ambulance licked across the front of Hannah Randall's house, illuminating the cracks in the upstairs curtains of all the neighbouring windows. Logan shot looks of condemnation up at a few of them, and watched them twitch in response.

Hamza, who it turned out had indeed been drinking orange juice, stepped out of the passenger side of the car, gave his stomach a reassuring pat as if to let it know the ordeal of the drive was finally over, then scurried after the DCI as he approached the front gate.

A Uniform was stationed just outside the garden. Logan didn't recognise him, but the constable nodded curtly and opened the gate as he and Hamza approached, then quickly closed it over again behind them.

Another officer opened the door before Logan could knock. He vaguely recalled seeing this one around at the Fort William Station at some point, although he couldn't even guess at her name.

'She's in the living room, sir,' the constable said, her voice low and sombre.

'How is she?'

'Not great. Her mum's with her, keeping her calm. Paramedics are here, too, checking her over.'

Logan leaned back and looked up at the house, then around at all the flashing lights. 'Can we get these turned off? It's like a circus out here.'

'I can sort that out,' Hamza said, backtracking along the path. He gave the officer guarding the gate a tap on the shoulder, then they both chose a different car and headed for it.

Logan glanced past the uniformed officer into the house beyond. 'She ready to talk, do you think?'

The female officer made a non-committal sort of noise. 'She's been talking to us. Not getting much useful out of her, mind you, though the mother's been a help. Maybe you'll have more luck, sir.'

'Aye,' said Logan, stepping past her. 'Maybe.'

Hannah looked up just briefly when Logan entered the living room. She was sitting in the middle of the couch, a woman in her fifties—her mother, presumably—pressed right up against her on the left-hand side, their hands clasped together on Hannah's leg.

Mrs Randall had the look of a crofter about her, with a reddish complexion and hair that looked like it had been ignored for some time. Her eyes were crinkled with a lifetime of laughter lines, and her teeth were so artificially white they could only have been a recently fitted set of NHS falsers.

'Who are you?' she demanded, glaring at Logan. She seemed to almost puff herself up until he produced his warrant card, at which point she returned to the job of squeezing her daughter's hand, and gently rubbing her back.

Across the room, the paramedics were in the process of packing up their kit. A bandage had been applied to one of Hannah's hands, and there were a couple of plasters on the side of her face, presumably to cover up smaller cuts.

What hadn't been covered was the purple-blue patch around her right eye that signalled the beginnings of what would soon be some not-insignificant bruising.

'Miss Randall. I came as soon as I heard,' Logan told her. He gestured to the armchair across from the couch, being sure to avoid the Ikea monstrosity beside it, this time. 'Do you mind?'

Hannah gave the briefest shake of her head, and Logan lowered himself onto the chair just as Hamza entered the room.

'It's fine. He's with me. That's Detective Constable Hamza Khaled. I'm Detective Chief Inspector Logan. Jack,' he told the older woman. 'You must be Hannah's mother.'

'Sandra. Yes,' she confirmed. 'Hello.'

'Hi, Sandra,' Logan began, then the paramedics jumped in before the conversation could get fully underway.

'Sorry. We're just heading off,' said the older of the two. He was almost Logan's height, but barely half as broad, with hair that was just clinging on and no more. He smiled down at Hannah. 'You sure we can't take you in and get you checked over?'

Hannah shook her head firmly. 'No. Thank you. I'm fine,' she said, although there was a shake in her voice that told Logan she was nothing of the kind.

The older paramedic gave her a thumbs-up. 'Right, well, if anything starts to feel worse, or you change your mind, just call the number on the card we gave you, all right? They'll get you straight in.'

Hannah glanced around, as if trying to remember what she'd done with the card, then nodded. 'Right. Thank you.'

'I'll see you out,' said Sandra, starting to rise. The paramedic waved her back before she could wrestle her way out of the couch's cushions.

'You're fine. We'll figure it out.' He smiled at mother and daughter, gave Logan a look that may have been a warning, then led his younger companion out into the hall.

Logan waited until he'd heard the front door close before saying a word. 'You've been in the wars,' he observed.

'Aye, you can say that again,' Sandra said. 'Bastards.'

'Who?' Logan asked. 'Who did this? What happened?'

Out of the corner of his eye, he saw Hamza flicking open a notebook, and heard the click of a ballpoint pen being extended with the push of a button.

Hannah huffed out a shaky breath and ran a hand through her hair. Beside her, her mother gave her a nudge.

'Well, go on, then,' Sandra urged. 'Tell them.'

'I've already told the woman. In the uniform. I don't know who he was,' Hannah said.

'He?' Hamza asked.

Hannah raised her eyes to meet his. 'Yes.'

'It's just… "bastards", you said,' Hamza replied, directing that part at Sandra. 'Plural.'

'I only saw one of them,' Hannah explained. 'But I heard someone down here.'

'You should see the mess they've made of the kitchen,' Sandra interjected. 'Trashed it, they have. And now we're not allowed to go in it because your lot have got it taped off. Can't even get a cup of tea.'

Logan's gaze went to the two half-empty mugs on the coffee table between him and the women. Sandra bristled like she was being accused of something.

'The policewoman had one of the neighbours make us some,' she explained. 'But, still.'

Hannah groaned, frustration furrowing her forehead. 'Forget the tea, Mum. They need to block off the kitchen so they can look for, I don't know. Evidence, or whatever.' She looked across the table at Logan. 'Right?'

'Aye. Aye, that's right,' he confirmed. 'Hopefully, it won't take too long.'

He sat back in the chair, relaxing a little in the hope it rubbed off on both women.

'Can you talk me through what happened, Miss Randall? I know you've gone over it, but it'd be useful for me to hear it from you in your own words.'

It was Sandra who jumped in to fill the momentary silence that followed. 'She was upstairs—'

'In her own words,' Logan reiterated. He smiled unconvincingly at the older woman. 'Please.'

Sandra's lips drew into a tight pucker. She clicked her tongue against the roof of her mouth once, but said nothing. Logan could see the strain on her face from the effort this was taking and almost felt bad about it.

Almost.

'Miss Randall?' he urged, his voice as soft and coaxing as it was ever likely to get. 'Tell me what happened.'

Hannah adjusted herself on the couch, shrugged, then adjusted herself again. She opened and closed her mouth half a dozen times during this process, as if about to start speaking, but then deciding against it at the last possible moment.

Finally, she found the words she'd been looking for.

'I was upstairs. In me and Brodie's... in the bedroom. I was just sitting there. Thinking, you know? About, well, everything. I heard a noise.'

'What kind of noise?' Logan asked.

'I don't know. A noise. Like a thump. Movement. Down here,' Hannah told him. 'I didn't think it was anything at first. Just sort of ignored it. But then I heard it again, and then he was... I just turned around and saw him there, and...'

She drew in air in a big, shaky breath. Her hands shook as they squeezed her mother's. Tears trailed down both cheeks as if racing one another.

'He was just there. Out of nowhere. Shouting at me. He... he had a knife. I thought, God, I thought he was going to kill me.'

Her voice grew fainter as her throat constricted. Sandra squeezed in closer and reached an arm across her daughter's shoulders, then pulled her in tight.

'It's OK. You're OK,' she soothed. 'You're fine now.'

'Did you get a look at him?' Logan asked.

Hannah shook her head. 'He had a mask on.'

'What sort of mask?' asked Hamza, his pen scratching notes onto the pad.

'Like a ski mask. Or like, you know the SAS? A black mask with eyeholes and a mouth.'

'A balaclava?'

Hannah gave the DC a nod. 'Yeah. That's it. A balaclava. I couldn't see much, and it all happened so quickly.'

'Anything else you can tell us about him?' Logan asked. 'Tall? Short? Fat? Thin? Anything at all.'

Hannah glanced up at the ceiling like she might find the answers written there somewhere. 'No. Just, I don't know, normal. He felt...' She gulped in a few steadying breaths. 'He felt heavy, though. When he was on top of me.'

Beside her, Sandra's eyes widened while the rest of her face appeared to crumple. 'On top of you? He didn't...? You weren't...?'

Hannah quickly dismissed the concern with a shake of her head. 'No. Nothing like that. He just... he pinned me down. Put his knee on my leg and slapped me a couple of times.'

'Oh, thank God,' Sandra exhaled. 'I mean, obviously that's bad enough, but it's not... at least he didn't...'

She left it there. There was no need to clarify.

'It must've been a very traumatic experience for you,' Logan said. 'And I appreciate how hard it must be to talk about it so soon after. Especially with everything else you're dealing with.'

Hannah made a non-committal sort of noise and didn't meet his eye.

'You said he was shouting at you. What was it he said?'

A frown. A pause that went on just a fraction of a second too long for Logan's liking.

'He wanted money. Jewellery. Stuff like that. He asked if I had a safe.'

'She doesn't,' Sandra said. 'Do you, love?'

Hannah shook her head. 'No. Nothing like that. I told him I didn't have any money, and he...' She gestured to the bruise forming around her eye socket. 'Well.'

'It must've been terrifying. You're doing great,' Logan told her. 'Did he say anything else? Anything that might connect him to Brodie?'

Hannah looked straight at him and shook her head. 'No. Nothing. Nothing like that. Just… he just wanted money.'

'Right. Yes. I understand. Just thought it was worth asking, considering the timing,' Logan said. He regarded the room around them. 'Did they get anything?'

Hannah's eyes retraced the route Logan's had taken around the living room. 'I don't… I'm not sure. Not that I've noticed.'

'No cash? Cards? Your purse or wallet?' Logan gestured to the thin gold chain around the young woman's neck. 'Jewellery?'

Hannah's hand went to the necklace as if trying too late to hide it. 'They ran when my mum appeared.'

'I couldn't stand the thought of her here on her own. Fulton stayed home with the wee one, and I came over. Thank God I did.'

Logan shifted his attention to Sandra. 'Did you see them? The intruders?'

'No, but I certainly heard them,' she said. 'They went out the back as I came in the front. Through the kitchen. Right racket they made.'

'Any idea how many of them there were?'

Sandra shook her head. 'Two. Three, maybe. Could be four. I don't know. Too much clattering for one.'

Hamza chimed in with a question of his own. He pointed to Hannah with the end of his pen. 'And you were still upstairs at that point?'

'Yes. In the bedroom.'

'But the man who attacked you had left?'

Hannah picked at a ragged piece of skin next to her thumbnail for a few seconds, before confirming. 'Yeah. He ran out when he heard the front gate. He panicked.'

Logan picked up the DC's baton and ran with it.

'Fast, then,' he said. When he saw the blank looks on the faces of both mother and daughter, he clarified. 'To get out of the room, down the stairs, and out through the kitchen before you got the door open, Mrs Randall. He'd need to be nippy.'

'Like I said, he was panicking,' Hannah replied.

'Aye. Fear can certainly spur people on, right enough,' Logan said. He jabbed a thumb back over his shoulder. 'I think you've given us enough for now. You should get some rest. We'll no doubt need to talk to you again tomorrow.'

'She'll be staying with us,' Sandra said. 'No way she's staying here.'

'Aye. I was going to suggest that. We'll need to search the place.' He offered Hannah a thin-lipped smile. 'Evidence. Like you say.'

–

The doors of the Volvo clunked closed. Hamza had barely settled into his seat when Logan spoke.

'Thoughts?'

Hamza looked back in the direction of the house as he reached for his belt. 'Well—'

'I don't buy it,' Logan said, before Hamza could finish replying. 'She's lying.'

'About the attack?'

'No. About the reason for it. When I asked her if it was about Brodie, she looked me right in the eye when she said no. That's the one and only time she's done that since I met her earlier. And for it to happen on the same day her partner's body turns up? Hell of a coincidence.'

'Suppose so, aye.'

'And, for a gang of burglars, they didn't take very much, did they? By which I mean they took hee-haw.'

Hamza shrugged. 'The mother arriving could've scared them off.'

'Maybe, but who turns over a kitchen looking for stuff to rob? Big telly in the living room. MacBook on the shelf under the coffee table. Handbag down the side of the chair I was sitting in. But what, they decide to make a grab for the Rice Krispies?'

He jabbed the button that started the engine. The Volvo spluttered into life as if caught off-guard, then settled into its usual throaty purr.

'She was literally wearing a gold necklace. She says the guy was on top of her. Even if he did panic—which I don't believe—he's come that far, he'd have at least grabbed that.'

'You don't think they ran?' Hamza asked. 'The mother said she heard them.'

Logan adjusted his rearview mirror. 'I'm not saying she didn't hear them. I'm saying it didn't happen like Hannah Randall says it did. How could it? He's upstairs, pinning her down, waving his knife about, making demands. He hears the gate opening, and then what? He turns into Billy Whizz?'

Hamza's brow creased. 'Who's Billy Whizz?'

'What do you mean, *who's Billy Whizz*?' Logan demanded, turning fully in his seat so he was facing the younger officer. 'Billy Whizz. The Beano.'

'Oh. Right. Aye. I never read The Beano,' Hamza said.

From the expression that settled on his face, Logan seemed to be even more incredulous about this than he was about Hannah Randall's story.

'What do you mean you never read The Beano? Who the hell didn't read The Beano?'

Hamza raised his eyebrows and puffed out his cheeks. 'It's a cultural thing, sir. Religious reasons.'

Logan winced like he'd just taken a low blow. 'Oh. Right,' he said, clearing his throat. 'I see.'

Hamza grinned. 'Nah, not really, sir. I just thought it was shite.'

Logan tutted.

'Aye. Hilarious. But, my point stands. There's no way some big knife-wielding mad bastard is going to be so freaked out by the sound of a gate opening that he'll sprint down the stairs, through the hall, into the kitchen, and out the back before the mother makes it up the path. What, was she crawling?'

He pointed through the windscreen at the entrance to the garden. 'Also, did you notice on the way out?'

'Notice what, sir?'

'That gate doesn't make a sound. Latch is knackered. It doesn't even shut properly.'

'So...' Hamza glanced down at his notebook. 'What happened?'

'That, I don't know,' Logan said. He jammed the gear-stick into reverse, and the road behind him was illumin-ated in a pale white glow. 'But I'm going to find out.'

'Give us something to do, I suppose,' Hamza said. His eyebrows raised. 'Oh! I got the bank statement from Fulton Randall. Showing the wages going in.'

'And?'

'Doesn't give us much more detail. I'm going to chase up the bank tomorrow,' Hamza said. 'But I will say that whoever the employer is, they're not skint. Nine grand a month he was on.'

Logan whistled through his teeth. 'That's no' buttons. What was he doing, running the place?'

'Beats me, sir. I just know that I'm in the wrong line of work.'

'Aye. You and me both,' Logan agreed. 'Get on the bank first thing. Find the company and let's speak to them.'

'Will do, sir. First thing.'

Logan eased the Volvo back from the squad car in front, then indicated to pull away from the kerb. Just before he did, he took a moment to fire a disparaging look in Hamza's direction.

'*Who's Billy Whizz?*' He tutted. 'I mean, *honestly.*'

## Chapter 21

Logan stood in the queue at the counter of J.J.'s Cafe, idly eyeing up a slab of Oreo brownie while he waited for the woman in front to finish placing her order.

Ben had volunteered to do the breakfast run on the way into the office, but Logan felt it was probably his shout after trying to coerce the DI into making the call to Vanessa the night before.

He opened the notes app on his phone as the woman in front moved off to take a seat, then he shuffled up until he was standing by the till.

'What can I get for you?' asked a man in a black apron. It had the word 'BOSS' emblazoned across the front in bold white letters, with 'My Wife is the' written above it in a much smaller font.

Logan read off the list that Ben had dictated to him, briefly considered adding on one of the brownies, then decided against it for the sake of his waistline. 'And no butter on one of the bacon,' he added, as the man behind the counter jotted down the order. 'One of them's a fussy bastard.'

Once he'd handed over the cash and been assured the order would be ready in a few minutes, Logan stepped aside to let the next customer in line through.

The place wasn't particularly big, but it was busy. Of the eight or nine tables, six of them were occupied, and there were a couple of others waiting for takeaway orders like himself.

A dark-haired woman was struggling to reach a high shelf on the wall along from the serving counter. A couple of angular wooden clocks were perched there, price tags hanging from the hands.

'You need a hand?' he asked, reaching up for one of the clocks. The woman smiled gratefully as he passed it to her.

'Thank you,' she said. She turned it over in her hands, examining its triangular frame.

'Ugly bugger of a thing, if you ask me,' Logan said. 'I wouldn't waste my money if I were you.'

The woman's smile became significantly less convincing. 'I made them,' she said.

The ground, to Logan's dismay, failed to open beneath him and swallow him up.

'Did you?' he asked. 'Well done.'

The woman took it in good grace, and her smile returned. 'Thanks. That's very kind of you. You want one?'

'I've nowhere to put it,' Logan said, although he could definitely think of a few places the things probably belonged. 'Otherwise, I'd be all over it.'

The woman laughed drily, then gestured to the top shelf. 'Get us that one down, will you? People aren't seeing them up there. I need to move them somewhere more visible.'

Logan almost suggested that perhaps people *were* seeing them and that therein lay the problem, but elected not to.

He handed her the second clock, and she set both down on a lower shelf that was just below Logan's head height, and just above her own.

'There. They can be found now.'

Logan regarded the newly positioned clocks, but he was distracted. Something the woman had said nagged at him. Niggled away. What was it?

'That's you,' said the man in the apron, presenting Logan with a white carrier bag that bulged with the boxes it contained.

'Right. Thanks. Aye,' Logan said, taking the bag. He looked back at the woman and her clocks, and something clicked into place.

'Good call on moving them,' he remarked.

She stepped back, hands on her hips, considering the clocks' new placement. 'Think they look better there?' she asked.

Logan answered honestly. 'No' really,' he said. 'But then, what do I know?'

And with that, he was out the door.

–

Once the rolls were divvied up and the tea was in hand, Logan perched on the edge of a desk by the Big Board and let them in on his theory.

'We know the body was moved. Buried somewhere, then shifted,' he said. 'I assumed that was because whoever killed Brodie was worried he'd be discovered, but given how and where he was reburied, that doesn't make sense.'

He looked across the faces of the others, their mouths all moving as they chomped through breakfast.

'I don't think the killer was worried the body would be found. I think he was worried it wouldn't be.'

Ben stopped chewing. 'What?' he said through the side of his mouth. 'You think they wanted it to be discovered?'

'I do,' Logan confirmed. 'I think he was moved there deliberately so someone would find him. Shallow grave, close to a well-used walking path. It's the only thing that makes sense.'

He took a bite of his own roll. Square sausage. Tattie scone. Wee daud of brown sauce. He wasn't a believer in Heaven, but if he had been, that roll would've been close to the perfect definition of it.

He thought some more as he chewed, then swallowed.

'The rescue. What became of that in the end?' he wondered. 'Did they find who they were looking for?'

Caitlyn washed down a mouthful of bacon with a gulp of tea. 'No, sir. Called off. They think it might've been a hoax. I checked up last night.'

'A hoax? Bastards,' Ben remarked, and all but Logan nodded their agreement.

'I'm not convinced.'

Ben raised his bushy eyebrows in surprise. 'You're joking. Wasting time and money, putting people's lives at risk. They're definitely bastards, Jack.'

'No, I mean I'm not so sure it was a hoax,' the DCI said.

Caitlyn appeared confused. 'Mountain Rescue team seem pretty confident, sir,' she said. 'You think there's someone out there?'

'No. What I'm saying is, I don't think it was just someone on the wind-up. I think it was deliberate. I think whoever made the call was trying to draw attention to the body.'

Hamza rubbed his tongue across his teeth, sweeping up the debris of his breakfast butty. 'Had to be the killer, then. Or someone who knew about it, anyway.'

'See if you can find out any details of the call. If they rang nine-nine-nine there should be a recording. Get me a copy.'

'Can I give that to Tyler, sir?' Hamza asked. 'I've got the bank thing to follow-up, and he's doing bugger all.'

DC Neish tried to protest, but his mouth was too full, and all he could do was extend a middle finger in the other DC's direction.

'I don't care who does it, just get it done,' Logan said.

'Oh, speaking of calls,' Ben said, perking up in his seat. 'A uniform sergeant was in here looking for you when you were getting the rolls in. Said he got someone to look into the phones last night, like you asked.'

Logan's legs stiffened, lifting him off the desk and into a standing position. 'And?'

Ben picked up a notebook, squinted, then held it at arm's length as he tried to read what it said.

'Did they find anything?' Logan demanded.

'Hang on. They found...' Ben shook his head. 'No. Nothing at all. No caller details.'

Logan sighed. He hadn't been expecting a result, but he'd been quietly hoping for one, all the same. He should've known better, though. Whoever was calling him was clever. Or, at the very least, not a complete idiot.

To be able to find out the direct-line numbers of all the phones in the office meant they were well-connected, too. Someone in the station, most likely.

Someone sitting in this very room?

No. He dismissed that last thought.

For now.

But Jinkies clearly had concerns about security, or he wouldn't have been taking all the precautions with the drug investigation. Probably worth having a word with him about it at some point. See if he had any suspects.

Something to look forward to.

'Why would the killer want the body found?' DS McQuarrie asked, jolting Logan back to the matter at hand. 'What would they stand to gain from that?'

'Glory, maybe?' Tyler suggested, finally managing to swallow down his food. 'Notoriety.'

'That can happen,' Ben said. 'Murderer kills someone, knows he should keep it secret, but also wants people to know what he's done, if not necessarily that he was the one who did it.'

Logan couldn't argue. He'd seen that often enough, read about it in old case files even more often. It was fairly standard for certain types of killer.

And yet, this felt different.

'I'm not sure it's that,' he said, pacing back and forth in front of the board. 'It doesn't feel like that sort of murder. I don't think anyone's in it for the glory.'

'What then? A warning to someone?' Hamza guessed.

'Guilty conscience?' Tyler suggested.

'Could be,' Logan conceded. 'Could be something else, too. We'll keep on it. Everyone had a chance to take a proper look over the full pathology report I emailed out?'

Most of them confirmed that they had. Tyler surreptitiously clicked to open his email inbox, and then side-eyed the screen.

'For those of you who haven't,' Logan said, spotting the DC's woeful attempt at subtlety. 'It confirms much of what we went over yesterday. Cause of death was not the dirty great knife wounds to the victim's torso, but the inhalation of a gritty, sand-like substance that we're working to identify. Teeth were smashed in and fingertips were removed in order, I think we can safely assume, to hinder identification.'

'We caught a break there,' Ben remarked.

'Not that big a deal, though, is it?' Tyler ventured, drawing his eyes away from the report on his screen. 'Town this size, local guy, he'd have been matched up in no time.'

DS McQuarrie nodded her agreement. 'That's another thing about the body disposal I don't get. Why keep him local? If you're trying to hide his identity, why dump him so close to home?'

'Feels pretty half-arsed,' said Tyler.

'Maybe it's whole-arsed,' Hamza suggested, which drew a confused look from the others for a number of reasons. 'I mean, maybe it was all planned. If they moved him so he'd be found, maybe they wanted him identified, too.'

'So, what's with the teeth and the fingers, then?' Tyler asked.

Ben looked up from his notes. 'We're assuming it was the killer who moved him. What if it wasn't? We know he was originally buried elsewhere, then moved. Maybe the original site was miles away. Maybe someone found out about the murder and wanted to, I don't know, bring it to our attention.'

'Could've picked up the phone,' said Hamza. 'Bit extreme to dig up a body and move it.'

'True,' Ben agreed. He looked down at his notes again. 'But it makes as much sense as anything else we've come up with.'

'We'll know more once we figure out where the first burial site was. Hopefully, we'll get a match on the sand in his lungs,' Logan said. 'I'll also draw your attention to the abdominal wounds. Any more thoughts on those?'

Tyler scrolled his mouse wheel, then grimaced at the sight of the pictures. 'Looks painful,' he remarked.

'Any thoughts other than the blindingly obvious?' Logan asked. 'And yes, it would've been painful. Done while he was alive. Although, from the report, it looks like he was lying on his back at the time, so it's possible he was unconscious.'

'Let's hope so, for his sake,' said Ben.

'Got to be the drugs thing, hasn't it, sir?' Caitlyn said. 'Too precise to be anything else.'

Logan agreed. 'They're surprisingly precise, actually. Whoever did this has likely done it before. Knows their way around the human body, anyway.'

Ben's chair creaked as he sat back. 'So, just so's we're all on the same page—we've got a young man, a recreational drug user himself, who travels extensively overseas for an employer we haven't been able to identify. He takes home... how much did you say, Hamza?'

'Nine grand a month.'

'Fucking hell!' Tyler spluttered. 'What was he, the Queen?'

'He takes home nine grand a month, and shortly after returning from one of these trips, he was murdered and had his insides cut open,' Ben concluded.

'And there's the rectal damage mentioned on the post-mortem,' Tyler announced, launching into his theory from the previous night. 'Could've been shoving stuff up his arse, too.'

'However he was doing it, presumably whoever killed him knew about it and took whatever he was carrying,' said Caitlyn.

'Maybe,' said Logan. 'Or maybe they didn't find it, and so they went to his house last night to look for it. I don't believe they were there to rob the place, regardless of what Hannah Randall might be trying to claim.'

'That all fits,' Caitlyn said.

'Should we bring her in?' Ben asked.

'Bagsy no' being the one to drive down and pick her up, boss,' Tyler said, visibly paling at the very thought of it.

Logan remembered his tea, which was sitting on the desk beside him, going cold. He picked it up and forced down an unpleasant gulp that made his lips draw back over his teeth. It was vile stuff, cold. Still, you didn't waste a cup of tea. It just wasn't done.

'Aye. Let's bring her in,' Logan said. 'But quietly. She's not a suspect, but she's also not telling us the truth. I want to know why, and I want her to tell us everything she knows about what Brodie was up to. Hamza, get on to the bank, see what you can find before she gets here.'

'On it, sir,' DC Khaled said, rolling his chair closer to his workstation.

'Tyler, get me that recording of the nine-nine-nine call.'

DC Neish blinked a couple of times.

'The mountain rescue callout. Keep up.'

'Oh. Right. Aye. Sorry, boss. Will do. You want me to finish reading the pathology report first?'

Logan tutted. 'No, I want you to get me the recording now, and I want you to finish reading the pathology report last night, when I sent you the bloody thing. Can you do that for me?'

Tyler regarded his screen, then arranged his features into a nonplussed sort of smile. 'Probably not that last part, boss,' he admitted. He reached for his phone. 'But, I'll see what I can do.'

# Chapter 22

Jinkies appeared momentarily surprised to see Logan in his doorway, but it quickly gave way to a look of smug satisfaction.

'Ah. Jack. Two tics,' he said, turning his attention back to the printed document he had been reading. He made a show of absorbing the contents, complete with nods, tongue-clicks, and the occasional utterances of, 'Uh-uh,' and, 'Mm-hm,' plus the occasional, 'Well, well.'

Logan endured it for as long as he could, which was almost a full twenty seconds, and a personal best.

'Sorry to interrupt, Hugh,' he said, stepping fully into the room.

The apology was partly sincere. He deeply regretted that he had to come and speak to Chief Inspector Pickering, but the fact he was interrupting the other man's working day offered at least some small consolation.

Jinkies made a show of sighing and setting down the paperwork he'd been reading, before clasping his hands on the desk and smiling benevolently.

'What is it I can do for you, Jack?' he asked.

'I'm going to need to look at the drug case CID's building. Against the Gillespies.'

Jinkies drew breath in sharply through his teeth. 'Hm. Well. As I explained, Jack, we're playing that one close to our chest.'

'Because you can't trust your own guys. Aye, you said. But, here's the thing, Hugh,' Logan said. He stepped in closer and leaned down with both hands on the desk. 'I don't care. I think that investigation may have a bearing on mine, so I'm going to need to see what you've gathered.'

'Let me think about it.'

'Fine.' Logan shrugged, checked his watch, then crossed his arms and waited. 'Take your time.'

Jinkies ejected a single mirthless, 'Ha,' then rolled his tongue around inside his mouth as he considered the request.

Finally, he leaned forward so he was hunched over his own clasped hands. 'Look, Jack. Between you and me? Fine. If it was just you, fine. Ben, even. I know you're both solid. I know I can count on you.'

He motioned to the door and lowered his voice. 'But the others? I don't know them. I don't know how... reliable they are.'

'If they weren't reliable they wouldn't be on my team.'

Jinkies raised an eyebrow. 'So, you trust them?'

'With my life.'

A smile tugged at the corner of the Chief Inspector's mouth. 'Did I detect a wee hesitation there, Jack?'

Logan uncrossed his arms. 'We're going to need to see the case you're building, Hugh,' he reiterated, his voice dropping into a warning growl. 'So, you can send it through to Ben, or—'

'Or what, Jack? You'll beat it out of me?' asked Jinkies, smirking.

'Or I'll ask Superintendent Hoon to put in a personal request for it,' Logan continued. 'And we both know that he won't just beat it out of you, he'll tear it out through your arse.'

Jinkies unclasped his hands and drummed them lightly on the desktop. 'Fine. Fine. I'll give you the summary. If you need to drill into the specific detail, we can discuss that at a later stage.'

It wasn't a complete surrender, but it was the best Logan was likely to get without expending a lot more energy than he was willing to. The summary would be enough to be going on with. For now.

'Fine. See that Ben gets it,' he said, turning for the door.

'Oh, Jack. Before you shoot off...'

Logan stopped and half-turned back. 'What?'

'If you're planning to bring in any of the Gillespies, run it by me first. I'd like to observe.'

Logan sucked in his bottom lip, then spat it out. 'Tell you what, Hugh,' he said. 'Let me think about it.'

–

'Got some information from the bank, sir. They won't give us much without a court order, but I was able to sweet-talk them a bit,' Hamza reported, catching up with the DCI outside Jinkies' office. 'I think the lassie liked the accent.'

'What, *your* accent?' Logan asked, struggling to hide his surprise. Hamza spoke with a thick Aberdonian twang. As accents went, it was not one that was renowned for its charm or sex appeal.

'Aye. Fit's wrang wi' my accent, like?' Hamza asked, really playing it up. 'It's a richt bonnie een this een, ken?'

Logan couldn't help but chuckle. 'Aye. Music to the ears. What did you get?'

'She told me it was a virtual bank account. Like, with some online service.'

'Like Paypal or something?'

'Similar, aye. Kind of. Actually, it's more like the Anti-Paypal. Sendfunds. Based in Central America and backed with Russian money. Or vice versa. No-one really seems to know which, but it doesn't really matter, because anyone can set it up from anywhere.'

'Any connection to Oswatt?' Logan asked. 'Beyond the name being on the transfer?'

'No, sir. And the name—Oswatt, I mean—is only in the reference field of the transfer. It was the bank woman who pointed it out. The sender's name is just a string of letters and numbers.'

Logan tutted. 'How did we not notice that before?'

'Dunno, sir. Just saw the name we were looking for and didn't think too much more about it. Sorry.'

Logan shook his head. 'Wasn't just you. We all did it. So, the account might not even be in the name 'Oswatt,' then?'

Hamza shook his head. 'Almost certainly not, sir. The thing about Sendfunds is it's not meant for businesses. It's for individuals. Their big gimmick is that they allow anonymous account opening, and encrypt all transactions. Think it started on the Dark Web before moving main-stream. CIA and FBI in the States are both—' He made quote marks in the air with his fingers. '—'Warning of the dangers' of it.'

'Untraceable global financial transactions. Aye, I can see why they'd be shiteing their kecks,' Logan said. 'Terrorist's dream come true.'

'And the rest,' Hamza agreed. 'It's pretty clever, though, sir, I have to say. You pay in via Western Union to account details that change every twenty-four hours, and the money appears in your own account a day or two later. From there it's all completely untraceable. Scammers' Paradise.'

Logan was beginning to get a picture of the service. It wasn't one that fit with a legitimate offshore energy company. 'So, the payments were coming from a personal account?'

'I think so, sir, aye. Not a hundred percent, but that's what it sounded like. She did say, though, that getting more information from Sendfunds is likely to be impossible. Like I say, secrecy is their big thing, and what with them being based abroad... Well, I don't fancy our chances.'

Logan agreed. A Central American online banking service was likely to be a brick wall too thick to even bother beating their heads against.

'Focus on the bank here. Get a request in and get Ben to escalate it. See if they can decipher that string of letters and numbers you mentioned. I want the name on the account that's been sending him the money,' Logan instructed. 'And chance your arm with the helpdesk again. Did you ask for a supervisor last time?'

Hamza confirmed that he had.

'Don't. Easier to put the wind up the front line staff. All we need is the name. Charm them, intimidate them, do whatever you can to get it. All right?'

'I'll see what I can do, sir.'

Logan clapped Hamza on the back. 'Good lad. Tyler got me that call recording yet?'

'Just waiting on it coming through, I think. He's got the transcript, but not the audio.'

He answered Logan's question before the DCI could even start to ask.

'Nothing really jumping out from the transcript. We got the call header, but the number was withheld. Audio should be through in the next few minutes, though.'

'They give a name?'

'Aye, but didn't ring any bells. Tyler's following up on it.'

'Right, good.'

The door from reception opened along the corridor. Logan turned to see Hannah Randall being escorted in by two uniformed officers. Her father, Fulton, walked beside her, an arm offered out for support that she was making no move to accept.

Her face was difficult to read. She was worried, yes, but angry, too, Logan thought. Maybe more of the latter than the former. Her eyes were red with shadowy bags hanging beneath the lower lids. She looked like she hadn't slept a wink all night.

They had that in common, at least.

'Mr Logan. Jack. What's all this about?' asked Fulton, his voice racing along the corridor ahead of the group. 'Hannah is... We're *all* very stressed and very tired. Couldn't this wait?'

Hannah looked irritated by Fulton's interjection. 'Dad. I told you. It's fine. You don't need to be here.'

'Well, I am here, Hannah. And I'm not going anywhere.'

Her eyes flicked upwards and she sighed, but voiced no further objections.

'Sorry for the inconvenience, folks,' Logan told them. 'I've just got a few questions. I'm hoping you can help clear some things up. I won't keep you any longer than absolutely necessary.'

He nudged open the door to one of the interview rooms, had a quick check inside, then motioned for them to enter. 'We'll grab a seat in here. Can I get you a drink? Tea? Coffee? I think there's some orange juice in the fridge, although I can't vouch for how long it's been knocking about in there.'

'Coffee wouldn't go amiss,' Fulton said. 'Hannah?'

Hannah shook her head.

'You sure?' Fulton pressed. 'Tea?'

'I'm fine, Dad! I just want to get this done and go.'

'Yes. Yes, of course, makes sense,' Fulton said. He smiled up at Logan. 'I'll still have a coffee, though, if it's going? Milk and one. Cream, if you have it, but milk's fine.'

Logan glanced at one of the Uniforms, who nodded and set off for the kitchen. Almost as soon as he'd turned the corner, another uniformed officer came around it. This one, Logan recognised.

'Detective Chief Inspector. Can I have a quick word?' Sergeant Jaffray asked as he arrived at the group.

He met Fulton's eye and they exchanged nods of acknowledgement, then he shot a smile at Hannah that went completely ignored.

'Of course, Sergeant,' Logan said, with just the vaguest suggestion of impatience. He asked the escorting constable to take the Randalls into the interview room and get them settled, then led Jaffray half a dozen big paces along the corridor away from the door.

'What can I do for you, Sergeant?'

'I just wanted to apologise about the phone thing, sir. I left a message for you about it. We couldn't get any information on who was calling last night.'

'Right. Aye,' Logan said. He glanced impatiently at the interview room. 'Not to worry. I was a bit stressed out last night. Thanks for trying.'

Jaffray relaxed a bit at that. 'No bother, sir. Always happy to help. If there's anything else I can do for you?'

'That's fine. Thanks,' Logan said. He started to set off along the corridor, then stopped a step or two in. 'Actually... The Randalls. You know them?'

The sergeant's smile remained fixed, but he leaned from left to right a little as he shifted his weight from one foot to the other. 'Everyone here knows Fulton,' he said. 'Through the rescue team. You soon get to know all the rescue boys, Lochaber and Glencoe.'

'And Hannah?'

That one was the sore spot, Logan thought. Jaffray's eyes went to the door, and his rocking increased for a few seconds before he fixed his feet more firmly to the floor. He cleared his throat before he spoke.

'Couple of years below me in school, sir. We're not friends or anything. She used to go out with a mate of mine, yonks back.'

Logan fixed him with a stare that bored into the sergeant like a drill. 'That it?'

Jaffray swallowed. He tried to smile, but it came out more like a grimace. 'Aye. Aye, that's it.'

Logan wasn't convinced by the other man's response and made a mental note to come back to it later.

'Right. Fair enough, then. Anything about them you think I should know?'

Jaffray put his hands on his hips and glanced at the ceiling, possibly seeking inspiration. He mulled the question over like that for a few seconds, then shook his head.

'No. Nothing I can think of. Hannah's got a kiddie. You know that?'

'Aye,' Logan confirmed. 'That relevant?'

The sergeant puffed out his cheeks. 'Um, probably not, no.'

He shot the corridor behind him a longing look. 'I suppose I'll just… If there's nothing else, sir, I'll just be…'

Logan dismissed him with a wave. 'Aye. I'm sure you've plenty to be getting on with.'

'You can say that again. Work, work, work,' Jaffray replied. 'Sometimes, I think it's never—'

'That'll be all, Sergeant,' said Logan.

Jaffray, to his credit, caught the cue to shut up, and hurriedly backed away along the corridor. He practically bowed as he retreated around the corner, and his disappearance was followed by a shout of, 'Watch it,' and a sudden yelp.

A moment later, the constable Logan had sent for coffee appeared, carrying a battered old tray with two mismatched mugs on top and what looked to be quite a disappointing plate of biscuits.

'Thanks,' Logan said. He prodded around at the biscuits—two soggy looking fig rolls and a single digestive—flared his nostrils, then took a mug in each hand. 'You're fine,' he added, dismissing the plate with a look that didn't just border on contempt, but full-on invaded it.

And then, with mugs in hand, he nudged the door to the interview room open with a knee and headed inside.

# Chapter 23

'Should I have a lawyer?' Hannah asked. She was sitting beside her dad, directly across the table from Logan, leaning back in her chair with her arms folded.

Fulton snorted out a laugh. 'A lawyer. Of course you don't need a lawyer.' He shot Logan a worried look. 'She doesn't, does she?'

'We can get you one if you like, but I'm sure it won't be necessary,' Logan said. 'You're not a suspect here, Miss Randall. Can I call you Hannah?'

She shrugged. Logan took it as her granting permission.

'You're not a suspect, Hannah. Not at the moment, anyway.'

Fulton sat up straighter in his chair. 'Not at the moment? What's that supposed to mean, "not at the moment"?' he asked. 'What are you trying to say?'

Logan took a sip of his coffee. It was the cheap stuff, and bitter. He briefly lamented dismissing the biscuits.

'We have no reason to suspect you were involved in Brodie's death, Hannah. Please, rest assured, I don't think that for a minute,' Logan told her.

This wasn't entirely true, in that he suspected everyone pretty much equally until he could prove they weren't involved, but there was nothing that set Hannah apart from anyone else at this stage.

From none of the frontrunners, anyway.

'I just want to go over what happened yesterday, and maybe clear up a couple of things that have come up. Inconsistencies, really.'

He set his mug down and indicated a button on the desk. 'I do have to record the interview, though. Standard procedure. There are also a couple of cameras in here,' he said, indicating them both with a point. 'And that's a one-way mirror. During interrogations, we usually have people sitting on the other side of the glass. This isn't an interrogation, so we don't.'

He smiled at them both in turn, his finger hovering over the button. 'Everyone OK with all that?'

Fulton looked at his daughter like he was asking her permission. She nodded, and he granted his own approval with a 'Fine. Of course. Whatever you have to do.'

Logan clicked the button, recited the usual spiel for the benefit of the tape, then forced back another sip of coffee. Fulton had taken a single gulp from his own mug, then set it down. Logan would be prepared to bet he had no intention whatsoever of going back to it.

It really was awful stuff.

'How you feeling this morning, Hannah? You get any sleep?'

'Not much,' she said. Her mouth was tight and puckered, like she was grudging every syllable it was forced to speak.

'Me neither,' Logan told her. 'Hotel beds. I hate them. I mean, it was comfy enough, but I can never nod off. See, when I'm in a hotel, it means I'm away from home, and when I'm away from home it's usually for a case and, well, the mind ticks over. Replaying stuff. Things people said.'

He set the mug down on the table with the softest of clunks.

'Things they didn't. Tick-tick-tick. Round and round, all night long.'

'Aye? Well, my fiancé was murdered, and my house was invaded by masked men with knives,' Hannah spat. 'So, sorry if I'm short on sympathy.'

'Hannah,' Fulton soothed. He smiled apologetically at the detective across the table. 'Sorry. She's just... she's upset.'

'Entirely understandable. I mean, who wouldn't be, after all you've been through? You're holding up better than most,' Logan said.

Another pause. Another sip. He regarded the young woman over the rim of the mug.

'How's the wee one? What was her name?'

'Carrie,' both Randalls said at the same time.

'Carrie. That's right. You mentioned. Have you said anything to her yet? About her dad?'

Some of the anger that had been shaping the lines of Hannah's body crumbled, becoming something more like grief. Her shoulders, which had been forced straight back, took on a forward stoop. She unfolded her arms and leaned her elbows on the table, supporting herself.

'No. Not yet.'

'There's no real rush,' Fulton said, placing a hand on his daughter's arm. 'She's used to him being away for a few weeks at a time.'

'Aye. Funny you should say that. That's one of the things I was hoping Hannah might be able to clear up for us. Brodie's trips. Specifically, where he goes, and why,' Logan said. 'The *where's* not too big a deal. We can get a list of the places he's been from his passport records. It's the *why* that really interests me, though. What's he been going abroad for?'

'Well, work, isn't it?' Fulton said. He looked from Logan to his daughter. Neither of them were looking back at him.

'Yeah. He travels for work,' Hannah said.

'Right. His work being…?'

'Offshore.'

'For Oswatt, right. French company, wasn't it?'

'Dutch,' Hannah corrected.

Logan clicked his fingers. 'Dutch. Right. Of course. Sorry.'

He clasped his hands loosely in front of him and leaned closer, confident and relaxed. 'See, the thing is, we haven't been able to get hold of anyone at Oswatt. In fact, we haven't been able to find any reference to Oswatt anywhere. And we've looked. Believe me, we've looked. But nothing. Not here, not in the Netherlands. Nowhere. Bit odd that, isn't it?'

'It's on the bank statements. Oswatt. I've seen it myself. I sent it to your man,' Fulton said.

'You're right. It's on the statement you sent. And thanks for that, by the way,' Logan said. 'But we talked to the bank. It's a virtual account from some Central American company. Not necessarily shady, but unusual for an alleged multinational energy company—who, again, we can find no record of—to be using it for their banking needs.'

He looked from one Randall to the other, before settling on the younger of the two. 'So, Hannah. Anything you'd like to tell me about Brodie's employer? Any additional information you can provide that will clear all this up?'

Hannah exploded into movement, leaning forward and throwing her hands up in the air. 'What does it matter? Who cares? He's dead. Brodie's dead. My daughter's father is *dead*! Who gives a shit who he worked for? It wasn't them that killed him, was it?'

Logan maintained his composure. 'How can you be so sure?'

Fulton ejected his second snort in as many minutes. 'Come on, what are you saying? He was murdered by an energy company?'

Logan shifted his gaze in the man's direction. 'You don't seem to get what I'm saying. As far as we can tell, there *is* no Oswatt. Brodie Welsh didn't work for an energy company, despite what appears to be a very elaborate attempt to make people believe that he did.'

His chair creaked as he shifted his weight a fraction. 'Now, if that's the case—if Brodie's job with Oswatt was some kind of cover—then that throws up a lot of important questions. Who did he work for? What was he doing?'

He fixed Hannah with one of his most probing looks. 'And who knew about it?'

There was silence in the room for a few moments, as Logan kept the pressure on. Hannah tried holding his gaze, but buckled quickly and looked down at the table. So, she did know. Maybe not everything, but some of it.

'Brodie's beyond being in any trouble now, Hannah,' he told her. 'We're not trying to point fingers, we're trying to figure out who killed him. That's the focus. That's all we want.'

'That's what we all want, Jack,' Fulton interjected. He put a hand on his daughter's back and rubbed it. 'Isn't it,

Hannah? If you know something, you have to tell them. For Carrie's sake. Tell him. Tell us.'

A tear fell on the table, leaving a tiny round puddle on the smooth wood. Hannah started to speak, but it came out as a croak. She coughed, clearing her throat, and then continued without looking up.

'He never said anything. Not really. When we got together, he just said he worked offshore. That he was away a lot. Lot of people round here work on the rigs, so I didn't think too much about it. Not to start with.'

She sniffed and wiped a sleeve across her face.

'But then, when we got engaged, I said we should set up a joint bank account. Put both our wages in. I was working at the school at the time. He wasn't keen, though. At first, anyway. Kept putting it off and putting it off. I thought he was just worried I'd run away with it all or something.

'When I got pregnant, though, I talked him into it. He agreed it was best. For the baby. So, we set it up. I got my wages paid in, but he didn't.'

Fulton frowned. 'But I saw them. On the statement.'

Hannah shot him a sideways glance. 'Not at first. I asked him about it, and he said he got paid in cash.'

'Cash?' said Logan. 'Nobody pays that amount in cash every month.'

'That's what I said,' Hannah replied. She pulled the end of her sleeve over her wrist and used it to wipe her nose. 'He got annoyed. Said I was accusing him of something. But then, after it had all calmed down—after *he'd* calmed down—he said he'd talk to the company and try to get it paid into the account.'

She shrugged. Her face was slack, her eyes dull, like she wasn't quite present in the room. 'And he did. It came in the next month, and every month since.'

'Always the same amount?' Logan asked.

Hannah nodded. 'Yeah. Why?'

'No overtime? Bonuses?'

She frowned, like this thought had never occurred to her. 'I mean, he did work overtime. He'd sometimes get called away at the last minute.'

'But no bump to the pay packet?'

'No. Not... no. Never.'

'Maybe it was...' Fulton began. His eyes searched the space in front of him, hunting for an explanation. 'He could've been on a fixed salary. Maybe the overtime wasn't paid, but covered in the normal wage. I mean, Christ, it was high enough.'

Logan agreed that this was a possibility. As someone who had put in hundreds of overtime hours without ever seeing a penny extra in his wages, he knew it wasn't uncommon.

'Can I see him?'

Hannah's question took the DCI by surprise. He should've been expecting it, of course. Been ready with an explanation as to why it wouldn't be a good idea. But the sincerity with which she asked, the big, wide, hopeful eyes, caught him on the back foot.

'Uh, aye. I mean, not right now, but maybe once all the tests have been...'

He saw her eyes well up again and her face pale, like the reality of it all had just been brought home for her once more. There, in that moment, she looked fifteen. A wee scared lassie who didn't know what to do.

'I can only imagine how hard this must be for you, Hannah,' Logan said. 'Truth be told, it might be a few days before you can see Brodie's body. Even then, I'm not sure I'd recommend it. It's your decision, of course, I can only advise, but I advise against it.'

Fulton took his daughter's hand in his. Judging by the look they shared, they'd already had this same conversation.

Hannah tried to speak, but all that emerged was a throaty wheeze. She looked to the ceiling, gulped down a few steadying breaths, then tried again.

'How did he die? Nobody's told me,' she said. 'How did he die?'

'Hannah. Sweetheart...' Fulton soothed, but she ignored him and fixed those big wide eyes on the detective across the table.

'Please. I have to know. I have a right to know. How did he die?'

Logan considered all the possible answers he could give to that question, including all the ways he might deflect it. In the end, he settled for the most direct.

'He suffocated.'

Hannah's lips thinned. Her eyes blurred. Beside her, Fulton sat up a little straighter, his eyebrows meeting in the middle.

'What? I thought they said he'd been stabbed?'

Logan glanced at Fulton just long enough to reply. 'He had. Yes. However, that wasn't the cause of death. He suffocated. Are you sure you want to hear this, Hannah?'

At the mention of her name, Hannah nodded. From the expression currently twisting the lines of her face, though, Logan doubted she was fully taking any of it in.

'Suffocated how?' Fulton asked. His hand squeezed his daughter's, the rest of him trembling at the very thought of it. 'With what?'

Logan looked between them both and shifted his weight in his chair. 'I'm not sure it's the right time to—'

'Tell us,' Hannah said. A command now, not a request. 'What happened?'

Logan let out a long sigh to signal that he thought this was a bad idea, before continuing.

'We believe Brodie may have been buried alive.'

Hannah didn't react quite the way Logan had been expecting. There were no sobs, or gasps, or cries of anguish. Instead, she went very still and very quiet, like her brain had shut down all non-essential functions so it could process this new information.

Fulton, on the other hand, physically recoiled. A noise emerged from somewhere within him, raw and primal. His bottom lip shook like a toddler with a burst balloon, and then he sat back suddenly and forcefully in his chair and clamped a hand over his mouth.

'Oh, God,' he whispered, choking back tears of his own. 'Oh, Brodie, no.'

# Chapter 24

Tyler was scrolling through a third page of search results when something icy cold was pressed against the back of his neck. He twisted in his chair, ejecting a surprisingly high-pitched 'Fuck off!' and throwing an arm out for protection.

He had expected to find Hamza standing behind him, probably pissing himself laughing. The sight that did meet him was far better.

Tyler jumped up, the cold spot on the back of his neck instantly forgotten.

'Sorry, couldn't resist,' said a young woman, holding a can of Irn Bru in one hand. From the way she said it, and the smirk on her face, she very clearly wasn't sorry in the slightest, but Tyler wasn't going to hold that against her.

'Sinead. What are you doing here?' he asked. He hesitated for a moment, overthinking it, then stepped in closer and gave her a slightly awkward hug.

She pressed the can against the back of his shirt, freezing him through the thin material.

'Argh! Quit that!' he said, although with far less venom in his voice this time.

'Sorry,' Sinead said again, arguably even less truthfully than before. 'Couldn't resist again.'

She pointed to an empty chair at the next desk over. 'Anyone sitting there?'

Tyler regarded the seat. 'Aye. The Invisible Man. We use him for undercover work.'

'His banter's still shite, you'll notice,' remarked Hamza. He was on the phone at his own desk, one hand over the mouthpiece. 'Hello, by the way.'

Sinead smiled back at the DC as she wheeled the empty chair over to Tyler's desk. 'Hi.'

Hamza took his hand off the mouthpiece, but didn't speak. From the way he bobbed his head and tapped a finger on his notepad, Sinead assumed he was listening to some catchier-than-usual hold music.

'Where's everyone else?' she asked Tyler as she sat down beside him.

'The boss is doing an interview. The others are...'

He regarded the Incident Room.

'Not here. Dunno where they've gone, actually,' he admitted, gesturing to his computer screen. 'I've been tied up with this. Trying to find someone who called in a missing climber report.'

'No joy?'

Tyler shrugged. 'Not really, no. He gives his name as Robert Smith, so searching mostly just brings up the guy from The Cure. You know? "Friday, I'm in—"'

He stopped himself from finishing the song title, smiled uncomfortably, then drew Sinead's attention to the screen again. 'He's the most famous one, obviously, but there are loads of them. I've found at least four living here in town. I've managed to speak to three of them, but can't find a phone number for the fourth.'

He gave his head a shake, then turned away from the computer. 'Anyway. What are you doing here? You're meant to be at home resting.'

'Yeah, but the thing is, it's really boring,' Sinead said. 'I've got nothing against "Loose Women", but there's only so many times you can watch it before you want to kill yourself.'

She considered this point. 'OK, maybe I do have something against "Loose Women",' she decided. 'So, yeah. I got bored, and Harris is away on his school trip for the next couple of days, so I thought I'd come down and say hello. See if you were free for lunch.'

Tyler groaned. 'I'd love to be, but...'

He indicated the screen, and then the room around them. 'Murder case, innit? All hands on deck.'

'Right. Aye. Of course,' Sinead said. 'Sorry, should've phoned ahead. Stupid.'

Brushing her hair back over an ear, she stood up, a plastic smile fixed on her face. 'I'll leave you to get on.'

'Or...' Tyler began. He took a Post-It from his desk and hastily scribbled down an address from the screen, then held it up for her to see. 'You could come with me and talk to this guy.'

Sinead sucked in her bottom lip. 'I'm not on duty. Is that allowed?'

'Fuck knows,' Tyler admitted. 'Probably not.' He tucked the address into the top pocket of his shirt and smiled at her. 'But I won't tell anyone, if you don't.'

Sinead gave a nod, then stepped aside. 'Fair enough, then. I'm in. Lead the way.'

Clicking off his screen, Tyler moved past Sinead and made for the door. Two seconds later, he yelped as an ice-cold can was pressed against the back of his neck.

'Sorry,' Sinead giggled. 'You just make it so tempting.'

DI Forde sat in the shadows on one side of the glass, half-reading Jinkies' report on the drugs investigation, and half-observing the conversation taking part in the room beyond the mirror.

It was nosiness that had brought him into the observation room, if he was being completely honest. But then, it was nosiness that had driven most of his polis career, including several of his biggest busts, so he didn't see any shame in that.

Ben flipped through a page of the report, scanned a couple of random paragraphs, then went back to earwigging on the events in the room next door.

Logan had insisted Hannah Randall wasn't a suspect, but Ben had wanted to take a look for himself. Watching her now, he reckoned Jack was probably right. If she'd killed him, she deserved an Academy Award for the performance she was putting on.

You got to know the guilty ones. You learned to pick up on all the little tics and habits that gave them away. There were dozens of them, hundreds, maybe, from the casting of an eye to the flaring of the nostrils. Usually subtle, and very easy to miss if you didn't know what you were looking for.

Hannah Randall hadn't displayed any of them.

That's not to say she wasn't hiding something—she was definitely hiding something—but had she murdered Brodie Welsh? No. Almost certainly not.

Ben turned to the next page in the report. It was dense with text, and the dim light of the room meant he'd have to squint to read it properly, even with his reading glasses on.

He'd come back to it.

Licking a finger, he turned a couple more pages until he found something marginally less trying on his eyes. It was still mostly text, but there were spaces between some of the paragraphs, at least. That sort of thing could go a long way.

Something buried in the writing on the page immediately nagged at him, but Logan had just delivered the bombshell about Brodie being buried alive, and Ben wanted to see how the Randalls reacted.

As was to be expected, both of them took it hard, albeit in their own individual ways.

Fulton was the most obviously cut up. Outwardly, at least. But Ben had seen that look on Hannah Randall's face on other people before, and was only too aware of the emotional turmoil that would be bubbling away below the surface.

His eyes returned to the page in front of him, practically of their own free will. At that first glance, something had jumped out at him. His subconscious had picked up on it, but the dominant part of his brain was struggling to find it.

He closed the report, holding the page between both thumbs, then opened it again in the hope that whatever he'd seen would appear again like magic.

It didn't. He angled the page towards the light from next door, and had just settled in to read the whole thing when he heard the door open behind him, and saw DS McQuarrie dimly reflected in the glass.

'Everything all right, Caitlyn?' he asked, turning away from the brightly-lit interview room. His eyes took a moment to adjust to the gloomier observation area, then settled on the DS.

'Fine, sir. It's just I found something that might be relevant to DCI Logan's interview. I was going to bring it to his attention, but thought I should run it by you first.'

'Sounds wise. He generally doesn't like to be interrupted unless it's...' Ben thought about where that sentence was headed, then clarified. 'Actually, he just doesn't like to be interrupted. What have you got?'

'It might be nothing, sir,' Caitlyn said. She held up a printout. 'Then again, it might be a pretty significant find.'

Ben peered at the sheet of paper over the top of his reading glasses. 'I'll swap you,' he said, offering up the report. 'See if there's anything on that page that, I don't know, jumps out.'

'That you back on the pop-up books again, sir?' Caitlyn asked, swapping documents with the DI. It wasn't great, as jokes went, but it was so rare for DS McQuarrie to make them that Ben laughed, more for encouragement than anything else.

'Make for more entertaining reading, I'm sure,' he said, smiling at her as he adjusted his glasses and considered the printout she'd given him.

The smile didn't hang around for long.

'Jesus,' he muttered. He looked back over his shoulder into the interview room, then back at the page before finishing with another 'Jee-*sus*' for good measure. 'How did we not know about this before?'

'Never followed up on, sir,' Caitlyn said, speed-reading the page of the report Ben had given her. 'No charges pressed. Everything denied.'

'I mean, aye. Fair enough. But, still an' all.'

Caitlyn nodded curtly. 'Aye, sir. Bit of an oversight somewhere.'

She turned the report back to him and jabbed a finger onto the page somewhere just below the middle. 'That what you're referring to, sir?' she asked.

Ben pulled back from the page a little and peered through his glasses and along his nose. The writing swam in the half-light, but a bit of squinting eventually brought it into focus and he blasphemed for a third time. This one was louder than the two before.

'Aye. That's it,' he said. Turning, he jabbed a finger against a button and bent in close to a microphone fixed in front of the window. 'DCI Logan,' he began, all his concerns about interrupting forgotten.

On the other side of the glass, the Randalls raised their eyes to the overhead speaker, where the voice had come from. Logan ignored it and looked straight at the mirror.

The voice hissed faintly through the intercom system. 'There's something I think you should see.'

# Chapter 25

'How do you say it? *Cor-patch*?'

Sinead tutted reproachfully and shook her head. 'Corpach,' she said, pronouncing the 'ch' as a soft sound at the back of her throat.

'Corpach,' Tyler said. 'Got it. Is that Gaelic?'

'Dunno.'

'What does it mean?'

Sinead shrugged. 'I don't know that, either.'

'"Ridiculously steep hill", maybe?' Tyler suggested, indicating the steep slope ahead of them with a nod.

He was behind the wheel of a marked police car, pulled in behind a row of parked cars, while he waited for half a dozen other vehicles to pass in the opposite direction, and was quietly dreading the hill start that awaited him once the oncoming traffic had cleared.

Once the final car had passed, he raised the clutch, depressed the accelerator, and—to Sinead's delight—stalled immediately.

'Don't,' Tyler said, seeing the glee on her face from the corner of his eye. He checked the handbrake, took the car out of gear, then started the engine again. 'Just don't.'

'I wasn't going to say a word.'

'Good. Let's keep it that way.'

With a not-inconsiderable amount of revving, Tyler drove on up the hill, muttering about not being used to the car as he growled it up the sweeping curve of the road.

'The address is up here on the right,' Sinead said, indicating a semi-detached house just ahead of them.

'There's nowhere to stop,' Tyler said, scanning for a space in the row of cars parked along the kerb.

'There's a car park further up. At the top,' Sinead said. Her voice was suddenly hesitant, like this was not necessarily the good news it might appear to be.

'OK, cool,' Tyler replied. He shot her a brief sideways glance. 'You all right?'

Sinead tugged on her seatbelt, which suddenly seemed to be too tight. 'Yeah. I just… I should've thought. When I knew we were coming up here, I should've thought.'

'Thought about what?' Tyler asked, as he pulled into an almost empty car park and nabbed himself the first available space.

Sinead raised a finger and pointed out of the DC's side window. A sign stood by an open gate, with the words: *Kilmallie Cemetery.*

'About that.'

It took Tyler a second or two to catch on.

'Shite. Your mum and dad?'

Sinead nodded, her eyes fixed on the sign. An archway of trees blocked her view of all but the first row of the graveyard's collection of headstones.

'I haven't been back since we moved to Inverness,' she said. 'I should've brought flowers.'

She let her gaze linger for a little while longer, then gave herself a shake and unclipped her belt. 'Anyway.'

By the time Tyler got out of the car, she was facing down the hill in the direction of the house they'd passed, her back turned on the cemetery. 'It's just down here,' she announced, not looking at him.

'Don't you want to...?'

'Murder investigation,' Sinead reminded him. 'All hands on deck. I can come back another time.'

'Right. Aye. Fair enough,' Tyler said. He put a hand on her arm. 'Or you could take five minutes now.'

Sinead glanced at him, then over to the graveyard entrance. 'I didn't bring flowers or anything.'

'I'm sure they won't mind,' Tyler replied. He flinched. 'On account of them presumably being nice people, I mean, not because they're... I don't mean...'

Sinead took his hand and gave it a squeeze. Her expression lightened. 'I know what you mean,' she said. 'And thank you.'

She squeezed his hand again, then interlinked their fingers. 'You sure it's OK?'

Tyler puffed out his cheeks. 'Have to meet the parents at some point, I suppose. Might as well get it out of the way.'

Despite everything, Sinead laughed as they started, hand-in-hand, up the hill. 'Aye, I suppose you're right,' she said. She bumped her shoulder against his. 'But just so you're forewarned, my dad is going to hate you.'

–

Ben and Caitlyn stood in the corridor along from the interview room, watching in silence as Logan read over the notes they'd drawn his attention to. He'd already echoed Ben's 'Jesus' a couple of times, and then elaborated on it with some quite creative swearing.

'And we're just finding out about this now? I'll murder Jinkies when I see him.'

'They didn't make any concrete link between them, sir. He's only mentioned in passing,' Caitlyn replied. 'But aye, surprising the Chief Inspector didn't bring it up.'

'Always said he was a useless bastard,' Logan remarked. 'Aye, to his face, like. No' behind his back.'

'Let's hope being a useless bastard is all it is,' Ben said. The way he checked the corridor around them and dropped his voice to a murmur made his meaning only too clear.

'You think he's on the fiddle?' Logan asked.

Ben frowned and double-checked that no one was listening in. 'I'm not saying that, Jack, no.' He tapped the report in the DCI's hands. 'But this is one hell of an oversight. I'm happy to accept that he's just inept. Or maybe he was going to tell us, but wanted to piss up around a bit first. But I think it'd be wise not to say too much in front of him until we know a bit more. That's all.'

'I'm still leaning towards "useless bastard" myself, but no harm in playing things close to our chest,' Logan agreed. 'No' like he's not doing the same with us.'

Caitlyn indicated the report with a look. 'You're going to mention them both to the suspect though, right, sir?'

'Hannah Randall isn't a suspect,' Logan replied. He tucked the paperwork under his arm, then exhaled through his nose. 'At least, not yet.'

—

'Here you go.'

Sinead turned to find DC Neish standing behind her with a bunch of flowers. It was an odd assortment—a real mish-mash of varieties, assembled with care, but very little skill. Around half of them looked fresh and new, a quarter had started to wilt, and the rest were at the stage of requiring hospice care.

'Where did you get that?' she asked him.

'I nicked them from a few different bunches,' Tyler explained. He saw the look of horror that flitted across her face. 'I just took the odd one here and there from a few of the bigger bunches, like. Nobody will notice.'

Sinead's eyes were still wide with shock, but she bit her bottom lip to stop herself smiling. 'Well, thanks. I suppose,' she said, accepting the bunch. 'And I take it back. My dad would absolutely love you.'

Crouching, she placed the flowers into the *Beloved Mum & Dad* holder that was pegged into the grass in front of the black marble headstone. 'There you go,' she whispered, adjusting the blooms in a futile attempt to make them look better. 'It's the thought that counts, right?'

She plucked a few blades of grass from the headstone, wiped a spot with her sleeve, then stood up and stepped back so she was beside Tyler.

'It must've been... I mean, I can't imagine,' the DC said.

Sinead swallowed and gave an almost imperceptible nod. For a moment, it looked like that would be her only response, but then she spoke, her words coming out slowly and hesitantly like she was having to slot them carefully into place.

'I was on duty when I got the call. I'd not long started. Back shift. I was on the speed gun on one of the straights through Glen Coe when I got the shout.'

She ground her teeth together, then clicked her tongue against the roof of her mouth.

'RTA. Two car collision. It was just up the road from where I was, so I was closest. I got there first.'

Tyler slipped his hand into hers. It felt limp and lifeless, and she showed no signs that she'd even noticed his touch.

'As soon as I saw the car, I knew. It wasn't an unusual car, either. Loads of them on the road. It could've been anyone. I told myself it wasn't them, in fact. Really tried to convince myself,' Her voice thinned, becoming softer, like a radio broadcast about to lose signal. 'But I knew it was. And then I saw this car sticker in the back window, and I had to stop telling myself that it wasn't. I knew it was them, and I knew there was no way anyone was walking away from that smash.'

'I'm so sorry.'

Sinead opened her mouth to say more, held it that way for several seconds, then closed it and wiped her eyes on her sleeve. 'Jesus, look at me,' she said, backing it up with a sound that approximated a laugh. 'What a state. I'm a greetin' mess.'

'Stop,' Tyler told her. 'It's no wonder. It's amazing how you've dealt with it all.' He tightened his grip on her hand. 'You're amazing.'

'Ah, shaddup,' Sinead said, hurriedly rebuilding the walls that had begun to crumble. She turned away from the grave and all the memories it held, and drew in a breath as she took in the scenery.

She and Harris had picked it specially. From there, you could look over the rooftops of Corpach, across Loch... what? Eil? Linnhe? She never knew where one ended and the other began. And from there up to Ben Nevis, with its snow-dusted peak.

It would've been quite breathtaking for the residents of the graveyard, had their breath not already been taken in a much more literal sense.

'Must be about the best view in town,' Tyler remarked, following her gaze.

Sinead couldn't argue. 'We wanted them to be some-where nice. Somewhere they'd have something to look at. Stupid, I know.'

'It's not stupid,' Tyler assured her.

'Aye, it is. They're dead.' She pulled on a smile. 'Sorry. Being a bit morbid.'

Tyler made a show of scoping out the graveyard around them. 'Wonder what brought that on?' he said. 'And it's not stupid. Just because someone dies, doesn't mean you stop caring about them. Doesn't mean you don't want them somewhere nice to...'

The words stopped coming. Sinead turned to see an expression of intense concentration furrow the lines of Tyler's face.

'What?' she asked. 'What's the matter?'

It took a moment for Tyler to come out of his daze. 'Hm? Oh. No. Nothing. It's nothing. Just a thought about the case. Not fully formed yet.'

'Are any of your thoughts ever fully formed?' Sinead teased.

'Yes!' Tyler protested. 'Usually. Occasionally.'

Sinead raised an eyebrow, and Tyler sighed dramatically. 'Well, OK, there was this one time...'

'I think even once is exaggerating,' Sinead said, then laughed at the look of mock outrage on his face. 'So, Robert Smith, then.'

'What about him?' Tyler asked, before the penny dropped. 'Oh! Our Robert Smith. I thought you meant the other one. Aye. Suppose we'd better. You ready?'

With a final look back at the headstone and its mismatched flower display, Sinead motioned down the hill in the direction of the gate.

'Aye,' she said. 'Lead the way, Detective Constable.'

# Chapter 26

It took three rounds of knocking before Robert Smith appeared at the door, and three full seconds for the expression on his face to switch from 'furious' to 'terrified'.

He was in his mid-to-late fifties, with a head that had grown up through his hair, relegating what was left of it to an unkempt ginger horseshoe that ran around the back of his head from one ear to the other. He'd managed to drag a few long strands across the top of his head and had plastered them in place with something greasy. Presumably, he thought this was better than just giving in and embracing his baldness.

It wasn't.

His outfit was unusual, given the time of year, and where they were in the world. He had on a tight-fitting Hawaiian shirt unbuttoned all the way down to where his beer belly started to curve outwards from the rest of him, and a pair of white shorts so small and tight Tyler wondered if they might constitute a criminal offence in and of themselves.

He'd answered the door all bluff and bluster, demanding to know what the bloody hell Tyler thought he was bloody well playing at, hammering on his bloody door in the middle of the bloody day.

It was only when he saw the DC's suit and the police car parked at the top of the street that the anger—and the 'bloodys'—fell away.

It wasn't until Tyler produced his warrant card that the beads of perspiration began to form on Robert's sizeable forehead.

'I don't... I'm sorry, I didn't mean to shout. I was just, I was in the middle of...' he stammered, before clamping his mouth closed, smiling weakly, and trying again. 'How can I help you?'

The door was open only a foot or so. Robert wasn't tall, but what he lacked in height he made up for in girth, and his bulk was firmly plugging the gap in the doorway, his body language making Tyler feel decidedly unwelcome.

'Do you mind if I come in, Mr Smith?' he asked. 'I've just got a couple of quick questions.'

Robert's eyes crept sideways until he was looking into the house. 'Uh. No. Sorry. I'm in the middle of something.'

'It won't take long,' Tyler insisted. 'I tried to phone, but I couldn't find a number.'

'We haven't got a house phone,' Robert explained. He seemed to notice his open shirt for the first time, and quickly clenched the patterned fabric together with one sweaty hand. 'I'm sorry, normally I'd invite you in, but it's just... I'm in the middle of something, like I said. Can you ask me here?'

Tyler peeked into the hallway over the top of the man's head. 'Is everything all right, Mr Smith?'

'What? Yes!'

'It's just, you seem a bit on edge, sir. If you don't mind me saying? You sure everything's OK?'

'Fine! Yes. Fine. God. Yes. Fine, fine. Just… just fine,' he replied, punctuating the words with bursts of forced, incredulous laughter. 'Dandy. Fine and dandy. All good.'

Tyler blinked slowly. Once. Twice.

'Right,' he said, dragging the word out. He looked into the hall again, trying to see further into the house, but Robert pulled the living room door shut.

'So, um, officer,' he said. Swallow. Deep breath. Mop of the brow. 'What was it you wanted to ask?'

Sinead stood just around the side of the semi-detached, listening to the conversation on the step. It had been her suggestion to hang back out of sight. She wasn't in uniform, or even on duty, and if Robert Smith turned into a person of interest, she didn't want technicalities to put the investigation at risk.

Of course, lurking around the corner listening in wasn't exactly a great look, either, but the man's point-blank refusal to let Tyler inside the house had piqued her curiosity.

The front garden, where Tyler was standing, was surrounded by a low hedge that was more brown than green, with patches of thinning almost as severe as the one on Robert Smith's head.

Sinead daren't get much closer to the front, or there was a very good chance Smith would see her, or at least hear her footsteps. Bad enough her being involved in his questioning while off duty, but it'd be so much worse if he spotted her skulking around at the side of his house.

Moving quietly, she sidestepped towards the back of the house, where a tall wooden fence surrounded the garden. There was nothing behind the garden but hillside. If you ignored the neighbours living in the other half of the semi-detached, it meant the garden was a quiet and secluded little spot. She could wait back there for Tyler to be done, then head back to the car with him. Nobody would see her. Nobody would know she was there.

Or, so she thought.

From beyond the fence, she heard a noise. A grunt. A groan, maybe.

She shifted position until she could see through one of the narrow gaps between the vertical planks of wood, and she felt her insides twist in panic. A man stared back at her from inside the garden. His eyes were dark, the rest of his face obscured by a tight-fitting black leather mask.

Around the corner, on the front step, Tyler had given up on his attempts to get inside, deciding it was best to just ask his questions and leave.

'It's about a phone call made to the emergency services in the early hours of yesterday morning, Mr Smith,' he explained, taking his notebook from his pocket.

Robert practically sobbed with relief. 'What, 999? Wasn't me.'

'They asked for the Mountain Rescue,' Tyler continued. 'And they gave your name.'

'Wasn't me. I don't know what else to tell you, mate. Wasn't me. I didn't phone—'

'Tyler!'

Sinead's voice was sharp and sudden and urgent. Tyler saw the look of relief on Robert's face be swept aside by one of raw panic.

'Shit, shit, shit, no!' Robert yelped. He shoved hard on the door, slamming it closed before Tyler could stop him.

The clack of a lock sliding home came a moment later, followed by a wail of anguish from the other side of the door.

Tyler gracelessly sprackled his way through the hedge and stumbled around the side of the house, but saw no sign of Sinead.

'Shite. Sinead!' he hollered, racing around the back, his head rapidly filling with a hundred different scenarios, none of them good.

He found her standing outside the back gate, one hand clamped over her mouth. At first, he thought this was because she was in a state of shock, but then he saw the lines creasing the skin around her eyes, and realised she was trying very hard not to laugh.

'What? What is it?' he asked. 'What's wrong?'

Sinead indicated the gate with a tilt of her head. 'See for yourself,' she urged.

Tyler looked the fence up and down, then leaned in closer, putting one eye to a gap.

It took him a second or two to figure out what he was looking at, but then he jumped back so suddenly anyone watching would've thought the fence had been electrified.

He bit his lip. His nostrils flared. He couldn't look at Sinead. He daren't, in case it set them both off.

'Oh God,' he whispered. 'You have got to be kidding me.'

# Chapter 27

Logan sat back at the desk with a bundle of paperwork and a half-arsed apology.

'Sorry about that. Something came up,' he said, setting the cardboard folder down beside his empty mug. He looked across the table at the Randalls, his finger hovering over the button that would start the tape. 'All set?'

'Will this take much longer?' Fulton asked. 'She'd... we'd both like to get back.'

'Hopefully you'll be on your way sooner rather than later,' Logan replied. 'I just have a couple of things left to go over, then we're done. All right?'

He shifted his gaze from one to the other, giving them time to object. Then, he pressed the button, rattled off the required legal spiel, and jumped right into it.

'Was Brodie ever violent towards you, Hannah?' he asked.

He saw Fulton stiffen in his chair, but ignored the movement and kept his sights on Hannah.

'What do you mean? Of course not,' Fulton said. He looked at his daughter. 'He wasn't, was he? You'd have said, wouldn't you? You'd have said.'

'No,' Hannah replied.

'Whose question were you answering there, Hannah?' Logan asked her. 'Just so we're clear.'

'Yours,' she said, her arms folded and defences fully deployed. 'No. He was never violent.'

The rigidity that had stiffened Fulton in his chair eased a little, but he was still sitting fully upright and alert.

'Right. I'm glad to hear that,' Logan said. He opened the folder and plucked out the top page of the paperwork within. 'It's just that we had reports from neighbours. Three separate incidents, in fact, over the past six months. They claimed they heard raised voices. Banging. Stuff being smashed. That sort of thing.'

'Well, they're lying,' Hannah insisted.

'Oh, no. They're not lying. Uniformed officers attended on all three occasions. You gave a statement each time saying it had been an argument. "Just an argument", you said. "No harm done".'

'Right. Well, it was that, then,' Hannah said. 'An argument. We argued. People argue.'

'They do. I've got an ex-wife. Believe me, I know,' Logan said. He consulted the sheet again. 'But, on one of these occasions, four months ago, give or take, the constable who attended—Constable Jaffray. I believe you know him. He's made sergeant now, as it happens. Don't ask me how. Constable Jaffray wrote in his report that there was blood on your face, and visible signs of a struggle having taken place inside the house.'

Hannah looked away, caught her reflection in the mirror, and looked back again. 'I can't remember.'

'That's all right, you don't have to. It's all written down,' Logan said, indicating the report. He leaned forward and paraphrased some of what he read. 'Neighbours say they saw you with a black eye in the days that followed. They also claim that during the argument, a female voice shouted—and I quote, "Fucking touch me again and I'll kill you".'

Logan set down the page. 'Any idea who that might have been, Hannah?'

Fulton had contained himself enough to sit silently while Logan read from the notes, his face gradually becoming paler. He craned his neck, trying to read the writing on the page, but Logan flipped it over while maintaining his unwavering eye contact with the woman directly across the table.

'Hannah?' Fulton began. She dismissed it with a scowl.

'It was nothing, Dad. We argued. I stormed off. I fell, all right? That's all.'

Logan clasped his hands together and leaned closer, as if about to share some big secret. 'I want to help you here, Hannah. I want to protect you.'

'Protect me? From what? From Brodie? I don't need protection from him. He's dead!' She wriggled uncomfortably in her chair. 'And, even if he wasn't, I wouldn't. He wasn't like that. We just... we argued sometimes. Like everyone.'

'Why didn't you say something?' Fulton asked, although it was whispered so quietly it might well have been rhetorical.

'I wasn't talking about Brodie, Hannah. I know you don't need protection from him. I was talking about his friends. Or colleagues, maybe.'

He saw it in her face, that tightening at the corners of the mouth, that subtle change around the lines of the eyes.

'How long had he been dealing?' the DCI pressed.

'Dealing?!' Fulton spluttered. 'What, drugs? Brodie? Brodie wasn't dealing drugs. Was he, Hannah? Not Brodie. Tell him.'

Hannah had gone back to picking at the loose skin around her thumbnail. A spot of blood welled up where she'd scraped too deep.

'I don't know. A while,' she said, her gaze cast down at the desk.

Fulton let his head roll back, buried his face in his hands, and made a succession of pained noises before sitting upright again.

'Right. No. This is… I think she should have a lawyer. This is, I don't know what it is. This is entrapment.'

Hannah tutted. 'Shut up, Dad. It's not entrapment, is it? He asked me a question, and I answered. All right? That's all. That's his job.'

Logan waited until the girl had finished drawing her father one of the dirtiest looks he'd ever seen, then pressed the advantage.

'How long a while? Roughly? Six months? A year?'

'I don't know. Since before I met him. Years,' Hannah said. 'I didn't know. Not at first. He never actually admitted it to me. Just deny, deny, deny. But I guessed. I figured it out.'

She sucked the blood from her thumb, regarded the wound, then went back to picking. 'Well, I thought he was shagging someone else to start with. I was actually relieved when I found out he wasn't.' She shrugged. 'I mean, not that I know of, anyway.'

'How did you find out?' Logan asked.

'I can't remember.'

Logan flexed his fingers, then clasped them again. 'Try.'

Hannah sighed and made a vaguely dismissive sort of gesture. 'Just things he said. I don't know. I heard him on the phone a couple of times.'

'Who to?'

'I don't know. And don't ask me what he said, either. I can't remember. It wasn't what he was saying, anyway, it was the way he said it. Cagey. But scared, too. Like he didn't want to say the wrong thing. When he realised I was listening, he hung up. Didn't say goodbye, didn't end the call, just hung up.'

'What did he say to you after the call?' Logan asked.

'Nothing.'

'Nothing?'

Hannah tutted. 'I don't know. He was angry. He shouted. We argued. He told me I was paranoid. Called me a psycho. That was it. We didn't talk about it again, but I knew after that. I figured it out.'

Fulton looked at his daughter as if seeing her for the first time. 'You knew? You knew he was dealing drugs with Carrie in the house, and you didn't say anything?'

'He wasn't dealing from the house, Dad, was he?'

'I don't know, was he?' Fulton bit back. 'You tell me! Was he?'

'No! Never. I never saw anything like that.' She turned back to Logan. 'Honestly. I knew. I mean, I suspected, but I couldn't prove anything. I never saw anything.'

She was putting a brave face on it, but Logan could tell she was ready to crumble. There was a scowl fixed on her face, but it was a mask that was slipping away, revealing the scared wee girl hiding behind it.

'Tell me about Sandy Gillespie,' he said.

The mask fell a fraction, giving a glimpse of the fear that flashed in Hannah's eyes at the mention of the name.

'What do you mean?'

'We believe Brodie met Sandy on a number of occasions over the past six months. We believe they may have been working together.'

'I don't know,' Hannah said. 'I don't know anything about him. I mean, you hear things, but I've never really had any dealings with him.'

'Really?' Logan asked. 'I want you to think very hard about that, Hannah. It's important. You've never spoken to Sandy Gillespie?'

The hesitation was tiny, but Logan had been watching for it.

'No. Not really. Maybe a hello in the shops. In passing.'

'And that's it?' Logan asked. He slid a sheet from the folder and watched Hannah's eyes get drawn to it.

'Wait. No,' she said. Her brow creased like she was struggling to recall something. 'Actually, I think he might've come to the house a couple of times. To see Brodie. I was in bed, though.'

Logan nodded and slid the sheet back into the folder. He wasn't sure what that particular piece of paper actually said, but it had served its purpose.

'Do you know why he came round? What they spoke about?'

Hannah shook her head firmly. 'No. Like I said, I was upstairs. With Carrie. I didn't see anything, I didn't hear anything, I don't know anything.'

'Are you quite sure about that, Hannah?' Logan asked.

'Yes. I'm sure.'

'Those people who came to your house last night. Could one of them have been Sandy Gillespie?'

There was no obvious physical reaction to the question. No widening of the eyes, no change to the colour of the cheeks, or to the shape of the mouth. Nothing to suggest shock or surprise.

'I only saw one. And I don't know. He had a mask on.'

'What about his voice? Did you recognise that?'

She shook her head, although with less conviction than the last time. 'No. Scottish, though. Pretty local, I'd say.'

Fulton interjected, leaning forward in his chair until he was practically inserting himself between his daughter and the detective. 'Wait, you think they killed Brodie, don't you? These drugs people. You think they killed him, and then came to the house.'

'It's one line of inquiry,' Logan confirmed. 'It's possible they may have been looking for drugs Brodie brought back from his last trip abroad. It would explain some of Brodie's injuries.'

He diverted his attention to Hannah. 'We know they weren't there to rob the place, Hannah. It's time for the truth now. Did they ask about Brodie? Did they ask about the drugs?'

Fulton wasn't done with his interjection yet and jumped in before Hannah could reply. 'Look, sorry. Is she under arrest? Is that what this is?'

Logan had a good idea about what was coming next. The look in Fulton Randall's eyes was one he'd seen countless times before.

'No,' he said, smiling patiently. 'She's not under arrest. She's just—'

Fulton's chair legs scraped on the floor as he got to his feet. 'Right, then. Come on,' he urged, motioning for Hannah to stand. 'We're going.'

Hannah looked from her dad to the DCI, then hurriedly complied. Logan sat back in his chair and folded his arms, demonstrating his disappointment without a word.

'If you want to talk to her again, then we'll have a solicitor present,' Fulton said. 'I'm not having you incriminating her, or pinning something on her she didn't do. I'm sorry, but I'm just not having it. Sorry.'

Logan said nothing as the Randalls bustled past him. He heard Fulton pulling on the door handle, and the little gasp of exasperation when he discovered it wouldn't open.

'Sorry, can you…? Can you let us out?'

Logan uncrossed his arms and sat forward.

'Hannah Randall and Fulton Randall are now leaving the room,' he said, then he terminated the recording with a jab of his finger, and reluctantly got to his feet.

After unlocking the door, Logan stood with a hand on the handle, blocking the way. Hannah wilted beneath his gaze as he looked down at her.

'Be careful out there, Hannah,' he said. 'If you feel like you're in danger at any point, contact us.' He pulled the door open, but didn't yet step aside. 'These people, whoever they are, are capable of some very nasty things.'

# Chapter 28

After seeing the Randalls out, Logan returned to the Incident Room to find DC Neish holding court in front of the Big Board.

Ben sat shaking his head in disbelief, while DS McQuarrie tried very hard to remain straight-faced. Hamza was taking a different approach, and was creasing up in his chair, literally holding his sides as if they might split at any moment.

It was the other occupant of the room who Logan acknowledged first. Sinead smiled at him as he entered, and he pulled an expression of mock outrage.

'Christ, are we letting anyone in here these days?'

'Looks like it, sir,' Sinead confirmed. 'How's it going?'

'Shite.'

'Usual, then?'

'Pretty much,' Logan said. He stopped between Ben and Caitlyn, and waited for Hamza to pull himself together. 'Obviously, I've missed something good,' he remarked, once DC Khaled had stopped giggling.

'You can say that again, boss,' Tyler said, grinning like the cat who'd got the cream. 'So, we were checking up on all the Robert Smiths in the area.'

Logan frowned. 'What, the singer? With the mad hair and the eyeshadow?'

'No. The 999 call,' Tyler said. 'To the mountain rescue. The name the caller gave was Robert Smith. Fake number, from what we can tell. But, there are a few Robert Smiths locally, so I checked them out to see if any of them had made the call.'

'Right. And?'

'They hadn't. None of them knew anything about it.'

Logan glanced down at Hamza. His eyes were wet with tears of laughter, and he was still trying to get his breathing under control. A quick look at Caitlyn revealed she was having to hold it together, too.

'Am I missing the punchline somewhere?' Logan asked. 'I mean, I enjoy a good joke as much as the next man, but I'm struggling to get this one. What's so funny?'

Tyler's face lit up like all his Christmases had come at once. He immediately launched into a lengthy and detailed explanation of the day's events that quickly set Hamza off again, and earned more disapproving looks from Ben.

Once Tyler had finished, Logan could actually feel his mouth hanging open. He quickly snapped it shut.

'You're joking!'

'Nope. Straight up, boss. Pardon the expression.' Tyler grinned. 'He had all these cameras set up, and these two lads were both going at her. One at one end, one at the other. They were all in their fifties, except one of the lads, who must've been mid-twenties at a push.'

'Jesus. And he was filming this?' Logan asked.

'Oh, aye. And none of your rubbish. Multi-camera set-up, boss. High-end. I mean, I haven't seen the final edit, obviously, but I'd be disappointed if it wasn't some top production quality stuff. He's like a Sex-Tape Spielberg.'

'His own *wife*, though,' Ben muttered. He had been shaking his head when Logan entered, and was still shaking it now. 'That can't be a healthy relationship.'

'She certainly seemed to be getting plenty out of it,' Tyler replied.

Ben scowled, like this only made it all that much worse. 'In the back garden, too. And on stone slabs, you say? Christ. Be murder on the bloody knees, that.'

This set Hamza off again. Laughter erupted out of him and almost caused him to roll sideways out of his chair as he tried in vain to contain it.

'What did you do? Did you arrest them?' Logan asked, raising his voice to be heard above Hamza's outburst.

'Not yet, boss,' Tyler said. 'Confiscated the footage and gave them a warning about indecency and ending up on the register. They tried to say the fence blocked the view from outside, so it wasn't indecent. I pointed out that the next-door-neighbour's house overlooked the garden and had a clear view of what was going on.'

'And? What did they have to say to that?'

Tyler smirked. 'One of the lads seeing to the wife *was* the next-door-neighbour. He said he didn't have any objections to it.'

'Jesus,' Logan said. He shook his head and cast disparaging looks at the others, like they were all somehow responsible. 'That's the Highlands for you, I suppose. I should probably just be thankful they were husband and wife and no' brother and sister.'

He waved a hand. 'Give the footage to Uniform. Tell them to follow up on it. Thankfully, it's not our problem. We've enough on our plate without some amateur Hugh Hefner to deal with, too.'

'Already passed it on, boss,' Tyler replied.

'Good,' Logan grunted.

'I hope you washed your hands, afterwards,' Caitlyn added, eliciting one final outburst of laughter from Hamza.

The others watched him in silence as he struggled to compose himself, tears streaming down his cheeks. His voice, when he finally spoke, was a high-pitched squeak of delight.

'*Murder on the bloody knees.*'

Logan's phone buzzed in his pocket. To his annoyance, he felt himself tense, dreading finding another *Unknown Caller* message plastered across the screen.

To his relief, there was a name there. To his delight, it was that rarest of things—the name of someone he actually liked.

'I'm just going to take this in the office,' he said, navigating between the desks and making for the door at the back of the room.

'Tenner it's the pathologist,' Tyler remarked.

Logan shot a look back over his shoulder. 'Tenner you'll be back in uniform this time next week if you don't get your finger out and get back to work,' he barked, and then he swiped the button that answered the phone and said, 'Hello. Superintendent Hoon? Always a pleasure to hear from you.'

After flashing a smirk at DC Neish, he entered the office and closed the door. The voice on the other end of the phone sounded confused. It also very much did not sound like Superintendent Hoon.

'Eh, no. It's me,' said Shona Maguire, her Irish twang unmistakeable.

'Aye. Yes, sorry. Long story,' Logan told her. He walked around to the other side of the desk and took a seat. 'How's it going?'

'Yeah. All right. Got a result in that might be interesting,' Shona said. 'I was going to email it but thought I'd better phone it through. And besides, nobody else has died under suspicious circumstances, so it was this or play *Angry Birds* again.'

'I'm honoured,' Logan said. 'So, what have you got?'

'Salt.'

'Salt?'

'Aye. Lots of salt. On his skin, in his hair, in the wounds. All over him,' the pathologist said. 'I tried to think of a joke about him being *a-salt-ed,* but I couldn't come up with anything decent. Also, you know, him being murdered and everything...'

'Not really appropriate.'

'Exactly. Not really appropriate. But, yes. Salt. Top to toe.'

Logan scribbled the word 'SALT' on the notepad on his desk, added a question mark, then drew a couple of circles around it.

'What's that about, then?' he wondered. 'You think he was buried in it?'

'I do,' Shona confirmed. 'I had Geoff Palmer help me look into it, and we reckon it's the type used to grit roads in cold weather. Which would fit with the sand and pieces of grit I found in his lungs.'

'I bet Palmer loved that,' Logan said.

'What's the matter? Jealous?' Shona teased.

'Jealous? Of that scrotum-faced bawbag? No' likely,' Logan countered.

'Right. Well, that's good, because he offered to take me out to dinner.'

Logan switched the phone from one hand to the other, buying himself time to formulate a suitably withering reply. At least, that was the theory. In reality, he couldn't come up with anything beyond, 'Oh. Right. Well... fair enough. That'll be... something.'

'I said "no", obviously,' Shona told him. 'I might be desperate, but I'm not Sex Pest Palmer desperate. I have some standards. Not many, and they aren't very high, but they're higher than that.'

Muscles relaxed that Logan hadn't felt tighten. 'Aye. Good. Standards are important,' he said.

'They are,' Shona said. She fell silent, then, like she was waiting for him to say something. Logan had plenty he wanted to say, he just couldn't work out which order to put it in, or how to begin.

'Right, well,' he said, just wanting to fill the silence. 'Thanks for the update. I'd best get back.'

'Right. Yeah,' Shona said, brightly. Too brightly, it could be argued. 'No problem. Any time. Happy to... you know. So, uh, bye, then.'

'Aye. Bye. And thanks again.'

'No bother. Like I say. Any time,' Shona replied. 'See you.'

'Right, then. See you.'

There was a knock at the door behind him.

'Boss?'

Logan hurriedly jabbed the 'hang up' button, then thrust the phone into his pocket, wheeling around on his heels in the same breath.

'Tyler. Yes. What is it?' he asked, making no attempt whatsoever to hide his annoyance.

'Sorry, were you in the middle of something?' DC Neish asked. His eyes went to the pocket with the phone in it, and one corner of his mouth curved into a smirk.

'I'm always in the middle of something, son. Now, unless you want my foot to be in the middle of your arse, what is it you want?'

'It's probably nothing, boss,' Tyler said, sidling the rest of the way into the office. 'It's just, I had a thought about how Brodie Welsh was buried.'

Logan made a 'hurry up' gesture with one hand. 'And?'

'Well, I was thinking, what if someone moved him because they cared for him? Like, even after they die, we want to know the people we care about are all right, don't we? I mean, not all right, obviously, but... all right. Like, we bring flowers. We spend a fortune on nice coffins, headstones, whatever. We want what's best for them.'

'I don't follow,' Logan said.

'I just mean, maybe whoever moved him was someone close to him. Someone who loved him, even. Maybe they wanted him found so he could be buried somewhere properly. Not guilt, exactly, just... I don't know. Respect, or whatever.'

'That suggests who? Hannah Randall?'

Tyler shrugged. 'Maybe. I don't know. Just an idea.'

It was an idea, all right. He'd give the boy that much. Logan tried slotting it into the bigger picture, but couldn't find a way to make it fit. Hannah Randall might arguably have had motive, but she didn't have the means to kill him. Not on her own, at least.

Whoever had killed Brodie knew about the drug dealing and how he brought the stuff into the country. They were looking for it inside him, which meant it was almost certainly the same people who'd come looking for it at the house later.

Which meant there was really only one viable suspect.

Or, to be more precise, one family of them.

# Chapter 29

The other two members of the Gillespie clan were no more attractive than their younger brother. Like Sandy, they were ugly inside as well as out, and the family resemblance was evident in their matching sneers.

DS McQuarrie motioned to them both in turn, their grainy, blown-up photos pinned to the Big Board for the rest of the team to see.

'Maureen Gillespie. Age forty-seven. De facto matriarch of the Gillespie family, on account of their actual mother refusing to have anything to do with any of them,' Caitlyn said, referring to her notes for the key points. 'Been in and out of prison over the years, mostly minor offences. She once bit the ear off a constable who was two weeks into the job, and then swallowed it in front of him.'

'Christ. And she looks like such an angel, too,' Ben remarked.

'Hell's Angel, maybe,' Hamza said.

'She did three years for that,' Caitlyn continued. 'Kept out of trouble ever since.'

'Or no' been caught, anyway,' Logan suggested.

'Aye. Not for want of trying, I'm sure,' Caitlyn said. She indicated the other mugshot. It showed a man whose age was almost impossible to determine, thanks to the mess of homemade tattoos etched all over his face. 'This is her brother, Thomas. Known locally as "Tam the Bam", which should give you a rough idea of the type of guy we're dealing with.'

'A poet?' Tyler guessed.

'Aye, we wish,' Caitlyn said.

'Jesus, look at the state of that coupon. He looks like my old desk from school,' Logan said. 'Scribble "Mr Fife is a prick" on his cheek, and he'd be a dead ringer. I bet if you turn him over, the back of his head is all dried chewing gum and bogies.'

'I'd say you shouldn't judge a book by its cover, but in this case, you can go right ahead,' Caitlyn told the team. 'Worst of a bad bunch by quite some margin. Convictions for robbery, GBH, sexual assault, and a dozen other crimes and misdemeanours. You name it, he's done it. The upshot of which is, he's currently doing a nine-stretch in Peterhead.'

'Almost restores your faith in the justice system, doesn't it?' said Ben.

'My gran lives in Peterheid,' Hamza announced. He glanced around at the largely disinterested looks this drew from the others. 'Aye, no' the prison, like. Just the town.'

'Great anecdote there, mate,' Tyler remarked, slow-clapping. 'Gripping stuff.'

Hamza scowled at his fellow DC, then cleared his throat and smiled apologetically at DS McQuarrie. 'Sorry, Sarge. Go on.'

'Looking at the case CID is building, Maureen and Sandy Gillespie have been bringing cannabis, cocaine, and heroin into the country from a variety of suppliers, via a range of different routes. They've then been offloading it to contacts across the UK. Very hands-off, they don't seem to be involved in anything close to street level.'

'They should be street level, though,' Ben observed. 'They *belong* at street level. How've they managed to get so high up the chain? Who's funded that?'

'Nobody seems to know, sir,' Caitlyn replied. 'They've got the cash to play with the big boys from somewhere, though, and now they're up there with the worst of them, if CID's investigation is right.'

'Any reason to think it isn't?' Logan asked.

Caitlyn shook her head. 'Solid enough police work, from what I can tell, sir.'

'Anything in there about Brodie Welsh?' Tyler asked.

'A couple of references,' Logan said, answering on the detective sergeant's behalf. 'Nothing major. The Gillespies were the focus. He's included in the report as a potential accomplice, but he makes a couple of cameo appearances. Nothing else.'

'There's a suggestion CID was going to try putting some pressure on him, sir,' Caitlyn said. 'Maybe bring him in and see if he would give them anything.'

Logan's eyes narrowed. 'Aye?'

It made sense, of course. It's what he would've done in the same situation. If the Gillespies had got wind of that, all the more reason to kill him. But how would they have gotten wind of it, if Jinkies was keeping the lid shut tight?

Clapping his hands on his thighs, Logan stood. 'Right, my turn,' he said, replacing Caitlyn at the board. 'As you know, I was interviewing Hannah Randall earlier, and she told me she believes Brodie was dealing, or involved in the drugs trade in some way, at least.

'From what we can figure out, he was trying to cover his arse by funnelling cash through a Central American online payment website, which allowed him to make transfers into his and Hannah's joint account, posing as an offshore company, Oswatt.'

'Which doesn't exist,' DS McQuarrie added.

'Stupid move, that,' Hamza said. 'Why not just use the name of an actual company? Why make one up?'

'Christ knows,' Logan replied. 'Less hassle, maybe? No danger of her phoning them up, or meeting someone else who worked for the company and asking questions. I don't know. I'm sure he had his reasons. The point is, he was taking cash payments—presumably from the Gillespies—sending it via Western Union to this payment provider, and then returning it to himself as a wire transfer.'

'It's almost clever,' said Ben. 'Were it not so bloody stupid.'

'Aye. We're not getting much back from the payment provider or his own bank, but he left enough of a trail that we can pretty much figure it out.'

'What about the home invasion, boss?' Tyler asked. 'Did she give you any more on that?'

'Yes and no,' Logan said. 'She couldn't say that the guy who attacked her was Sandy Gillespie.'

'Couldn't, or wouldn't?' Ben asked.

'That's the big question. There was definitely a reaction to his name—she's scared of him—but all she could give us on the attacker was that he sounded local. I asked her what they were really there for, told her we knew they weren't out to rob the place.'

'And?' asked Ben.

'And that's when her dad jumped in and said she'd had enough. We want to interview her again, she's going to have a brief with her,' Logan said. He shrugged in begrudged acceptance. 'Can't blame them, I suppose. I'd do the same in their shoes.'

After that, Logan told them about the salt on Brodie's body, and the possibility that it had been buried in a pile of road grit somewhere. Hamza made a note to find out where the council stored its winter supplies of the stuff.

Tyler's investigation into the various Robert Smiths had drawn a blank. If any of them had called in to report someone missing out on the hills, they were all denying it now. No alarm bells had rung while speaking to any of them—or none that didn't involve homemade pornography, at least—and the only conclusion he could come to was that the name had been as fake as the number.

'Which either makes it one hell of a coincidence, or whoever made the call wanted the body found,' Logan said. 'And I don't believe in coincidences.'

'Assuming that's the case, and assuming it was the Gillespies that killed him,' said Hamza. 'Why would they want him found?'

'If we can figure that bit out, we've got the bastards,' Logan said. 'Gillespies or otherwise. We still don't know if it was the killer who moved the body, or someone else with their own motive. Either way, it's the key to putting this thing to bed, so I want everyone working on it.'

He clicked his fingers and pointed to DC Neish.

'Have you listened to the 999 recording yet?'

Tyler nodded. 'Aye, sir. English accent, but put on, I think. Not a voice I recognise.'

'Email it over and I'll have a listen later,' Logan instructed. 'In fact, email it round to everyone. CID, too. See if they recognise it. Maybe we can get a name.'

'Maybe, sir, aye,' said Tyler, although he sounded doubtful. 'I'll get it sent out. Jinkies, too?'

'Aye, Jinkies, too,' said Logan, then: 'Wait.' His eyes darted from side to side. His lips moved silently as if working on some difficult mental maths. 'Aye. Bugger it. Send it to him, too. Mark it urgent. I'll have a listen, then go talk to him about it myself.'

'I'm assuming you'll be wanting to talk to the Gillespies?' said Ben. 'You running that by Jinkies first?'

'Away and shite,' Logan said. 'He might think he's the big I-Am, but we know different. But yes, in answer to your question, I think it's high time we had a more in-depth chat with the Gillespie clan.'

'What about the CID investigation, boss?' Tyler asked.

'We'll just have to take our chances. This takes priority,' Logan said. He jabbed a thumb at the mugshots. 'Anyone got a preference?'

'Bagsy no' the ear biter,' said Hamza.

'Fine. Caitlyn, you and Hamza go bring Sandy back in. Tyler, you're with me.'

'Hold on, we're not going for the biter, are we, boss?'

'Afraid so,' Logan told him. 'If it's any consolation, I've always hated your ears, anyway. More than the rest of you, I mean.'

He picked up his coat from where it had been abandoned across a desk, and gave Ben a nod that the older man understood only too well.

'I suppose I'll smooth this all over with CID, then, will I?' DI Forde asked.

'Aye, that's an idea,' said Logan, in a way that suggested the thought had not even occurred to him. 'You do that, then. Thanks.'

Ben rolled his eyes. 'Any time,' he said, then he stood with a creak and watched as the rest of the team piled on out through the door.

CID was not going to like this. They weren't going to like it one little bit.

# Chapter 30

Fulton Randall indicated left at the roundabout by the police station, waited for a couple of cars to pass, then pulled away with a heavy foot that loudly revved the engine and kangarooed the car into a series of brief lurching jumps.

'Shit. Sorry,' he said.

It was all he said, in fact, until they were passing the leisure centre a mile or so up the road, and had left the station and its interview room far behind.

'So.'

It wasn't a question, exactly. It wasn't much of anything. It was an invitation, he supposed, to a conversation he wasn't sure how to have.

In the passenger seat beside him, Hannah continued to stare ahead through the front windscreen. A smir of rain was falling, and the car's automatic wipers flicked lazily across the glass, eliciting a screech from the too-dry rubber.

'Anything you'd like to tell me, Hannah?' Fulton asked. Probing, but gentle. Like a tongue carefully testing a hole in a tooth, braced for the very real possibility of pain.

'No. Nothing.'

Fulton tore his eyes off the road ahead and shot her a sideways look. 'What? After everything in there? There's nothing you want to—'

'Dad!'

He faced front again and jammed a foot down on the brake, bringing the car to a stop just a few inches from the one in front. A couple of vehicles ahead, an elderly couple crossed at the traffic lights outside the hospital.

'After all that. Brodie. *Drugs*. There's nothing you want to say?'

'I've said everything, haven't I?' Hannah snapped. She crossed her arms and squeezed herself in against the passenger door, as if trying to put as much distance between herself and the conversation as possible. 'You heard me say everything.'

'Oh, I heard. I heard,' Fulton said. He crunched down into first gear as the lights changed, then pulled away when the traffic started moving. 'I just can't believe I'm only hearing now. I mean, what were you thinking? He was dealing drugs, and *you knew*? Carrie in the house, he's dealing drugs, and you knew? I mean, Jesus Christ. What were you thinking?'

She glanced at him for the first time since getting in the car. 'Just leave it, Dad, all right?'

'No! Not all right. You were living with a drug dealer!' His hands tightened on the wheel. His jaw clenched as his back teeth ground together. 'And he hit you.'

There was no reply from the passenger seat. Fulton took the bypass turnoff, heading south out of Fort William.

This wasn't how he'd envisioned this conversation. He wanted to stop the car, to look at her, to put his arms around her, if she'd let him. Instead, he slowed as he approached yet another roundabout, and then accelerated smoothly across it.

'Talk to me, Hannah,' he pleaded. 'He hit you, didn't he?'

'Jesus, Dad.'

'Just say it, sweetheart. You can tell me.'

Hannah turned her head sharply and stared out of the side window, watching all the big B&Bs and hotels of the Golden Mile go blurring by. She flinched in surprise when her dad's hand patted her on the leg.

'It's fine. You don't have to tell me if you don't want to. Sorry, I shouldn't have pressed you,' Fulton told her. He gave the leg a squeeze, then returned both hands to the wheel. 'It's just… you're my wee girl, you know? I know you think you're all grown up—and you are—but you're still my wee girl. I worry. We both do. Me and your mum.'

Hannah said nothing until the last of the guesthouses had been replaced by trees and hillside.

'It only happened twice,' she said, not turning.

The leather of Fulton's steering wheel creaked beneath his grip.

'It was my fault.'

'Don't you say that. Don't you ever say that!' Fulton managed to grunt. She still hadn't looked round, and so didn't see him drawing a sleeve across his eyes to wipe away the tears that had sprung out of nowhere.

He cleared his throat. Once. Twice. Bringing his voice under control.

'What happened?'

Hannah watched the world whizz by, her breath fogging the rain-flecked glass. 'Doesn't matter now,' she said. 'He's gone.'

'I just wish you'd told me. I wish you'd said something sooner.' Fulton exhaled, a deliberate attempt to ease some of the tension he could feel building across his chest and shoulders. 'At least it's out in the open now. No more secrets, eh?'

There was a squeak as Hannah wiped her breath-cloud off the window. 'Yeah,' she said. Her eyes met those of her reflection. 'No more secrets.'

# Chapter 31

Caitlyn's fingertips tapped on the steering wheel as she waited for the stream of oncoming traffic to pass so she could make the turn.

The tapping was not particularly unusual. Hamza had seen it often enough. It was a recurring tic of hers, usually appearing when she was growing impatient. Which was often.

Today, though, it was different. It wasn't the usual tap-tap-tap of irritation. There was a beat to it. A tune, almost.

He almost said something when the voice in his ear spoke again. Leaning forward in the passenger seat, he pressed his notebook against the dash and started writing, just as Caitlyn took the turn.

'Shit,' he muttered, as the pen drew a line straight across the page.

'Sorry!' Caitlyn said. He glanced at her and caught her smiling in a way that made him think she'd done it on purpose.

'No, not you. Sorry,' Hamza said into the phone. 'Go on.'

He listened, heart slowly sinking, as the Highland Council employee on the other end reeled off the answer to the question Hamza had posed earlier.

'Right. And there's no way that...? No. No, gotcha. Thanks for getting back to me. You, too. Thanks.'

He stabbed a finger against the screen and muttered a couple of the milder curses below his breath.

'Good news, then?'

Hamza shot the DS a suspicious look.

'What?' she asked, raising an eyebrow.

'What's wrong with you?' Hamza asked.

Caitlyn took her eyes off the winding road ahead for a moment. 'Eh? Nothing.' She nodded at the phone in his hand. 'What did they say?'

Hamza threw the phone a dirty look like it was somehow responsible for the information he'd been given.

'Council grit storage is covered by CCTV. People kept nicking it, so they beefed up security a few years back. Every depot has full camera coverage, highly visible, signs everywhere. They're going to go through the footage, but—'

'Nobody's going to be stupid enough to stuff a body there,' Caitlyn concluded.

'Exactly,' Hamza said. He sighed. 'I suppose I should phone the boss and let him know.'

'Yeah. You'd better.'

Hamza regarded the phone for a while, then tapped an icon. 'I'll text him.'

The sound of a clucking chicken came from the seat beside him. The bottom half of his face broke into a smile, while the top half frowned deeply.

'What is up with you lately?' he asked.

'What? Nothing,' Caitlyn said.

'You're acting weird. You're not dying, are you? Because, I can't deal with that.'

'Aw, thanks,' Caitlyn said.

'The conversation, I mean.' He gestured to the door handle. 'I mean it, if you tell me you've got six months to live or something, I'll jump out.'

Caitlyn laughed. Even this was out of the ordinary.

It wasn't that she was usually miserable, exactly, she was just a little… stiff. Less inclined to join in with joking as the rest of them, maybe. Hamza had always put it down to her being fiercely ambitious. Tyler reckoned she had a poker up her arse. All things considered, Hamza thought his instinct was probably more accurate.

Recently, though, she'd seemed different. Not less driven, exactly, but less fierce in the way she went about it, maybe. Lighter.

Happier, dare he say?

'I'm not dying. I promise,' she told him. 'It's nothing. Honest.'

She shuffled more upright in her seat, adjusted her rearview mirror, then indicated the car's satnav. 'Now, stick in Gillespie's address, will you? We'll be arriving in Kinloch shortly.'

–

'Christ. Aye. This is more like it.'

Tyler sat forward in the passenger seat of the Volvo, eyes wide as he watched the scenery go rolling by.

Half of the sky had been smeared with blobs of wispy, grey cloud that clung to the tops of the hills and mountains rising steeply on the left. On the right, a bright, clear blue was fighting back, driving the gloom away and revealing a landscape that looked straight out of *Braveheart*.

During the drive south, they'd passed a couple of waterfalls, an impressive gorge, and the former home of disgraced TV and radio personality, Jimmy Savile. Sure enough, it had 'paedo' scrawled all over its whitewashed stone exterior, in a variety of creative spellings.

'Peedo' had been Tyler's favourite, and had started him on a monologue in which he imagined a world where the principal ingredient of the modelling putty, 'Playdo,' was urine. This particular flight of fancy went on for almost a full minute before Logan had politely instructed him to 'Shut the fuck up.'

'Aye, no' bad, is it?' the DCI said, lifting his eyes from the road for a moment and briefly taking in their surroundings.

'I always wondered why people came up here on holiday,' Tyler said. 'I mean, no offence to the place, but it's not exactly jumping, is it?'

'People don't come here for "jumping",' Logan pointed out. 'They don't want "jumping", they want...' He motioned to the sprawling landscape that stretched out ahead of them. '...that.'

'Aye. That's what I'm saying, boss. I get it now,' the DC said. 'I understand. I've learned something today.'

'First time for everything,' Logan said. It was such an open goal that he almost felt guilty for taking the shot, but he knew Ben would never have forgiven him if he'd passed it up.

The car crested a little peak in the road, then dipped down suddenly on the other side. Tyler wriggled uncomfortably and took a steadying breath.

'Need to do something with the roads, though.' He looked ahead, then turned in his seat and glanced back at the road already travelled. 'I think Sinead's parents were killed round here somewhere.'

'Bit further up, I think,' Logan said. 'Rannoch Moor sort of area.'

Tyler blinked, gazed blankly at the landscape, then nodded as if he knew where that was. 'Right. Yeah. Down this way, I meant.' He blew out his cheeks. 'Can't imagine it. Can you?'

Logan gave a single shake of his head. No. He could not.

'How is she? After everything.'

'She's... aye. Doing all right. Itching to get back on the job, though.'

'That's a good sign,' Logan said. He'd seen too many good officers scared off by one bad experience. Not that he blamed any of them. He envied the buggers, if anything.

Logan side-eyed Tyler, who was being uncharacteristically reserved.

'You don't think so?'

'No. I mean, yeah. I do. I think it's great,' the DC said. 'It's just, is it not a bit soon? After what happened.'

'She's obviously made of stern stuff,' Logan said. They caught up with a Corsa pootling along the road, and he eased the Volvo past it without slowing. 'If she thinks she's ready, then she's ready.'

'Maybe. You're probably right,' Tyler said. 'I'm just worried, I suppose, boss. Can't help but think it's a bit soon for her to be getting back into uniform.'

'Maybe she shouldn't, then,' Logan said.

Tyler blinked in surprise. 'Oh. What? You agree with me? Magic. Maybe you can help convince her?'

'No, I can't. That's not what I'm saying,' Logan replied. 'If the lassie thinks she's ready, who the hell are we to say otherwise? I'm just saying, maybe she shouldn't be back in uniform.'

'I don't...' Tyler began, and then the penny dropped. 'Oh. Right. Gotcha.'

He went back to looking out at the scenery, giving the idea some thought.

After a while, his eyes went to the satnav, and the little triangle that ploughed smoothly through a flat, unremarkable patch of green that didn't even bother trying to do the place justice.

'Not long now,' Logan said.

'She's proper arse end of nowhere, isn't she?' Tyler observed. 'Be annoying if she's not in, after all this.'

He looked out at the scenery again. 'Still, nice to get out of the office, eh?'

Logan checked his mirrors, then turned off the main road. A long, narrow dirt track stretched out ahead of them, all potholes and puddles. The Volvo lurched violently on its suspension as Logan guided it up the winding incline.

'Actually,' Tyler swallowed, one hand slipping onto his stomach, the other gripping the handle of the door. 'Is it too late to take that back?'

—

'Mummy!'

Hannah bent and scooped up Carrie as she came running across the living room, her bare feet pit-patting on the laminate flooring.

'Oh, look! Dinner!' Hannah cried, dipping the girl backwards until her head was pointing to the floor and giggles came tumbling out of her.

'No! I'm not dinner!'

'No? You *smell* like dinner!' Hannah said, adopting a gruff voice. She snuffled furiously around Carrie's neck, ratcheting her laughter up until it was a series of high-pitched squeals of delight. Hannah licked her lips and smacked them together. 'Do you *taste* like dinner, I wonder?'

'Nooooo!'

'For God's sake, don't keep me in suspense!'

Hannah stopped trying to eat her daughter, and instead looked over to her mother. Sandra stood in the kitchen doorway, a dish towel twisting over and over in her grip. 'What did they say?'

Fulton looked very deliberately at Carrie, then back at his wife. 'Probably not the time.'

Sandra tutted. 'Right, well, you come through here and tell me, then,' she ordered, retreating into the kitchen.

Fulton locked eyes with his daughter and they shared something that was in spitting distance of being a smile.

'All right, spud?' he said, giving Carrie a tickle on the way past. His touch caught her by surprise and she jumped in her mum's arms, then exploded into laughter.

After following his wife into the kitchen, Fulton closed the door, muting the sounds of merriment from the living room.

Sandra stood with her back to the draining board, vigorously drying a plate. Behind her, the window looked out onto the steep slope that led from the house down to the main road.

The snow would start making its way down from the higher peaks soon, turning the track into the usual winter ordeal.

Still, it was worth it for the view.

'Well?' Sandra demanded. 'What did they say? What was it about? Do they know who killed Brodie?'

Fulton exhaled. 'No. I mean… I don't know. Maybe,' he said. Crossing to her, he gently removed the plate from her hands and set it down on the worktop. 'There's a few things we need to talk about. Things that came up.'

Sandra said nothing. Not vocally, anyway. Her eyes asked a hundred questions she wasn't sure she wanted to know the answer to.

'Brodie wasn't who we thought he was,' Fulton told her. 'He was involved in drugs.'

'Drugs? What do you mean *drugs*?'

'I don't know. He was dealing. Or importing them, maybe. Bringing them into the country. That's what the trips abroad were about.'

'He was working abroad. He was at work. For the oil people.'

Fulton gave a little shake of his head. 'It was a cover story. There was no oil company.'

Sandra's back bumped against the edge of the worktop as she took a stumbled step backwards.

'Did she know? Did Hannah know?'

Fulton winced. 'Aye. No. I mean… she suspected, aye,' he said. He took a breath, bracing himself for his own reaction as much as his wife's. 'He got… Brodie. He got violent. With Hannah.'

The change to Sandra's face brought tears whooshing to Fulton's own eyes. She shrank before him, one hand fumbling blindly for the edge of the worktop like it was the only thing in the world that could keep her on her feet.

He lunged for her, arms surrounding her, pulling her in close. She pressed her hands against his chest, like she might be about to push him away, but then let them both fall to her sides and just leaned there against him, her legs grateful for the support.

'When?' she whispered.

'It doesn't matter,' Fulton told her. He sniffed and blinked back his tears, staring out of the window at the neat garden, and the wilderness beyond its boundaries. 'She's OK now. That's the main thing.'

Sandra tried not to ask the question. She didn't want to ask it, didn't want to know the answer, didn't want to think about what that answer might mean.

She asked it, anyway.

'Did she kill him?'

Fulton stepped back and stared down at his wife in shock. She looked older than she'd looked just a moment before, as if just saying those words out loud had taken years off her life.

'What? No. No, of course she didn't,' he whispered. 'Don't be so ridiculous!'

This time, she threw herself at him, her arms tightening around him as she sobbed against his chest.

He smoothed her hair and held her close, as his eyes travelled to the kitchen door. The giggling was louder than ever now. Happy and carefree.

'Of course, she didn't,' he muttered.

*Don't be so ridiculous.*

# Chapter 32

The track up to Maureen Gillespie's house was the longest mile of Tyler's life.

By the time they reached the end of it, his guts were churning, his arse was aching, and he had half a mind to arrest the woman just for the state of her driveway. *Nauseating a Police Officer. Five years, minimum term.*

It wasn't even like the place was worth the effort. From a distance, it had looked like a quaint cottage set on the hillside. Up close, it could more accurately be described as a shack. Tyler himself had less generously proclaimed it, 'a heap of shit,' on the final stretch of the ascent. Now that they had arrived at it, he'd seen nothing that might change his mind.

He flexed his fingers, chasing away the numbness that had been brought on by his vice-like grip on the door handle during the drive up, then stepped out into a pool of dirty water that covered his foot all the way up to the ankle.

'Great,' he muttered. 'We're in a puddle, boss.'

'Fine my side,' said Logan, stepping down from the car onto the pock-marked dirt track.

The house was through a narrow gate and up a short path. It was made of wood that had once been painted white, but which had been stripped almost naked by years of wind and rain. The same weather conditions were likely responsible for the building's distinctive slouch, and the way its roof sagged in the middle.

A brick chimney rose up from the aged slate roof. It looked old and tired, like it had been standing for decades before the rest of the house was built around it. There was no smoke rising from it, although given the condition of the brickwork that was probably for the best.

Tyler splashed through the puddle, catching up with Logan as he strode through the open gate and onto a path that was little more than a track worn through overgrown grass.

'I thought it looked rough from down the hill,' he said. 'But it's worse up close and personal, isn't it?'

There was no need for a response. The question was obviously rhetorical, as there was no way that anyone in their right mind could argue against Tyler's point. It wasn't just that the house was a state, it was the area around it, too.

Bits of old scaffolding and broken guttering lay abandoned in the long grass. A couple of fence panels were rotting on the ground, bugs swarming through the damp and decay.

Twin wheelie bins—one blue, one green—were the most modern thing in the house's vicinity. Both had overflowed with beer cans and black bags, vomiting the contents into the tangle of weeds and bracken that surrounded them.

'Handy she's all the way out here,' Tyler remarked. 'Imagine some poor bugger having to live next to all this.'

'Aye, I doubt she'd win herself any Neighbour of the Year awards,' Logan agreed. He pointed around the side of the house. 'Go keep an eye on the back door, will you? I can't imagine she'll leg it, but just in case.'

'You be all right on your own, boss?' Tyler asked, which earned him a withering look from the DCI. 'Right. Aye. Fair enough. I'll go watch the back.'

Logan waited until Tyler had disappeared around the side of the house before he made his approach. The house looked empty, felt cold and unwelcoming, and he got the feeling that this would turn out to be the wasted journey DC Neish had joked about.

His phone chirped in his pocket as a message was received. That made sense. If Maureen was running a drug empire from out here, she'd need network access. The house must be in one of the rare phone signal oases that popped up along the route through the glen.

Logan checked the message as he walked the last few feet to the house. Hamza. Dead end with the council. Disappointing, but it had been a stretch, so not exactly a shocker of a result.

As he started to tap out a reply, he saw the signal bars drop away to zero again.

'Some bloody oasis,' he muttered, then he returned the phone to his pocket as he arrived at the front door and rapped his knuckles on the peeling wood. It wasn't the full-on Polis knock. Not yet. No point spooking her, if he could avoid it.

He waited. A mile down the track, he heard the distant rumble of a truck heading south along the A82. From somewhere closer, he heard the calling of birds and the soft swish of the bracken blowing in the breeze.

From within the house, he heard nothing.

He tried again, louder this time. The side of the fist, as opposed to the knuckles. 'Maureen? We know you're in there. We'd like a word.'

No movement. No answer.

No great surprise.

'DC Neish. Any sign?' he called. His voice sounded too loud in the comparative silence of his surroundings.

'Nothing here, boss,' came the reply.

Hunkering down, Logan opened the letterbox and peered through into the bare bones of a hallway. Flies looped in the air down by the door at the far end. Late in the year for them, unless conditions in the house were especially ripe.

The curtains were drawn across the windows, blocking Logan's view of inside. There was a slight gap where one set met in what he guessed was the living room, but it was too narrow, the room beyond it too dark, for him to be able to see anything.

'Reckon she's not home,' announced Tyler, appearing around the corner. 'Back door's locked. I was able to see into the kitchen—I wish I wasn't, but I was. No sign of anyone in there, just a big pile of dirty dishes. I tell you, boss, I don't know if she's a murderer, but she's definitely a clarty bastard.'

Logan stepped back and gave the house another once-over. There was no denying that it felt empty. Abandoned, even. If it hadn't been for the build-up of rubbish in the bins, he'd have sworn nobody had lived here in months.

And yet, something about the place was nagging at him. Some detail he'd subconsciously picked up on was telling him not to leave. Not yet.

It was Tyler who spotted it.

'There's a hole in the window, boss.'

Logan followed the DC's outstretched finger until he saw it. A round hole in the bottom corner of the glass, fracture lines splintering off from it like the legs of a squashed spider.

There were fragments of glass on the sill below the hole, outside the window.

'Shot came from inside,' Logan muttered.

'Shot?' Tyler's head tick-tocked between the DCI and the hole. 'What, like with a gun?'

'Aye. That's a bullet hole,' Logan told him.

Tyler practically ducked. 'Shite!' he ejected in a worried whisper. 'So someone might be in there? Armed?'

'Have to be helluva timing on our part,' Logan said. He pushed down the front door handle. It was unlocked and opened inwards with a nudge.

The smell that rolled out went some way to confirming Logan's suspicions, but he had to see it. He had to know.

'Christ, it stinks,' Tyler wheezed, covering his mouth.

'Stay out there,' Logan instructed. 'Keep your eyes open.'

Tyler retreated gratefully, blew the last of his breath out through his nose to clear the stench away, then gulped down some fresh air.

Inside, Logan wrestled a hand into a rubber glove as he clumped along the bare wooden floor of the hallway. He heard the hum of the flies from inside the room, felt the stink of what was to come forcing its way through his airways and down his throat.

He creaked the living room door open, and there she was, spread out across the couch.

Maureen Gillespie.

Or, what was left of her.

# Chapter 33

Hamza tapped his phone screen to wake it, then swiped to the messages.

'Anything back from the Chief?' Caitlyn asked him, flicking the handbrake switch and turning off the car's engine.

'Nothing, no,' Hamza said. 'Signal's pretty weak, though. He might not have got it. Not a big deal, though. Not exactly breaking news.'

'No,' Caitlyn agreed. She peered ahead at a house just along from where she'd parked the car. 'That one, is it?'

Hamza consulted his notebook, glanced at the numbers on the two closer houses, then nodded. 'Aye. That's it.'

He unclipped his seatbelt. 'Fingers crossed he's in.'

'Hopefully,' Caitlyn said, unfastening her own belt.

Hamza had just started to open his door when she spoke again.

'I've met someone,' she said. The words came out of her in a sudden rush, like she could no longer hold them back. She blushed when Hamza turned to face her, and tried with mixed results to wipe the smile off her face. 'Sorry. That's not appropriate. Forget I said—'

'Like *met someone* met someone?' Hamza said.

Caitlyn's smile rallied. She nodded. The movement was quick and mouse-like, and not like her at all. Hamza wholeheartedly approved.

He closed the passenger door. 'That's great news, Sarge! Congratulations. I knew there was something different.'

'You'll make a fine detective one day,' Caitlyn told him. She tilted a hand from side to side and scrunched up her nose. 'Or, well, average.'

'I can but dream,' Hamza said. 'Who is he? Is he on the job?'

Caitlyn's smile took a bit of a dunt. 'No. They're... I mean... *she*. Not he.'

'Oh,' said Hamza. He felt his eyes start to widen and fought to keep them regular sized. 'Oh! Right. I... gotcha. I didn't think you were... I mean, I didn't think you weren't, either, I just... wow.'

He punched her playfully on the arm, and both of them immediately hoped the other would never mention those last few seconds ever again.

'Good for you, Sarge,' Hamza said. 'I'm really... that's great.'

'Thanks. And sorry. Shouldn't have said anything. Not very professional.'

'Come on, seriously? I told you about my fungal nail infection,' Hamza reminded her.

'In some detail, yes, fair point,' Caitlyn said. 'Well, thanks. I just wanted to tell someone. It's early days, but... yeah.'

'So, is she on the force?'

'No. God, no.'

Hamza nodded his understanding. Being polis was one thing. Being in a relationship with one? He couldn't imagine much worse.

'And she's all right with you doing it?' he asked.

Caitlyn nodded. 'Aye. She's fine with it.'

'Well, give it time,' Hamza said, which drew a staccato laugh from the DS.

'Aye, that's true.'

She opened her door and stepped out onto the pavement.

'Well, come on then,' she urged. 'Let's get a shifty on. He's not going to arrest himself!'

Hamza got out of the car and joined her beside it. 'Happy you is weird, Sarge,' he said. 'Good weird, though,' he hastily added. 'Just… it's going to take some getting used to.'

Caitlyn screwed up her face. 'New relationship. The novelty will wear off soon enough. I wouldn't bother getting too used to it.'

Sandy Gillespie's house was in darkness when they opened the gate and headed up the path. It was barely after three, but the nights were drawing in, and several of the surrounding houses had some lights on.

'Reckon he's home?' Hamza asked.

'Fingers crossed,' said Caitlyn, taking the lead. She hammered out a rhythmic knock on the door, then listened.

'I can't hear anything,' Hamza remarked, then the barking of a dog from somewhere inside the house almost made him jump out of his skin.

'Well, we know the dog's home, at least,' Caitlyn said. 'Think we can convince it to open the door?'

She glanced at the upstairs windows. The curtains were open, but the rooms beyond the glass were in darkness.

Knocking again, she gestured to one of the downstairs windows. 'Take a look.'

Hamza picked his way across the gravel surface of the garden, carefully avoiding the half dozen dauds of dog shit scattered like landmines across it.

Cupping his hands, he peered into what turned out to be the living room. It was messy, but otherwise pretty unremarkable. An Xbox lay on the floor, wires trailing across the stained carpet to a large flatscreen TV. 4K, Hamza reckoned. Nice bit of kit.

He was about to report the place empty when he caught a glimpse of movement over by the door, there one moment, gone the next. A shadow, cast by someone out in the hall. Too big to be a dog.

'He's in there,' Hamza whispered.

Caitlyn stepped closer to the door, raised a fist and hammered against the wood. Thud-thud-thud.

'Mr Gillespie? Mr Gillespie, open the door, it's the—'
*Bang.*

Around halfway down the door, a foot-wide section of the wood exploded outwards. The air behind Caitlyn became a fine mist of red. She made a sound—a gulp, a gasp—as she was propelled backwards off her feet.

A switch flicked somewhere, grinding the world into agonising slow motion.

Hamza watched helplessly as Caitlyn sprawled through the air. He followed her flight, his own feet rooted to the ground, as she tumbled back and hit the path with a damp thack.

He stared at the mess of raw flesh that was her stomach. Gawped as she coughed and choked, blood hiccupping up over her chin and running in rivulets from both sides of her mouth.

Her eyes met his. Wide. Desperate. Pleading. The world returned to full speed—faster, even—and he moved, dropping to his haunches and hauling her away from the door.

Blood poured from her, *fountained* from her. Hamza felt it, wet and warm, as it cascaded over his hands.

'Shit, shit, shit. Sarge. Caitlyn. Fuck!'

She gagged. Spluttered. Convulsed there in his arms.

'No, no, no, no!'

He heard movement—the creak of a door slowly opening—and threw himself over her, shielding her body with his, bracing himself for whatever came next.

'What happened? What's going on?'

The voice had come from elsewhere. Not Gillespie's house. Somewhere behind him.

A man in a dirty vest stood framed in the doorway of a neighbouring house, his dinner balanced on a plate in one hand. He was mid-chew when he saw the woman on the ground, and almost choked as he swallowed it down.

'Fucking hell.'

'Ambulance! Call an ambulance!' Hamza bellowed. Caitlyn trembled beneath him, her teeth chattering together, her blood pooling between the gaps in the gravel. 'Officer down!'

## Chapter 34

'Anything, boss?'

Logan angled his phone down so he could see the screen. The signal he'd picked up earlier hadn't shown face again since, and he didn't want to go traipsing through Maureen Gillespie's house to look for a landline.

She'd been dead for a few hours, by Logan's reckoning. Five or six, maybe. No more. Her death had been swift, judging by the way in which her brains had exploded from the back of her head.

What had come after death would have been far more time-consuming.

Logan squinted at his screen. 'Bugger all. You?'

Tyler took another look at his own phone, rotated a full one-eighty on the spot, then shook his head. 'Nah, nothing.'

With a tut, Logan angrily stuffed the phone in his coat pocket, as if this would somehow teach the thing a lesson.

'I'll take a drive down the hill and phone it in from there,' he said, setting off for the car. 'You wait here and guard the scene.'

Tyler couldn't hide his disappointment. 'Seriously, boss? It's freezing. And, it's not like there's another way up. Nobody's going to get past us without us seeing. As scenes go, it's already pretty guarded.'

He had a point, much as Logan hated to admit it.

'Fine. Get in.'

'Nice one,' Tyler beamed, hurrying after him.

It was only when they were both back in the car and Logan was wrestling it through a tight five-point-turn that Tyler remembered the condition of the track. A track which he'd now have to endure twice more.

'Shite. Actually, maybe I should stay. Just in case,' he suggested.

Logan had just ejected a particularly world-weary sigh when the Volvo's speakers announced a call coming through on his mobile. The dash display flashed up the caller's name.

*Ben Forde.*

'Must've picked up the signal,' Tyler remarked, just in case the DCI had been unable to figure that out on his own.

Stopping the car, for fear of losing the signal again, Logan tapped a button on the steering wheel, and the ringing was replaced by a crackle of static.

'Ben?'

Ben Forde's voice was a broken hiss of interference.

'Ben? You're breaking up. Say again.'

Tyler's phone bleeped in his pocket. He fished it out while Logan tried to decipher another string of garbled pops and hisses from the speakers.

'I'm not getting you, Ben. I'm going to try to...'

'—ello? Ja—'

Tyler's incoming message notification chimed again.

Again.

Again.

'Christ, I'm more popular than I thought,' he mumbled, tapping the notification.

The sound from the speakers crackled again, then fell silent. Ben's name disappeared from the screen.

'Bloody thing,' Logan muttered, sliding the car into first gear.

'Boss.'

Logan turned and saw it on the DC's face. Something had happened. Something terrible.

'What is it?' he asked. 'What's happened?'

'It's DS McQuarrie, boss. It's Caitlyn,' Tyler croaked. He started to say more, but his breath got stuck somewhere between his lungs and his voice box. He turned the phone instead, letting Logan read the words on the screen.

'Oh, Jesus,' the DCI whispered. He jammed his foot down on the accelerator and the Volvo lurched off from a standing start, churning the ground with its back wheels. 'Oh, God, no.'

–

By the time they arrived, the circus had descended on the street. Neighbouring houses had been evacuated, and cordon tapes had been set up at either end of the road, half a dozen Uniforms standing guard at each end.

Logan screeched the Volvo to a halt behind a row of police cars and vans, their lights painting the darkening street in overlapping shades of blue.

'Where is she?' he barked, jumping out of the car without bothering to shut off the engine, and startling a uniformed constable.

'Sir?'

'Fuck's sake! DS McQuarrie. Where is she?'

Ben Forde stepped out from the back of one of the vans.

'It's all right, son. I've got it,' he said, dismissing the constable with a wave. 'I think I saw one of the local journalists poking his nose around. Away and tell him to piss off, will you?'

The Uniform nodded. That, he could handle.

'Yes, sir. On it, sir.'

Ben watched the constable go scuttling off in search of anyone with a camera, then turned back to Logan.

'Where is she?' the DCI demanded. 'What's the story?'

'Ambulance took her about fifteen minutes ago. I've sent Hamza into the hospital with her. He didn't want to leave her. He's pretty shaken up.'

'What the hell happened?'

Ben threw a scowl in the direction of Sandy Gillespie's house, and the gaping hole in its front door.

'Shotgun, we think. Close up from the other side of the door. He must've been standing just inside. Shot her clean through the wood.'

Logan sucked air in through his teeth. 'Bad?'

Ben nodded. 'Bad. Aye.'

'But not *bad* bad, though, right?' Tyler asked. 'She's going to be all right, isn't she?'

Ben opened his mouth, then shrugged. It wasn't much of a movement, but it seemed to drain him of almost all his strength.

'Jesus Christ,' Tyler whispered, running both hands through his hair. 'Jesus Christ.'

'Is it Gillespie?' Logan asked. 'Is he still in there?'

'As far as we know, aye,' Ben confirmed. 'But he's not talking to anyone, and we daren't send anyone in. Armed Response are on their way. Be here within ninety minutes.'

'Ninety fucking minutes,' Logan said, spitting the words out as if the ETA was some sort of personal insult. He stared over at the house, fingers flexing in and out, making fists.

'His sister's dead,' Tyler told Ben. 'Maureen. Up at the house. Someone shot her, then cut her open.'

Ben looked unsurprised. Or unbothered, maybe, like it was way down his list of concerns.

'Right. So, whoever was higher up the chain came looking for their missing gear,' he deduced. 'And she didn't have it.'

'Aye. And my bet is that wee bastard in there knows what happened,' Logan said, stabbing a finger in the direction of the house. 'And he thinks that whoever came for Maureen is going to be coming for him, so he holed himself up with a gun and waited for them.'

'And Caitlyn went and got caught in the middle of it,' Ben said. He squeezed the bridge of his nose between finger and thumb. 'Christ Almighty, what a mess.'

A movement at the corner of Logan's eye caught his attention. Sergeant Jaffray stood a few feet away, raising his hand like a nervous schoolboy.

'What?' Logan demanded, making him jump. 'What is it?'

Jaffray lowered his hand. 'Um, just to let you know, he's still not answering,' the uniformed sergeant said. 'We've got his mobile number, too, but it's switched off.'

Logan's glare became too much for him to cope with, and he shifted his attention to DI Forde, instead. 'I didn't know if you wanted us to have a go with the megaphone again, sir?'

Ben deferred to Logan with a raising of his eyebrows. 'Jack?'

Logan paced back and forth on the pavement, a few steps one direction, then a few steps back.

No. Not paced, exactly. He prowled, his gaze fixed on Gillespie's house like a predator on its luckless prey.

'We're sure he's in there?'

'Hamza reckons so,' Ben replied. 'Nobody saw him come out.'

'And ninety minutes for AR?'

Ben nodded. 'Aye. Bit less now, but near enough.'

'Right. Fuck it,' Logan said. He shrugged off his coat and let it fall to the ground at his feet, his eyes never leaving Sandy Gillespie's front door. 'Megaphone.'

Sergeant Jaffray looked down at the DCI's open hand.

'You deaf, son? What are you waiting for? Get me the damn megaphone!'

'Right, yes. Right,' Jaffray blurted, practically jumping out of his skin.

He scurried into the back of the nearest van and returned a few seconds later with a battery-operated loudhailer. Logan took it, hefted it from hand to hand, checked the wrist strap was firmly attached, then nodded his approval.

'Right. Good. This'll do,' he said, turning away from the sergeant like he'd suddenly ceased to exist.

'What are you going to say, boss?' Tyler asked.

Logan rolled up one of his shirt sleeves. 'Say?' He switched the megaphone to the opposite hand and rolled up the other sleeve. 'Who said I'm going to say anything?'

He set off in the direction of the house, then stopped when Ben caught him by the arm. 'You should have a vest on, Jack.'

Logan looked down at himself, then back at his friend. 'Aye. I probably should,' he agreed.

Ben puffed out his cheeks, shook his head, then released his grip on the DCI's arm. He, Tyler, and half the Lochaber area force watched as Logan marched across the street, threw open Gillespie's gate and set off up the path.

'What the hell's he doing?' Tyler asked.

Halfway up the path, Logan swung the megaphone by its strap and launched it at the living room window like the hammer of Thor. The street was filled with the sound of breaking glass, which was swiftly followed by a shout of panic from inside the house.

Logan was at the door a second later, inside a half-second after that.

Ben exhaled as he watched the DCI break into a run and go storming up the hallway.

'What he does best, son,' he said. He folded his arms and waited for the fireworks. 'He's doing what he does best.'

# Chapter 35

Sandy Gillespie was sweeping the shotgun across the living room, the weapon shaking in his hands, when the dog started going bananas in the kitchen, and he realised that he'd been played.

He spun, yelping in fright, finger just starting to tighten on the trigger of the shotgun when a man—no, not a man, a *beast*—came barrelling into the room like a force of nature: raw, and violent, and unstoppable.

Gillespie didn't recognise him. His anger disguised him, twisting his features into something monstrous. Rage radiated off him in rolling waves, stumbling Sandy back a pace as he desperately tried to bring the barrel of the gun into the gap between them.

The intruder was big. Bigger, in that moment, than anyone Gillespie had ever seen. Bigger than anyone who'd ever lived, he thought. Not a man. Not even a beast. A giant. A *god*. Fire and fury made flesh.

A bear-sized fist cracked against the side of his head. A wrecking ball. A juggernaut. An express train.

Pain exploded through his skull, filling it up, blinding him. The floor lurched beneath his feet like the deck of a storm-ravaged ship. He grabbed for the gun that was no longer in his hands, grasped for the air that was suddenly swooshing around him. And then he howled as his nose burst open on the carpet, and a broken tooth caught at the back of his throat.

He heard the breathing of the beast, raw air rasping in and out through its snarling maw. He saw the gun lying on the floor, just beyond his reach. One good lunge would do it. One kick of the legs, one swift grab, one single shot, and it would all be over.

The beast spoke then, each word booming out of him like the tolling of some terrible funeral bell.

'I dare you, son. I fucking dare you.'

The floorboards whimpered as the beast took a step back, giving Gillespie room to manoeuvre. Giving him a chance.

'Do it,' the voice urged. 'Go for it. Pick it up.'

Gillespie stared at the weapon. So close. Right there.

'*Pick it up!*' The voice was a roar, all rage and spit, and hot, fiery dragon breath.

When Gillespie didn't move, a clawed hand caught him by the back of the neck and dragged him closer to the gun. He hissed and whimpered as his broken nose and chin were burned across the rough carpet.

'There you go. Go on, what are you waiting for? It's right there,' the beast told him. Sandy felt himself rise up an inch or two, before he was slammed down again onto his face. The floorboards gave another creak as the beast retreated a couple of paces. 'Pick it up. Do it. This is your one and only chance. Now or never, Sandy. Do it!'

Gillespie wheezed, coughed, and spat out the broken tooth. For a moment, he just stared at it as it lay there in a puddle of blood and spit, not quite comprehending what it was, or how it had got there.

The beast growled.

The dog barked.

Sandy Gillespie's legs twitched.

And then, with a banshee yell, he grabbed for the gun.

–

The shotgun's roar reverberated out from inside the house, shaking the remaining windows in their frames. Everyone but Ben Forde ducked for cover, and then they all listened to the sound of furniture breaking, something heavy hitting something hard, and then a desperate, terror-stricken scream that gargled into silence.

'Shit, shit. What do we do?' Tyler hissed, raising his head just enough to peer over the bonnet of Logan's Volvo. Despite the racket, there was no sign of movement from the house. 'Do we go in? What do we do?'

Ben shook his head. 'We don't go in, no. Relax, son. It's all under control.'

DC Neish chewed on a thumbnail, his gaze going from Ben to the house and back again.

'But… the gunshot, boss. He might be in trouble. He could be hurt.'

'Aye, well, that'll be his own stupid fault, won't it?' Ben said.

His phone rang, sharp and shrill, making half the officers in earshot jump with fright. He hurriedly checked the screen, and the name on it made his stomach flip itself all the way over.

DC Khaled.

Hamza.

'Like I said, son. Nothing to worry about. It's all under control,' Ben reiterated, then he tapped the answer button, pressed the phone to his ear, and braced himself.

It was almost six minutes later when Logan finally emerged, shoving a bloodied and babbling Sandy Gillespie in front of him. Gillespie's legs were barely holding him up, but the threat of the detective at his back forced them to carry him down the path, through the gate, and out onto the street beyond.

He shuffled, zombie-like, off the pavement and onto the road, the spiralling lights of the polis vehicles dazzling him.

All around them, Uniforms watched in silence as Logan steered the bastard towards Ben and Tyler with a well-placed shove to the back.

'Keep walking,' the DCI barked, drawing a little whimper and a burst of speed from the man in front. A bubble of blood burst on his lips. He spluttered, choking on the taste of his own broken nose.

A slab of a hand on Gillespie's shoulder jerked him to a stop at the kerb. His eyes went from Ben to Tyler and back again, half-panicked, half-pleading with them for protection. Neither of them made any move to help him. Judging by the look on DC Neish's face, in fact, Gillespie would be safer staying in the hands of the senior officer.

'Arrest this gentleman, will you?' Logan said. He gave Gillespie another shove that sent him tumbling to the pavement at Ben's feet. 'And get him out of my sight.'

Ben drew in a long, steadying breath. He shot Tyler the briefest of looks, and the DC took a half step forward, putting himself between Logan and Gillespie, blocking the way.

Logan looked between them, studied them, read their bodies and their faces, and understood. He knew, in that moment, what had happened. He knew what the charge was going to be, and wished he could somehow stop the words before they came tumbling out of Ben's mouth.

He couldn't, though. It was too late. The damage was already done.

'Sandy Gillespie,' DI Forde intoned, not even looking at the snivelling bastard at his feet. 'I am arresting you for the murder of Detective Sergeant Caitlyn McQuarrie.'

# Chapter 36

A hush hung over Fort William Police Station. Smothering it. Stifling it. It invaded every corner, from the reception where Moira silently sat, to the empty interview rooms.

It pushed down hardest on the Incident Room, focused mostly on the Big Board, where Caitlyn had most recently worked her own particular brand of organisational magic.

Ben and Tyler sat at their desks, staring blankly at nothing in particular, lost in thoughts they were still too numb to think. Logan sat through the back, in his private office, the blinds drawn and door shut tight. He'd been in there since they'd got back.

'Give me a minute,' he'd said.

That had been three hours ago.

Somewhere, far off in the building, a phone rang. It echoed along the silent corridors long enough to make Ben tut in irritation, then was silenced. Somebody answered, or someone rang off. Ben didn't care which. It had stopped, and that was the main thing.

'Still can't believe it.' Tyler's voice was low and lifeless. Not shocked, or angry, but flat and matter-of-fact. 'Still can't believe she's gone.'

Ben nodded. He wished he had some words of wisdom to offer. Some comfort for the lad, but he didn't. The reality of it was, it happened. He'd lost other colleagues over the years. Friends. Family, almost. Tyler would, too. That was just the way of it.

You grieved. You processed. You moved on.

Somehow, you moved on.

'That prick been brought in yet?' Tyler asked. This time, his voice wasn't flat, or level, or matter-of-fact. There was anger there, raw and fierce.

'Still at the hospital,' Ben replied.

Sandy Gillespie had sustained some injuries during his arrest by Logan. Nothing major. Nothing that couldn't be explained away by a violent tussle over a firearm. A couple of broken fingers, a shattered nose, a cracked rib. He'd heal. He'd recover. Physically, at least.

'Under guard, though?'

'Oh, aye. Uniform were queuing up. He's no' going anywhere. Be tomorrow before we can question him, though.' Ben shot a look at the shuttered office. 'Maybe for the best.'

Tyler followed the DI's gaze. 'The boss going to be OK?'

Ben's reply took a moment to come. 'Aye. Jack? Aye. He'll be fine,' he said, although there wasn't a lot of conviction in it. 'He'll just be taking some time to process. It's been a long day.'

Tyler couldn't argue with that. He checked his watch. After eleven. He stifled a yawn for as long as he could, then relented to it.

'Sorry,' he muttered, once it had passed.

Ben caught the contagion and covered his mouth with both hands as he yawned, too. 'You've got me started now.' He got to his feet and took his jacket from the back of his chair. 'Come on. Home time. Nothing else we can do here tonight. Tomorrow's going to be a big one.'

Tyler didn't need to be told twice. He jabbed the button that turned off his computer monitor, then got to his feet.

'You heading to the hotel, or up the road, boss?' he asked.

Ben had been wondering that very same thing. The hotel was close, and the thought of climbing into bed was tempting. But after everything that had happened, he had a longing to be at home, to be with Alice. Just to see her, say hello, argue about something insignificant. Pretend everything was normal, just for a while.

But everything wasn't normal. Not by a long shot.

And there was still work to be done.

'Hotel,' Ben decided. 'You?'

Tyler, it turned out, had been having a similar debate with himself, and had come to the same conclusion as the DI.

'Much as I'd like to go home, hotel for me, too,' he said. 'Going to see this through, boss. For Caitlyn's sake.'

Ben nodded his approval. 'Aye. For Caitlyn's sake,' he agreed.

Because, that's what you did. That's what you had to do. You grieved. You processed.

Somehow, you moved on.

'Any word from Ham?' Tyler asked.

'I sent him home. Aye, *home* home,' Ben replied. 'Told him to take a few days, and that we'd call him with any questions.'

'Sounds sensible.'

'Aye, well. Some of us have to be,' Ben said, stealing the briefest of glances at Logan's office door.

Fishing in his pocket, Ben dug out his car keys and tossed them to DC Neish. 'Here. Go wait in the car. I'll check on himself, then be out.'

'No bother, boss,' Tyler said. He looked the closed door up and down, then mouthed an almost silent, 'Good luck,' before leaving.

Ben didn't approach the office. Not yet. He eyed it warily, instead, like it was the lair of some great and terrible dragon. He wasn't scared of Logan. Not by a long shot. He could give as good as he got, and the DCI knew better than to try any of his shite.

He was afraid, though, of what else he might find lurking in the corners of the office. The grief. The misery. The guilt and self-blame.

It was fair to say that Logan disliked most people. Actively despised many of them, in fact. When something happened to those handful that he *did* like—especially those he considered his responsibility—the fallout could be painful to witness.

He knocked on the door, softly at first.

'Jack? Jack, it's me.'

There was silence for a while, then:

'I'll just be a minute.'

'Aye, well, you said that three hours ago,' Ben told him. 'I think your watch might be knackered.'

There was a sigh, heavy and sullen.

'It's open.'

Light spilled into the darkened office when Ben opened the door, making Logan hiss and blink. It pushed away the shadows and reflected in the bottle of amber liquid standing open on the DCI's desk.

A single measure was missing from the bottle, presumably having found its way into the *Cadbury's Creme Egg* mug that sat in the dead centre of the desk, an inch or two from Logan's hand.

'Jesus, Jack. Where the hell did you get that?' Ben asked.

Logan didn't look up, his gaze fixed like a tractor beam on the mug. 'Does it matter?'

'Yes, it matters! Of course, it matters! What are you thinking?'

'What am I thinking? What am I *thinking*? I'll tell you what I'm thinking. I'm thinking I sent Caitlyn to that bastard's house,' Logan said, tearing his eyes from the mug. 'I'm thinking that one of my decisions has once again led to the death of a… of a *fucking excellent* police officer. That's what I'm thinking, Detective Inspector. If you must know.'

His fingers crept around the mug. He lifted them off one at a time, then put them back, like the surface was too hot to hold onto for long.

'Why? What are you thinking?' he muttered.

'Oh, you know full well what I'm thinking, Jack,' Ben said, shooting the bottle a look of distaste.

'I don't. I don't have a clue. Enlighten me.'

'I'm thinking, "Look at the state of this selfish bastard",' Ben said.

Logan snorted a derisory laugh. 'Oh, is that—?'

'I wasn't finished,' Ben snapped. 'I'm thinking we lost a very good officer today. One of the best I've ever worked with. I'm thinking we've lost a real asset and a good friend, and I refuse to just stand here and watch as we lose another. I won't.'

Logan's shoulders straightened. His chest inflated like he was preparing for a fight.

But then, with a sigh, it all collapsed, and he sat there behind his desk looking smaller than Ben had ever seen him before.

'You're right. No. You're absolutely right,' Logan said. 'I wouldn't ask you to do that.'

His fingers stopped their dancing and tightened around the mug.

'So, shut the door and turn the lights off on your way out,' Logan instructed. 'And I'll see you on the other side.'

–

Sandy Gillespie surfaced groggily from the latest in a series of short, restless sleeps. For a moment, he couldn't remember where he was, but then a selection of aches and pains cut through the brain fog, and the metal bracelet around his wrist rattled where it was fastened to the hospital bed.

What time was it? There was a clock on the wall, but the room was in near-total darkness, making it difficult to see. Before he'd fallen asleep, light had been flooding in through the little window in the door, but someone must have pulled the curtain and covered it while he slept.

He squinted at the clock for a while, trying to force his night vision to kick in. Just after three, he thought. Or possibly a quarter past one.

They'd taken his watch. His clothes, too. Swabbed him down and taken his prints, and only then allowed him to receive treatment. He should sue. He should fucking sue. Take the bastards for all they were worth. Police brutality, that's what it had been. No question.

Pain burned through his ribcage, and he grimaced. That big bastard had done a number on him. He'd caught him off-guard. Caught him panicked. If he ever saw him again, the shoe would be on the other foot. Yes, next time, things would be very—

'Hello, Sandy.'

Gillespie made a sound. It was not a sound he had intended to make, and not one he was particularly proud of. It was somewhere between a yelp and a squeal, like a puppy whose tail had just been trodden on.

The voice had come from the darkest corner of the room. There was a shadow there, big and bulky, imposing itself against the background of black.

*Shit. Oh, shit.*

'How the fuck did you get in here?' Gillespie demanded. His voice was an unsteady tremble, fraying around the edges. 'You shouldn't be in here.'

'Doesn't matter how I'm here, Sandy.'

Gillespie's eyes were adjusting to the gloom, and saw Logan come stepping from the shadows. He had his coat on, his hands shoved deep down in the pockets. The coat and the stance made him look even larger and more intimidating than before.

'What matters—what you should be concerning your-self with—is *why* I'm here.'

Gillespie swallowed. He pulled on the handcuff, but his hand remained trapped.

'Why *are* you here?'

Logan didn't answer. Not right away. Instead, he crossed to the end of the bed and leaned on it, his big hands wrapping around the metal frame.

'Honestly? Your guess is as good as mine,' the DCI admitted. 'I was wide awake and at a loose end. Thought I'd swing by and see how you were doing.'

Gillespie shot a look to the door. The corridor light seeped in at the edges of the curtain. From there, strapped to that bed, it may as well have been another world.

'You can try shouting, if you like,' Logan said. 'See how you get on. I dare you.'

Gillespie dismissed it with a shake of his head. He remembered very clearly what had happened last time the detective had dared him to do something. The multitude of aches currently ravaging his body were making damn sure of that.

'Don't hurt me.'

Logan chuckled drily. 'I'm not here to hurt you, Sandy. I wouldn't dream of hurting a man like you, who knows all his rights. And risk you getting away with everything on some technicality? No.'

Sandy said nothing, just watched in nervous silence as Logan turned to look at the monitoring equipment by the bed. As the detective turned, something in his coat pocket chinked against the bed's frame. Glass. A bottle.

Christ, was he drunk? Sandy tried to wriggle out of his cuff, again, but he knew he was wasting his time.

'Your sister's dead,' Logan said, almost absent-mindedly. He turned his attention away from the hospital machines, and back to the bed. 'Maureen. We found her.'

Sandy nodded. As suspected, this was not news to him. 'How?'

'Have a guess.'

'I don't know.'

'I didn't ask if you knew. I told you to guess,' Logan said. His tone was dangerous, like another wrong response might ignite him and blow the whole room to kingdom come. 'So, please. Humour me. Guess.'

'Shot,' Gillespie said.

Logan feigned surprise. 'Well done. Spot-on. Some guess there, Sandy. Shot. Through the head.'

He formed a gun shape with two fingers and took aim at the man in the bed. 'BANG!' he barked, and Gillespie's heart monitor spiked as he jumped. 'Shot dead. Right through the forehead. Close up, they reckon. Downward angle, suggesting she was on her knees. Pleading.'

Gillespie chewed on his bottom lip, biting back whatever response was trying to come out.

'Nasty business,' Logan continued with a sad shake of his head. 'And then, after she was shot, she was cut open. Like Brodie Welsh, only with less care and attention. Brutal, it was. Very messy.'

Gillespie squirmed in the bed. He looked away from the detective, hiding the tears welling up in his eyes.

'Fuck you,' he whispered.

Logan straightened. 'Aye. Probably best not to dwell on it, right enough. Nasty business. Because, think about it, Sandy, if someone did that to her and didn't get what they were after, just imagine what they'll do to you.' He flashed the wee scrote a smile that was all teeth. 'And just think how easy it was for a clumsy big bastard like *me* to get to you in here.'

He gave that a few moments to sink in, then headed for the door. 'So we'll maybe see you at the station tomorrow. If you're feeling up to it. With a bit of luck, we'll be able to put all this unpleasantness to bed, once and for all.'

He opened the door, letting the light in. Gillespie blinked and shielded his eyes with his free hand.

'Wait!' he called, before Logan could leave. 'The, eh, the cop. That woman. I didn't know she... she wasn't meant to...' He shrank beneath Logan's gaze, his voice becoming a squeak, like air escaping the neck of a balloon. 'I'm sorry.'

Logan clicked his tongue against the roof of his mouth, then nodded. 'Aye. You will be, son,' he said. 'You will be.'

He swallowed, his grip tight on the door handle like he was wrestling with himself over whether to stay or go. Was he finished here, or was he just getting started?

The weight of the bottle in his pocket pulled his coat down at one side.

And Logan knew what he had to do.

# Chapter 37

Ben Forde was the first one into the Incident Room the next morning. He'd promised Tyler a lift in at eight, but he'd been awake half the night, and by the time the clock showed seven, he was already halfway to the station.

'Jack?' he called, as he stepped into the room. The main bulk of the place was empty. The desks were untouched, their stacks of paperwork and evidence bags all exactly as they'd been left the night before.

The office blinds were still shut, the door still closed. Ben muttered a few of the more minor expletives below his breath, ran a hand through his thinning hair, then began his approach.

'Jack? It's me. You awake?'

There was no reply from within the office. Ben stopped by a window and tried to peek through the gaps at the edges of the blind, but the room beyond was too dark for him to see much of anything.

He swore again, with a little more venom this time, then knocked on the door.

'Jack? You in there?' he asked. He knocked again, louder this time. 'Wakey wakey. Come on.'

He gave it a few seconds, then tried the door handle. Locked.

*Shite.*

Ben's heart skipped into a higher gear. He gave the door the classic polis knock this time. *Thump-thump-thump.*

'Jack! Stop arsing about and open the door!'

He rapped his knuckles on the window, hard and fast and sharp. He called out again, close enough to fog the glass and loud enough to shake it.

'Jack! Open the bloody door!'

Ben listened, straining to hear over the sound of his blood whooshing through his veins. He gave it to the count of ten, before concluding that radical action was needed.

'Right. Fine. Don't say I didn't warn you,' he called, then he stepped back, angled his shoulder towards the door, and lunged.

It had been a number of years since Ben Forde had last put in a door. They had been lighter back then, he thought, as pain went radiating down his arm and across his back. Flimsier.

He tried again, putting all his weight behind the second attempt. The impact was harder, the pain more severe. The bastarding door remained firmly shut.

Back in the day, he'd have put it in with a couple of well-aimed kicks, but the lock was at waist height, and there was no way he was getting his leg that high without risking permanent injury.

'You'd better be lying dead in there,' Ben hollered at the office, then he took three big paces back, sucked in a couple of deep breaths, and charged.

His first instinct, when he heard the crack, was that he'd broken a bone. Certainly, that was what the agony that exploded across his shoulder suggested.

But then, he was stumbling into the office, the door swinging open and pouring light into the darkness.

Ben crashed awkwardly into Logan's desk and had to grip the edge to stop himself sliding right over the top of it.

The office was empty. No Logan.

Straightening, Ben gingerly moved his arm around, testing for damage. It throbbed, but there were no sudden sharp stabbing sensations that would suggest anything serious. That was something.

The *Creme Egg* mug was still on the desk. Ben stole a look inside. Just like the office, it too was empty.

He groaned. 'Ah, bollocks.'

This was bad. This was very bad.

He turned to leave, and then stopped and walked around to the other side of the desk. There was a bin there, tucked away under the desk, a round metal pail lined with a plastic bag.

The gold-coloured top of the whisky bottle jutted up above the rim, and Ben's heart fell all the way down to his feet.

'Christ. The whole thing?'

There was no saying where the DCI would be now. No saying what he'd be doing, or who he'd be doing it to. No saying what damage he might inflict on the ongoing investigations, or—

'You all right in there, Benjamin?'

Ben turned to find Logan looming in the doorway, a paper cup in each hand, a white paper bag poking out from a coat pocket.

'Jack! Where the hell have you been?'

'Cafe along the road. Got us rolls.' He regarded the broken door frame. 'Problems?'

'Problems? Aye. What? Aye, problems. I was shouting, but you didn't answer me.'

Logan frowned. 'I wasn't in.'

'Well, no. I mean, aye. I know that now, obviously,' Ben replied, throwing his arms up in exasperation. 'I nearly broke my shoulder getting that open.'

'I'm pretty sure there's a spare key somewhere,' Logan said. He held out one of the cups. 'Here. Coffee. I'm assuming you didn't get much sleep.'

Ben resisted for all of three seconds, before tutting and accepting the cup. 'Aye, and whose fault is that?'

He sat in Logan's chair and took a sip of the coffee. It was blisteringly hot, and he set the cup down on the desk to let it cool. A white paper bag landed next to it.

'Square sausage and a tattie scone.'

'Making amends for something, Jack?' Ben asked, opening the bag. His stomach gurgled as the smell wafted out, and he realised he couldn't remember the last time he'd eaten.

'Aye. Something like that,' Logan admitted. He sat in the chair across from the DI and opened up his own paper bag.

'How'd you know I'd be in here early?'

Logan tapped the side of his head. 'Mind like a steel trap, Benjamin,' he said. 'Also, you've become a right predictable bastard in your old age.'

He looked, Ben had to admit, remarkably fresh. Much fresher than the DI himself felt, that was for sure. There was none of the bleariness Ben had been bracing himself for, no bloodshot eyes, or gravelly voice. No shouting, or staggering, or out-of-character declarations of love.

He was, as far as the DI could tell, stone-cold sober.

'I went to the hospital. To see Gillespie,' Logan announced, and Ben almost choked on his square sausage.

'Jesus Christ. You did what?'

'I know. I know,' Logan said. 'I wanted to...' He gestured vaguely with his roll. 'I don't know. I thought it'd help.'

'Help who, exactly? Not the case, that's for sure. Not us. Not Caitlyn.'

Logan stuffed his mouth with bacon butty and chewed.

'And did it?' Ben asked. 'Help, I mean?'

Logan made a weighing motion, then forced down a swallow. 'Helped me realise I was being an arsehole,' Logan said.

Ben grunted. 'Huh. Well, that's something, I suppose.'

There was a sound from out in the Incident Room. The squeak of a door opening.

Both men turned just as Hamza peeked tentatively into the inner office.

'Did I no' tell you to take a few days off?' said Ben.

Hamza shifted his weight from one foot to the other. 'Aye, sir. You did. But... well. You know.'

Ben nodded. He knew. Of course, he knew.

'Coffee's on your desk,' Logan said. 'Bacon roll. Crispy, no butter. Right?'

Hamza smiled, albeit faintly. 'Cheers, sir.'

The door squeaked again out in the Incident Room. 'Morning, Detective Constable,' Logan announced.

Tyler appeared beside Hamza, thumbing sleep from his eyes. 'Morning.' He shot Ben a slightly accusatory look. 'And cheers for the lift, boss.'

'I thought you'd be sleeping.'

Tyler yawned so wide he almost swallowed his face, then gave a shake of his head. 'Couldn't. Not really. I got a taxi in.'

'Go get some caffeine and grub in you, son,' Logan said. 'I left it on your desk.'

Tyler rubbed his head, smoothing down a clump of hair that had been sticking up. 'Right. Nice one. Cheers, boss.'

'How'd you know?' Hamza asked. 'That we'd be here?'

Logan tapped the side of his head again, but this time said nothing.

'Go get stuck in, lads,' Ben told them. He picked up his own cup and took a sip. 'Then let's get to work.'

He and Logan waited for the DCs to leave the office, then Logan stood up and dusted the breadcrumbs off his crumpled shirt. 'I'm going to go get cleaned up,' he announced. 'Then we'll crack on. All right?'

Ben raised his paper cup. 'See if you can find some deodorant, while you're at it. No' putting up with you smelling like that all day.'

Logan raised an arm, sniffed, and then pulled a face. 'Aye. I take your point,' he said, then he pointed to Ben, installed behind the office's desk. 'Don't get too comfortable in that seat, by the way.'

And with that, he was gone.

Ben waited until he heard the Incident Room door squeaking for a third time, then he set down his cup.

It took him a moment to prepare himself mentally, but then he rolled the chair back, leaned down, and took the whisky bottle from the bin.

Full. All the way to the top.

He sat back, exhaling, and shot a grateful look at the ceiling. He hadn't touched it. He hadn't given in. Aye, he must've been tempted, but he'd handled it. He'd resisted. He'd coped.

You grieved. You processed. And then, you moved on.

Ben gathered up the paper bags, drained the last of his coffee from his cup, and tossed them into the bin beside the bottle. That done, he took out the plastic bag and tied the whole thing tightly at the top. Double knot. Better safe than sorry.

'Just dealing with this,' he told Tyler and Hamza as he crossed the Incident Room with the bag in hand. 'And then, we'll get started.'

Tyler swallowed a bite of breakfast and indicated the bag with a nod. 'What is it, boss?'

Ben glanced down at the bag, its weight swinging it back and forth in his grip. 'Nothing to worry about,' he said. 'Nothing to worry about at all.'

## Chapter 38

Hamza couldn't bring himself to look at the others. Not yet. Not now. He had picked a spot in the gap between Logan and Ben, and was committing to it fully with a thousand-yard-stare.

'It just came out of nowhere. I thought... I mean, I saw a shadow moving in the house. I told Caitlyn. DS McQuarrie, I mean. I told her, and she knocked, and then... it just happened. Out of nowhere.'

He frowned, like he still couldn't quite understand exactly what it was that *had* happened.

'Bang. Or boom. Aye. More a boom. Not a gunshot, an explosion. And there was... behind her, there was this mist. Red. Just so... just so red. It was like it was swirling in the air there, like a firework, or something. And then, she was on the ground, and I just grabbed her and pulled her out of the way of the door.'

He sniffed, his stare still fixed on a spot only he could see. 'I didn't know what to do. I panicked. Totally bottled it. Just started shouting for help. For someone to help her. For someone to do something, because I... I didn't know. I didn't know how to. I didn't know what to do.'

DC Neish put a hand on Hamza's shoulder. 'You're all right, mate.'

'Tyler's right, son,' Ben added. 'You got her help. You kept her safe until the ambulance came. There's nothing else anyone could've done. Nobody could ask any more of you, not me, not Jack, not Caitlyn. You did her proud.'

Hamza sniffed again and drew one of his shirt sleeves across his eyes. 'She, eh, she'd met someone. Recently.'

'What, like, a guy?' Tyler asked.

'A girl. A woman, I mean.'

'Aye? Wow! She was a dark horse, wasn't she?' Tyler remarked.

'Do we know who she is?' Ben asked.

Hamza shook his head. 'No. She didn't say. It was quite new, I think. It's why she'd been acting differently.' He shrugged. 'Why she'd been happy.'

'I get it, Hamza,' Logan said. It was the first time he'd spoken in several minutes, and it snapped the DC out of his stupor. 'I understand why you feel guilty. And you're right to.'

Hamza's eyes grew a fraction larger. 'Sir?'

'Not because it's your fault, or because you did anything wrong. It isn't, and you didn't. You're right to feel guilty because you're a good copper, son. You're a good man. And good men, in these circumstances, feel guilty. They feel like they should've done more, or should've acted sooner, or should've worked some miracle that would've somehow saved the day.'

He glanced over at Ben, who gave him the briefest of nods in response.

'You're right to feel all that, because you're a good man, Hamza. But it wasn't your fault. You did all you could, and nobody thinks otherwise.'

Hamza didn't look entirely convinced, but he gently cleared his throat. 'Thanks, sir. Appreciate it.'

'Has Hoon spoken to her family yet?' Logan asked, turning to DI Forde.

'Her parents, aye,' said Ben. 'They're on Orkney. He's got a liaison working with them and making arrangements. Funeral will be up there, he thinks.'

'I'd like to speak to them, too,' Logan said. 'But I want to have some news for them first. What time are we getting Gillespie in here?'

Ben glanced up at the clock on the wall. 'Doctor said he's all ours from around one. His solicitor is on standby.'

'Right. So, we've got plenty of time, then,' Logan said, standing. He fished in his pocket until he found his car keys. 'Who's up for a wee road trip?'

–

Forty minutes later, Logan, Ben, Tyler, and Hamza stood in the shadow of Buachaille Etive Mor, listening to the distant rumble of passing traffic, and the irregular flapping of the plastic cordon tape.

The area had been meticulously searched by the Scene of Crime team, and all forensic materials taken away to be tested and catalogued. There was no reason the bridge and the path past the SMC hut couldn't be opened now—at least one climbing organisation was already demanding it, in fact—but Logan had insisted the place be kept cordoned off for another day or two, while he and the team continued to work on the case.

Of course, Brodie Welsh's murder wasn't the all-consuming urgent matter it had been just a day ago. There were two other murders to throw into the mix now, although from where Logan was standing, they were both pretty clear cut.

Sandy Gillespie had killed DS Caitlyn McQuarrie. Maureen Gillespie had been killed by someone she was involved with in the drugs trade. They'd get a name from her brother, sooner or later, and from there it should be straightforward enough. There was no great mystery to either.

Unlike Brodie Welsh.

Sure, Maureen and Sandy were probably responsible for his death. That made sense. It was clean. Easy.

Too easy, though?

Why move the body? Why stage the call-out? Why want him found? The main thrust of it—the actual murder part—that made sense, aye. But the rest? Sandy Gillespie was going to have to go some to make all the pieces fit the jigsaw.

Still, the evidence was there. The way Brodie had been cut open suggested someone who knew about his drug trafficking, and Logan was prepared to bet the footprints found around the grave would be the same size as one of the Gillespies'.

They had the motive, too, if they thought he was trying to cross them, or otherwise becoming a liability. Maybe they'd gotten wind that Hannah had seen through Brodie's cover story. Or maybe he'd been taking more of a cut than he was meant to. In that line of work, reasons to get yourself murdered were usually in abundance.

It made sense. The Gillespies, or someone working with them, must've done. It made sense.

And yet...

The sound of DI Forde's voice pulled the brake on Logan's train of thought and dragged him back to the here and now.

'Much as I enjoy getting out of the office, Jack, I can't help but wonder what we're doing out here in the freezing cold?' He gestured over the bridge at where Brodie's body had been discovered. 'Something new come up?'

Logan shook his head. 'No. I just wanted us to go over it one more time before we talk to Gillespie. See if we can make some sense of it. Also, aye.' He inhaled deeply through his nose. 'I thought we could do with getting out in the fresh air. Clears the head.'

'Here! Boss!' Tyler gasped. He pointed up beyond the mountaineering club hut to where an animal stood watching them, its antlers raised to the sky. 'Is that a moose?'

Ben snorted. 'A moose? No, it's not a moose. It's a stag.'

'Shite, aye. That's what I meant,' Tyler said. 'Stag.'

'Jesus. Is that where he's up to now?' Logan asked. 'Basic animal identification? They grow up so fast.'

Ben chuckled, then went back to addressing the DC. 'Aye, son, that's a stag. You get plenty of them out here.'

He put a foot up on a rock and gestured south along the A82.

'I mind one incident a while back. Christ. Eighties, maybe? I was in uniform. Couple of lads were tearing up the road from Glasgow, and a stag jumps out in front of the car. Just throws itself out in front of them, too close for them to stop. They plough right into it. Heavy bugger of a thing. Smashes the front of the car in. Headlights gone, windscreen cracked. The works. Lot of damage.'

'What about the stag?' Tyler asked.

'Killed. Big beast, it was, too. It's dead, but it's no' in bad nick. So, these lads, they reckon it'll fetch a few quid. At the butcher in town, like. Maybe pay for the car repairs, even. So they fold down the back seats.'

'Haha! No way!' Tyler laughed.

'They fold down the back seats,' Ben continued. 'And they manhandle it in. It's an estate, so there's a bit of room, but it's a tight fit. Like I say, it's a big bugger. Takes them a good twenty minutes of shoving it back and forth, but they eventually get it in the car, get the boot shut, and set off.'

'And did they manage to sell it?'

Ben shook his head. 'No. Halfway up the road, it woke up.'

'What?!' Tyler spluttered. 'Seriously?'

'Seriously. Wasn't dead, just stunned. It went from fully spangled to wide awake, like that,' Ben said, clicking his fingers. 'They stopped the car and jumped out, then stood at the side of the road and watched as it kicked its way out of the back. Took it three minutes. Wrote the whole car off, then it just gave them a dirty look and wandered off.'

'That's mental,' Tyler remarked.

'Aye, well, you don't mess with nature,' Ben said. 'That's the lesson I took away from it, anyway. That and never buy a Lada Riva Estate.'

They all stood watching the stag on the hillside for a few minutes, none of them saying a word. The animal padded back and forth through the heather, paying them very little heed.

Occasionally, it would glance their way, but it seemed more curious than concerned. It would watch them for a while, mouth moving up and down as it chewed, then turn its attention to something else.

'He's a big lad, isn't he?' Ben observed.

'Aye. He's a beauty,' Hamza agreed. He smiled faintly as he watched the animal go about its business. 'Caitlyn would've loved seeing that.'

None of the others corrected him. They didn't have to.

'She wouldn't, would she?' he said. 'She'd just tut and roll her eyes, and ask us if we planned taking our fingers out of our arses and getting back to work anytime soon.'

Logan laughed drily. 'Aye. That sounds more like her style, right enough.' He gestured back across the car park, to where the Volvo stood. 'We should get up to Maureen's. Forensics have been and gone, and I'd like to do a walk-through. See if anything jumps out before we talk to Sandy. We're assuming someone else killed her, but there's no saying that wee bastard didn't do her in himself. He might've been trying to frame her for...'

His voice trailed away into a thoughtful silence. He looked across the bridge to the site where Brodie Welsh's body had been found.

'Everything all right, Jack?' Ben asked him.

Logan blinked, frowned, then nodded. 'Aye. Grand,' he said. He tore his eyes from the cordoned-off square of dirt. 'Everything's just grand.'

–

Maureen Gillespie's house held no real surprises. Logan had already seen the SOC report, although he'd figured out most of it himself on his initial look at the scene.

There were no signs of damage to the doors, which suggested either Maureen had left her doors unlocked—possibly, with the remote location, but unlikely given the company she would've been keeping—or had let her killer inside.

The bullet hole in the window had been caused by a stray shot, most likely. The room where Maureen's body had been found was in a real mess, and some minor injuries to her hands, arms, and neck suggested there had been a fight before the fatal shot had been fired.

The house had been turned upside-down, much like Maureen's own insides had been. There were no prints other than those of Maureen herself, and a few from Sandy, mostly on dirty glasses piled up by the sink.

Whoever had turned the place over had been prepared. They'd planned it enough to come equipped with gloves, at least, and there was a distinct lack of any physical evidence as to the killer's identity.

It would all come down to Sandy Gillespie, then, and whether he was feeling brave enough—or lucky enough—to speak out. The thought of offering that bastard protection stuck in Logan's throat, but he had a nasty feeling that's what the future would hold.

Aye, they'd get him for Caitlyn's murder, but he'd end up somewhere nice and cushy in return for selling out the bigger fish. He'd be detained, aye. Incarcerated. But he wouldn't be punished. He'd never be truly punished.

Not in the way Logan would like.

While DCs Neish and Khaled took a look around outside the house, Ben entered the living room at Logan's back.

'All right, Jack? Find anything?'

'No.'

Ben cast his eye across the room, sucked air in through his teeth, and shook his head disapprovingly. 'Not a bad wee house, too. Untidy, aye, and it could do with some work. Bit out of the way, too, but no' bad.'

'Aye, the bloodstains on the floor give it a certain ambiance, right enough,' Logan said. He dropped onto his haunches by the window and studied the hole for a moment, then turned and followed some invisible line in the air. 'There,' he said, pointing to an upturned armchair.

The bottom had been split open, and judging by the amount of stuffing on the floor, the cushions had, too.

'There what?' Ben asked.

'That's where the bullet came from. Shooter was sitting down.'

Ben frowned. 'Thought you reckoned they were fighting.'

'Aye. But the angle points to that chair. So, maybe they'd been fighting, Maureen knocked them onto the chair, then they pulled the gun and shot at her. They missed, but it bought them time to get back up and set about her.'

Ben considered this. 'That works, I suppose,' he said. 'Although, do we know Maureen didn't fire the gun? Aye, no' through her own face, but the window. She could've fired first, whoever was in here got the gun off her, and—'

'No. They checked her hands. No residue,' Logan said. 'Whoever killed her brought the gun with them and took it away afterwards. Same with the knife used to cut her open. Wounds don't match anything found in the house. It was all premeditated. Someone came here expecting to kill Maureen Gillespie, and then to gut her like a fish.'

'And she let them in,' Ben said. 'She just opened the door and let them walk right in. Someone she knew, then.'

'Aye,' Logan said. He took another look around the room, then shoved his hands in his pockets and headed for the door. 'And someone she trusted.'

# Chapter 39

Logan regarded the solicitor like she was something he'd discovered sticking to the sole of his shoe.

'I'm sorry?' he said, in a tone that practically dared her to repeat the words she'd just said.

She gladly accepted.

'My client will not be taking part in any interview in which you are a participant,' she said, meeting Logan's angry glare with one of practised indifference. 'You can try to stare me down all you like, Detective Chief Inspector, but you physically assaulted my client not twenty-four hours ago, and then proceeded to pay him a midnight visit in hospital while he was recuperating.'

She snapped her gaze in Ben's direction. 'Were you aware of that? That DCI Logan snuck into Mr Gillespie's room last night? Threw his weight around a little.'

'Bollocks, I didn't throw anything around,' Logan protested.

'But you admit you entered his room without any sort of permission or clearance?'

Logan threw Gillespie a dark and dirty look. The bastard had been watching him, but quickly looked away when Logan caught his eye.

'I paid him a visit, yes. I wanted to inform him of what had happened to his sister.'

The solicitor clasped her hands on the desk between them. 'Yes. Well. You should consider yourself fortunate that we're granting you any sort of interview at all. We have not yet ruled out the possibility of pressing assault charges.'

'Charges?' Logan said. He felt Ben's hand on his arm but ignored it. 'Your client—' He jabbed a finger in Gillespie's direction, making him shrink in his seat. 'That jumped-up wee arsehole right there, went for a gun. A gun, might I remind you, Miss...'

'Grey.'

'...that he'd already used to shoot and kill one of my officers.'

'Allegedly,' the solicitor added.

Miss Grey was irritatingly composed for someone so young. She was early thirties at most, and had put herself together with well-rehearsed care and attention.

She wore an old-fashioned pinstripe suit—shirt, tie, jacket, and trousers—that was maybe a half size too big for her, but it all felt like a deliberate style choice, like she'd had it tailored too big on purpose. The outfit was perfectly matched by her short, meticulously sculpted quiff.

When he'd first seen her, Hamza had suggested the look might be some sort of feminist statement about being a powerful woman in a man's world. Tyler, on the other hand, reckoned she was a part-time Elvis impersonator.

Logan couldn't care less who or what she was. He was just annoyed by the fact that she clearly knew what she was doing. She had him over a barrel.

She knew that, too.

'I was defending myself from your armed client,' Logan said. 'I'd consider that justified use of force.'

'You broke his nose, and two of his fingers, knocked out three of his teeth, and cracked a rib. He also sustained extensive bruising to the arms, back, throat, and neck, plus psychological damage still to be assessed.'

'Psychological damage my arse!' Logan spat. 'He killed one of my officers.'

'Allegedly,' the brief reiterated.

'He went for the shotgun. He was going to shoot me!'

'After you goaded him into it, Detective Chief Inspector. Yes? That is what happened, isn't it? You told him to pick it up. Dared him to.'

'If I dared him to jump off the Erskine Bridge, would he do that, too?' Logan asked. He eyeballed Gillespie across the desk. 'Because I'm game to put it to the test, if you are.'

Miss Grey smiled and ejected a dry little laugh from the back of her throat. *Ha*.

'I'm the Senior Investigating Officer on this case, sweetheart. You don't come in here and lay down the law. That's my job.'

'Right. I see. Well, I think in that case, we're done here,' the solicitor said, reaching for the briefcase she had tucked beside her seat. 'We came here in good faith, but I refuse to allow my client to be questioned by the man who physically assaulted him, then turned up drunk at his hospital bed in the middle of the night attempting to intimidate him.'

Logan felt Ben's eyes on him.

'I wasn't drunk. I hadn't been drinking,' he protested, as much for DI Forde's benefit as for the woman across the table.

'I'm afraid that my client disagrees.'

'Aye, well your client's a nasty wee murdering bastard, and I don't care what he thinks, quite frankly.'

The solicitor set her bag on her knees and gave a single shake of her carefully coiffured head. 'I could almost forgive it, had you been drunk. Alcohol and grief. Never a winning combination. A lapse in judgement could perhaps be overlooked in those circumstances. But if you say you were sober... no. That's unacceptable. Sandy.'

Gillespie looked around at the sound of his name, caught off guard.

'Huh?'

'We're going. Come on.'

Logan's stare practically pinned Gillespie to the chair, but a sharp, 'Sandy!' from Miss Grey dragged him out of it and up onto his feet.

'We'll be in touch,' she said.

They were almost to the door when Logan relented.

'Fine.'

Miss Grey stopped. She stood motionless for a moment, controlling the smile that threatened to take over her face, then turned. Logan hadn't moved, and the solicitor found herself watching the back of his head as he spoke.

'I won't participate in the interview,' he told her, his voice flat and measured. 'DI Forde and another member of the team will question Mr Gillespie without me present in the room. I trust that will be acceptable?'

The solicitor nodded without bothering to consult her client first. 'It's a start.'

'Right, then,' Logan said. He got to his feet. The movement was slow and filled with a calculated sort of menace, like a monster rising from the deep. 'The pair of you, sit your arses down, and let's get on with it.'

# Chapter 40

Logan stood as close as humanly possible to the observation room window, as if trying to convince himself he was right there in the room next door where the action was, rather than just standing here, helplessly watching on.

'You make a better door than a window, Jack.'

Logan didn't give Jinkies the satisfaction of a response. The one-way mirror was plenty big enough for the Chief Inspector to see through, even with Logan standing slap bang in the middle of it, so close his breath was blurring the glass.

'You sure about sending your man in there?' Jinkies continued. 'Bit wet around the lugs, isn't he? For a case like this, I mean.'

'He'll be fine,' Logan grunted.

'I'm happy to partner up with Ben in there. Take the lead on this one. I do know a thing or two about Mr Gillespie's activities, after all, and I've crossed swords with the brief before, too. She's tough. Needs a firm hand.'

'It's fine, Hugh,' Logan said, trying not to physically recoil at the thought of Jinkies' 'firm hand'. 'It's all under control. The lads know what they're doing.'

He waited, poised on the balls of his feet, for Hugh to put himself forward again. The one-way mirror was largely soundproof, but it wasn't perfect. Logan wondered how loud a bollocking he could give Jinkies without everyone next door getting an earful of it, too.

Fortunately, they didn't have to find out, as the Chief Inspector wisely decided not to push the suggestion any further.

'Well, if you change your mind, you just have to ask,' he said. 'We're all invested in this one, Jack. We all want justice for DS McQuarrie. And, if we can get him to confess to Brodie Welsh, too, so much the better. If we get something there, I'll talk to Fulton and Hannah. God knows, they could do with a result.'

'Bit premature to be running to them, isn't it?' Logan suggested.

'Fulton is a good friend of the station, Jack. He deserves to be kept in the loop.'

Logan didn't bother to reply. Any breath spent on a conversation with Jinkies was a breath wasted, in his opinion. It was bad enough that he'd invited himself in to observe the interview, Logan didn't feel any obligation to humour the bastard with conversation, too.

Hamza sidled up to the glass beside Logan, drawing a 'tut' and a sigh from Jinkies, followed by the sound of a chair being dragged across the floor.

'You think Tyler's up to it, sir?' Hamza asked. He kept his voice low, less concerned about the people on the other side of the glass hearing him as he was the man behind him. 'Gillespie gave him the run-around before.'

They both watched DC Neish set his notebook and pen down on the desk in front of him, as Ben Forde recited all the usual stuff about recordings and tapes.

To the casual onlooker, Tyler looked relaxed and confident. Logan and Hamza both knew him well enough to see through it, though. It was there in his movements and the lines of his face. He was nervous.

'He's going to be fine,' Logan said, although it wasn't clear whose concerns he was trying to put to rest. 'Ben's taking the lead, he's just there to make up the numbers.'

He raised his voice a little, making sure Jinkies could hear. 'Besides, he's a better copper than we give him credit for. They'll nail this bastard to the wall.'

'I hope you're right, Jack,' Jinkies said. 'Now, scootch over a bit, will you? You're blocking the show.'

–

A few feet away, beyond the glass, Tyler shot a surreptitious glance at his reflection, placed a second pen on the table beside the first, then clasped his hands in a manner that mirrored the body language of DI Forde.

Across the table, the solicitor, Miss Grey, sat with her own pen poised above a leather-bound notepad, a slightly impatient expression on her face. She looked like she was already waiting for a chance to jump in, before either of the detectives had even started their line of questioning.

She was going to be hard work, Tyler thought. His eyes briefly went to her slicked-up quiff and her stylishly oversized suit and tie.

Yes, definitely hard work.

'Mr Gillespie. Can I call you Sandy?' Ben asked. He was smiling and relaxed, as if chatting to a friend of a friend. 'I'm Ben Forde. I'm one of the detectives brought in to work on the Brodie Welsh case. I'm sure you're familiar with it.'

'My client isn't here to talk about that case,' Miss Grey interjected. 'He's here to answer questions relating to the death of Detective Sergeant...' She checked her notes with a glance. '...Caitlyn McQuarrie.'

*She didn't even know her name.* At least four men in the immediate vicinity shared that thought at exactly the same time. *She didn't even know her name.*

'Aye. I know. But, to be honest, we don't have a whole lot of questions about that,' Ben said. 'Not directly, anyway. You see, we know he did that one. We've got witnesses. He was the only person at the scene. Forensics have his fingerprints on the gun, and gunpowder residue on his skin and clothing. No, that one's pretty open and shut. We're confident of getting a conviction there, aren't we, Detective Constable?'

Tyler nodded, his eyes fixed on Gillespie. 'Yes, boss.'

'Would you say we're confident, or very confident?' Ben asked.

'I'd say we're supremely confident, boss.'

Ben's eyes widened in surprise and delight, then he turned his attention back to Gillespie and his solicitor.

'*Supremely* confident of a conviction. You hear that, Sandy? Supremely confident that you'll be found guilty of murdering a police officer. Plus all the usual stuff about owning an unlicensed firearm, assault with intent, and so on, and so on.'

Ben frowned as if struggling to recall some detail. 'What's the maximum sentence for murder these days? Miss Grey, can you remember?'

The solicitor sighed, clearly unimpressed by the DI's theatrics.

'Mandatory life sentence, isn't it, boss?' Tyler interjected.

Ben slapped the edge of the table. 'That's the one! Of course, life doesn't mean *life*,' he said, smiling benevolently at Gillespie. 'I'm sure you know that. You'll get out eventually, after whatever minimum term the judge decides to set.'

He leaned back, the confused expression returning. 'What was that one that was just set recently?' he asked. 'Set a new record.'

'Thirty-seven years, boss,' Tyler told him.

'Thirty-seven years,' Ben repeated. He whistled quietly. 'Thirty-seven years.'

'Minimum,' Tyler added.

'Good point, son. Good point. No saying he'll get out after that. No saying he won't do forty.'

'I'm sorry,' the solicitor interjected. 'I was under the impression my client was here to answer questions, not to sit in on a personal and, if I might add, highly speculative conversation between two officers who really ought to know better.'

She looked at them both reproachfully, like a disappointed teacher. 'Now, my client will require pain medication within the next forty-five minutes, as a direct consequence of the beating inflicted upon him during his arrest. I suggest, if you have questions, you ask them soon.'

Ben held both hands up, conceding the point. 'You're right, you're right. No more messing around. Down to business.'

On the other side of the mirror, Logan held his breath.

'Did you murder your sister, Sandy?'

Gillespie clearly hadn't been expecting that one. He opened his mouth, shot his brief a blank look, then spluttered out a series of incredulous sounds that he eventually followed up with a 'What?'

'Your sister. Maureen,' Ben said. 'Did you kill her? It's not a difficult question, son. It's a yes or no answer.'

'No! No, I didn't kill her.'

Ben tapped on Tyler's notepad. 'Jot that down, will you, DC Neish? "No". Make a note of that.'

He waited until Tyler had followed his instructions, then continued.

'Right, well, who did?'

'I don't... I don't know!'

'You don't? But you knew someone had killed her, right?' Ben pressed. 'That's why you were holed up in your house with a shotgun, isn't it? That's what you told DCI Logan yesterday. You were, quote, "protecting yourself", unquote. You mistook DS McQuarrie for an invader. You thought she was someone coming to kill you, like they'd killed your sister.'

Gillespie adjusted himself in his chair. 'Right...'

'So, you knew about Maureen. About her being dead. How?'

'What do you mean?'

'How did you know Maureen was dead? You got a psychic connection? Did her ghost tell you?' Ben asked.

'What? No.'

'Then how did you know? Either you killed her, or you know who did. That's the only way you could've known to prepare for them coming after you, too, Sandy. That's literally the only two options.'

'No. I mean, that's not...' Gillespie caught the look from his solicitor, and then cleared his throat. 'No comment.'

'Did you kill Maureen?'

'No comment.'

'Did you go to her house, get in a fight, and kill her?'

'No comment.'

'Did you shoot your sister in the head, and then mutilate her dead body?'

Gillespie bit his bottom lip so hard all the colour drained out of it.

'No comment.'

'You gutted her like a fish, Sandy. You carved her up. Your own sister.'

'No! I didn't!' Gillespie spat, slamming his hands on the table. 'It wasn't me! All right? It wasn't me, it was...'

He crammed a hand in his mouth and bit down on the knuckle, stopping himself.

'It was who, Sandy? Who killed her? Who did all that stuff to her?' Ben asked, his voice becoming coaxing and gentle. 'We're all ears. Aren't we, son?'

'We're one big ear, boss,' Tyler said, picking up on the cue.

'Who was it? You can tell us. We're all friends here.'

Gillespie's chair creaked as he leaned his weight back. 'No comment,' he whispered.

It was Ben's turn to take on the look of a disappointed school teacher. 'Fine. OK.' He nodded slowly. 'Fine. We'll park that for now. We'll come back to it. I can see it's a sensitive subject,' he said. 'How about you tell me about Brodie Welsh, instead?'

'I didn't kill him, either, if that's what you're getting at,' Gillespie said. 'Don't try to pin that one on me, an' all. I had nothing to do with it.'

'I never said you did,' Ben replied, adopting a shocked expression that suggested the thought had never crossed his mind. 'He was a friend of yours, wasn't he? I'd imagine you must've been pretty cut up about it all.'

Ben shot a sideways look in Tyler's direction. 'No' as cut up as he was, mind you. Same thing again as Maureen. Cut right open. Guts split wide.'

'Nasty business, boss.'

'Aye, you can say that again,' Ben said, shuddering as he turned back to Gillespie. 'Of course, Brodie was neater than Maureen. The killer, they took more care with him. It was less… God. What's the word?'

'Aggressive?' Tyler suggested.

'Demented, I was going to say. Less frenzied. Less… *visceral*. Brodie? Now, Brodie's wounds were nasty, but they were business-like. Professional, almost. Maureen, though? Yikes. There was emotion put into that. Passion, you might even say.'

Gillespie flinched like he was imagining the scene. Or perhaps remembering it.

'Is there a question coming, Detective Inspector?' asked the solicitor. 'Or are you going to continue to taunt my client about the death of his sister? Because, if it's the latter, I can't see that being looked favourably upon in court, can you?'

'Had you met Detective Sergeant McQuarrie before, Sandy?' Ben asked. 'Before you shot and killed her, I mean.'

The change of direction caught Gillespie off-guard, and he responded with a slightly bemused shake of his head.

'Shame,' Ben said. 'Although, to be quite honest, you'd have hated her. Exceptional police officer. Liked to do things by the book, and didn't mince her words. She'd have had you down as a lanky streak o' pish at first glance. She did, in fact. She pulled your mugshot and put it up on the board we've got. You know, like in the films? Where we track the investigation?'

Ben smiled at the thought of it. 'I never tended to bother with them myself, but DS McQuarrie, she loved a Big Board. Always kept it perfect. Everything on there. Photographs, maps, statements, the works. She put you up there for us. You and Maureen. She had the measure of you right away, Sandy. Before she'd ever clapped eyes on you in person, she could see you for what you are.'

'Could she?' Gillespie said, his nostrils flaring. 'And what good did that do her?'

Through the glass, Logan saw Ben's smile solidify and hold in place. He wasn't going to give the bastard the satisfaction.

'Did Maureen see you for what you are, too, Sandy? In the end, I mean? Is that why you killed her?'

Gillespie snorted and folded his arms across his chest.

'I told you, I didn't kill her.'

'You want to know what I think happened?' Ben asked. He gestured to the solicitor. 'You might want to make a note of this. You too, son.'

Tyler picked up his pen and placed the nib against the paper. 'Ready when you are, boss.'

Ben leaned forward and lowered his voice as if letting the others in on a secret. 'I can't take all the credit. DCI Logan, he came up with it. I was dubious at first, I'll be honest with you, but it does kind of make sense.' He smiled at Sandy. 'Ready? Right, then, pay attention, and then you can tell me if we're getting close.'

# Chapter 41

Logan and Hamza had been joined at the glass by Jinkies, and a DS from CID who'd been investigating the Gillespies for drugs trafficking, and who was not overly impressed that his thunder had been stolen.

As they'd stood listening to the questioning, Jinkies had been emitting little mutters, groans, *mm-hms* and other verbal diarrhoea that did nothing but get on Logan's tits.

The CID man, DS Lowrey, had remained stoic and silent throughout. It was the only reason Logan continued to tolerate his presence in the room.

'Here's what we think happened, son.' Ben's voice sounded a little tinny over the observation room's speaker system. 'It's a bit complicated, so just ask if you lose the thread, all right?'

He gave Gillespie a few seconds to respond, then pressed on.

'Right, then. Here goes. We believe that Brodie Welsh recently returned from a trip abroad, and had been carrying drugs inside his body on behalf of you and Maureen, just as he'd been doing on a regular basis for the past few years.'

'No comment.'

'We believe you and Maureen were acting as middlemen, buying what Brodie—and no doubt others— brought you, and selling it up the chain to someone else outwith the area. Alternatively, rather than being freelancers, as it were, you were under the direct employ of this mystery person or persons. They provided the funds, you arranged the supply, and you were handsomely rewarded for your efforts.'

Ben raised his eyebrows. 'How am I doing so far?'

Gillespie shot his brief a sideways glance, then looked back at the DI. 'No comment.'

'Now, it strikes me—and please, don't take offence here—but it strikes me that Maureen was the brains of the outfit,' Ben continued. He looked to Tyler for his input. 'Would you agree with that assessment, DC Neish?'

'Aye, boss. Aye, I'd agree.'

'I mean, I never got the chance to meet her, personally, but from what I've read and heard about her, I'd say she was the boss. Out of the two of you, I mean. Would that be a fair assumption?'

Gillespie ignored the question, and Ben didn't bother to waste any time forcing the issue.

'What size of feet are you?' he asked, instead.

'What?'

'Feet. Shoes. What size?'

Gillespie looked down, like the answer might be written at the bottom of his trousers. 'Eight. Why?'

'And Maureen?'

Sandy shook his head. 'I don't know. The same?'

'Big feet for a woman,' Ben remarked. He turned to Tyler. 'That's not sexist, is it?'

'No, you're fine, boss,' the DC replied.

'Thanks.' Ben rolled his eyes in Gillespie's direction. 'Can't be too careful, these days. Too easy to accidentally offend someone, and then all hell breaks loose.'

'What do Maureen's feet have to do with anything?' Gillespie asked.

'Doesn't matter. Forget it,' Ben said. 'So, here's what I think. What *we* think, I mean. Me and the rest of the team.'

He tipped Miss Grey the wink and indicated her notebook. She stared back at him with professional disdain.

'We think that you and Maureen discovered Brodie had been scamming you. Pinching a bit off the top. Keeping a wee bit for himself and punting it locally,' Ben said. 'We think you waited until he'd come back with a shipment, you both confronted him about what he'd been up to, then you killed him and cut him open, hoping to retrieve what he had on him.'

'That didn't happen,' Gillespie said. 'That's shite.'

'But you didn't retrieve it, did you, Sandy?' Ben continued, glossing right over the objection. 'You went through all that bother of cutting him open, and the stuff wasn't there. That's why you went round to the house. You and Maureen. That's why you broke in and trashed the place, terrorising Hannah Randall in the process. You were looking for your gear, weren't you?'

The answer came through gritted teeth. 'No comment.'

'Must've been pretty desperate to put yourselves at risk like that,' Ben mused. 'I mean, it's taking a big chance that she could recognise you.' He turned to Tyler. 'What do you reckon would motivate someone to put themselves at risk like that?'

'Fear, boss.'

'Fear. Exactly. I couldn't have put it better myself, son,' Ben said. 'Fear. Fear that the folk up the chain were going to come looking for the shipment you were supposed to bring them. Had they already been asking about it? Had they been making noises about what would happen if you didn't find it?

'I mean, that's why you trashed Hannah Randall's house, isn't it? Fear of them up the chain. And that same fear's why you killed Brodie Welsh.'

Gillespie's lips were desert-dry. He flicked his tongue across them, with little effect.

'No comment,' he croaked.

'Do you think that's helping your case, son?' Ben asked, sitting forward. He waved vaguely at the solicitor without looking at her. 'Is that what she advised you to do? "No comment" over and over? You're aware this is being recorded, yes? The cameras aren't just for show, you know. They work. They're recording everything, same as the tape.'

Ben let that bed in for a moment, before continuing. 'How do you think that's going to play to the jury? Local man murdered. Father. Aye, gone off the rails a bit, but whose fault was that? They'll see his girlfriend in the gallery. Wee daughter, maybe. And all they'll hear is you giving it "No comment". How do you think that'll go down? Like a lead balloon, if you ask me.'

He sat back and shrugged. 'But hey. What do I know? I'm no' the one with all the fancy letters after my name. If she thinks it's worth the gamble, far be it from me to argue.'

Inside the observation room, Jinkies let out a little snort. 'It's quite the technique, isn't it?'

'Aye,' Logan mumbled.

'I mean, I'm not sure how effective it's likely to be when it comes to—'

'Hugh?' Logan said, tearing his eyes away from the scene in front of them.

Chief Inspector Pickering turned, a half-smile playing across his face. 'Yes?'

'Gonnae shut the fuck up?'

'I'm *sorry*?'

'Seriously. If you're not muttering to yourself, you're making clicking noises with your tongue, or tapping your teeth, or some other bloody thing. Even your breathing is annoying me. I'm trying to concentrate here, and all I'm getting is—' Logan inhaled and exhaled deeply like he was trying to stop himself hyperventilating. 'It's like getting a dirty phone call from Darth Vader.'

Logan eyeballed the Chief Inspector, whose face was still frozen in a mask of shock, daring him to respond. It was only when Ben Forde's voice came over the speaker again that Logan turned his attention back to the room on the other side of the glass.

'So, I'm going to ask you again, son. And I want you to think very carefully about the response. Did you murder Brodie Welsh?'

'You don't have to answer that,' Miss Grey said.

Gillespie coughed quietly. 'No. No, I didn't kill Brodie,' he said. 'But...'

'But what?' Ben asked.

'Maybe, I don't know, maybe Maureen did.'

'Maureen?'

Gillespie nodded. 'She didn't say anything, so I don't know. But maybe. She made us go to the house, anyway. She told me how much shit we'd be in if we didn't find the gear. Said what they'd do to us.'

In the room next door, Jinkies and DS Lowrey both blinked in surprise.

'Did he just...?' Lowrey asked. 'Was that a confession? To dealing, I mean? Did he just own up?'

Logan waved the man into silence as Ben continued the questioning.

'So, you think Maureen killed Brodie?' he asked. 'That'd be handy, wouldn't it? For you, I mean.'

Gillespie's eyes narrowed in confusion. 'What?'

'Well, it conveniently gets you off the hook, doesn't it? She kills Brodie, then she goes and gets killed herself, meaning she's not here to answer for it. You get to walk free.'

Tyler opened his mouth, but Ben beat him to it.

'Or you would, had you not shot and killed Detective Sergeant McQuarrie yesterday afternoon. I mean, we know that one. We can take that one as a given, can't we?'

On the other side of the glass, Logan and Hamza watched for it. Waited for it. Held their breath and prayed for it, even.

'Right, Sandy?' Ben urged.

And there it was. The nod. The acknowledgement. The acceptance.

They had an eye witness, forensic evidence, and now, in that nod, a confession.

Regardless of what else they got him for, regardless of what else he'd done, Sandy Gillespie was going to jail for the murder of DS Caitlyn McQuarrie.

And, if there was any justice in the world, he'd rot there for a very long time.

Ben shot a fleeting look at the mirror, then steered things back to Maureen and Brodie. He'd come back to Caitlyn later, of course, and cement the confession. But it was there on the video for all to see, and anything else was icing on the cake.

Logan wheeled around, turning from the glass.

'Did we get him, sir?' Hamza asked. 'Did we get him on Caitlyn?'

'Aye,' Logan said. 'Aye, we got the bastard.'

Hamza gave the DCI a quick look up and down. 'You all right, sir?'

'Fine. Aye. Great,' Logan said, hurrying past the younger officer. 'Just going to get a cup of tea. Anyone else want one?'

'Aye, go on then, Jack. I wouldn't say no to a—' Jinkies began, but Logan was through the first of the observation room's two doors, and it was already clicking closed behind him.

# Chapter 42

Logan stepped out into the corridor, ran his hands through his hair, and breathed out. It felt like he'd been holding that same breath since the phone call telling him Caitlyn had been shot. It was a relief to finally get rid of it.

Back in the interview room, Ben would be sticking to the plan. The discovery of Brodie's body pointed the finger of suspicion firmly at the Gillespies. They had to know that. Sandy was now putting it all on his sister, but what if that had been his intention from the start? What if the body was meant to be found so that the Gillespies—Maureen Gillespie, in particular—would be suspected?

Ben would be quizzing Sandy now. Had he done it? Had he killed Brodie and tried to pin it on Maureen? If so, why? And did that mean he'd killed Maureen, too?

Logan's eyes fell on the vending machine in the corridor. The tea from it was like dishwater, but he didn't want to be gone too long, and a traipse to the kitchen to boil the kettle felt like a step too far.

He begrudgingly jabbed the black coffee button, concluding that it was the most palatable thing on offer, and waited while the machine hissed and whirred into life.

'Come on, come on,' he muttered, glancing back at the observation room door.

He felt bad about leaving Hamza in there with Jinkies, but he'd needed to step outside for a minute to compose himself, to take a moment's comfort from the knowledge that Caitlyn was going to get justice.

Now, though, he was itching to get back. He wanted to know what else Gillespie had to say, to get to the bottom of everything, and square it all away.

Had he tried to frame his sister for killing Brodie? It was the only explanation that fit, even if it had to be battered in a bit around the edges. Why else move the body? Why else put it somewhere it would deliberately be found, if not to stitch someone up?

And yet, there was no evidence to imply that the Gillespies had fallen out. Nothing to suggest why Sandy would deliberately try to frame his sister for Brodie's murder.

It could've been the next man up the chain, but that wasn't generally how it worked, in Logan's experience. Everyone dealt with the person below. You had a problem with the man two links down? You got the link between you both to handle it. You didn't skip over them. It was too risky, too easy to get yourself found out. Why put your face out there where it didn't need to be seen? Plausible deniability, that was the name of the game.

The Gillespies had to have killed Brodie. Then, when they'd failed to deliver the gear he'd been carrying, the people above had come after the Gillespies themselves. The chain had been maintained. It made sense. It all fit neatly together.

Or it would've done, had the body not been moved. Which brought him right back around to a stitch-up. Sandy had been quick to point the blame at Maureen in the interview. Was that a spur-of-the-moment survival instinct, or part of some bigger plan he'd had in place from the start?

If you ignored the bit about the body being moved, it was completely plausible that the Gillespies had murdered Brodie Welsh. And yet, it didn't feel right. Not in his gut. Not deep down, where it counted.

If Logan could get in there with Sandy Gillespie himself, he'd get the truth out of the bastard. One way or another, he'd make him spill everything.

The rattling of coffee into a plastic cup came to a stop. With a final hiss and a puff of steam, the vending machine released its grip on the cup, and Logan reached in to pick it up.

He had just got a hand around it and turned in the direction of the observation room door when a vaguely familiar voice called out to him.

'DCI Logan? Do you have a minute?'

Sergeant Jaffray bustled along the corridor, a couple of traffic cones clutched under one arm, a length of cordon tape trying its best to escape from beneath the other.

'What is it, son?' Logan barked. 'Kind of busy here.'

Jaffray regarded the coffee cup in his hand for a moment, then nodded so enthusiastically he almost dropped his traffic cones.

'Right, yes. Right. I just wanted to apologise, sir.'

Logan rifled through his memory, trying to recall what the sergeant had to be sorry for. Beyond being a useless bugger, anyway. He drew a blank.

'For what?'

'For everything, you know, with Mr Randall.'

Logan felt his eyebrows bump together above his nose. 'What?'

Jaffray took a breath and straightened himself up. 'I've been bracing myself for it since he was in. Kept waiting for you to come give me a bollocking. And, well, my nerves

can't take it. I thought it best to get it out in the open.
I'm sorry.'

Logan took a step closer. 'I'm not following, Sergeant.
What are you talking about?'

'Oh. Right. I thought…' Jaffray's eyes darted shiftily
along the corridor like he was looking for a way out. 'It's
nothing. Forget it.'

Logan took another step, so he was now towering
above the smaller officer. He leaned in, bringing his face
close enough to Jaffray's that his breath made the sergeant's
eyebrows twitch.

'What are you talking about?' Logan growled. 'What
were you going to say about Fulton Randall?'

Jaffray shifted on the balls of his feet. 'I, uh, it was an
accident. Slip of the tongue, really. I didn't mean to tell
him. I thought he already knew.'

'Knew about what?'

The sergeant was positively squirming now. His traffic
cones slipped out from under his arm and hit the floor
with a thack that echoed along the corridor.

'About Brodie and Hannah,' he said. 'About the
domestic.'

Logan blinked, stepped back, mind racing.

'What? You told Fulton that Brodie had attacked
Hannah?'

'Like I say, it was an accident, I thought he—'

'When?'

Jaffray's mouth flapped open and closed. One of
Logan's hands clamped around his upper arm, the fingers
almost meeting around the other side.

'*When?*'

'At… at the time, sir. Couple of days after it happened.'

*At the time*. Jesus Christ.

'What about the drugs stuff? Did you tell him that, too?' Logan asked.

Jaffray's eyes searched the DCI's face. 'Drugs stuff, sir? I don't... what?'

'The dealing. The Gillespies!'

Nothing changed on the sergeant's face to suggest he had the faintest idea what Logan was talking about.

'What about the Gillespies?' he asked, but Logan didn't hear him. Didn't listen. There was another voice in his head, instead. An echo of one, at least.

*Fulton is a good friend of the station, Jack. He deserves to be kept in the loop.*

Logan's coffee cup hit the floor as he turned on his heels.

'Bastard!' he ejected, then he stormed across the corridor, threw open the door to the observation room, and charged inside.

# Chapter 43

Ben Forde was drilling Sandy Gillespie about his relationship with his sister when the mirror shook in its frame.
The corresponding thud from the other side caught the
attention of everyone in the room, and all four of them
turned in time to see the glass pane shaking for a second
time.

'Problems, Detective Inspector?' asked Miss Grey.

Ben and Tyler exchanged glances.

'Eh, no. Just a… I'll just…' Ben hovered his finger
over the button on the desk. 'Interview suspended at two-
seventeen PM. DI Ben Forde leaving the room.'

He jabbed the button, shot Tyler another look, then
hurried out, just as something heavy was slammed against
the other side of the glass once again.

Gillespie and his solicitor both watched DC Neish
expectantly. He smiled as casually as he could. 'Probably
just… the wind,' he said. 'Nothing to worry about.'

Miss Grey sniffed. 'Yes. Well. I think we'll have a
break here. My client needs a break. We can reconvene
tomorrow.'

Tyler half-laughed, like he thought the woman was
joking. As he watched her pack her notes into her
briefcase, though, he realised she was being serious.

'Wait, what? You can't just go.'

'I think you'll find we can,' Miss Grey said, fastening the straps of her bag. She motioned for Sandy to stand. 'We can continue tomorrow, at a mutually agreed time. For now, though, Mr Gillespie and I will be—'

'Sit down.'

The firmness of Tyler's voice cut through the solicitor's bustling. She looked up from her briefcase straps, one sculpted eyebrow raising quizzically.

'I'm sorry?'

'You heard me. Sit down. We're not finished.'

'I didn't say we're finished, I said we were taking a break.'

Tyler sat forward in his chair, and fixed the solicitor with a look that Logan would have been proud of.

'We'll decide when we take a break. Not you. We've got your client for another...' He checked his watch. 'Twenty-two-and-a-half hours.'

The solicitor opened her mouth to correct this, but Tyler got in first. 'I think we can safely say a senior officer will extend the usual twelve-hour period, don't you?' he said. 'I can't imagine getting DCI Logan to agree to that will pose a problem.'

He smiled, not unkindly. 'So I suggest you use this short interlude wisely, Miss Grey. Clear your calendar. Phone home. Let everyone know you're not going to be available, because you... we... have a very long night ahead of us.'

He looked from the solicitor to her client and back again, then cast a meaningful look at their chairs.

They resisted. For a while, anyway. It was Miss Grey who caved first. She sat down heavily, like a sullen teenager after a telling-off. Sandy muttered something below his breath, then plonked himself down, too.

Tyler nodded approvingly at them both, then rubbed his hands together. 'That said,' he began, beaming from ear to ear. 'Who fancies a cuppa?'

–

Tyler entered the observation room to find Ben, Hamza, and one of the guys from CID trying to prise Logan's hands from Jinkies' throat. The Chief Inspector was pinned against the one-way mirror, the tips of his toes barely touching the ground.

'Jesus. What's going on, boss?'

'Get over and give us a hand here,' Ben barked. 'Jack! Jack, let him go! You're going to kill him.'

'That's the general idea!' Logan hissed, but then he released his grip and stepped back, hands raised. Jinkies crumpled to the floor, coughing and spluttering, his eyes practically bulging out of his head.

'I'll have… your job… for this, Logan,' the Chief Inspector wheezed.

'*My* job? Oh, you think so, Hugh? You think that *you'll* have *my* job? When I'm done with you, you won't even be left with your bloody pension, never mind your career!'

'What's happened?' asked Ben, setting himself up as a barrier between both men. 'What the hell's this about, Jack?'

Logan stabbed a finger at the man on the floor. 'You want to tell him, Hugh, or will I?'

Jinkies rubbed his throat. The skin was red and raw, but his breath was gradually returning. 'I don't know what you're talking about.'

'Fulton Randall. You told him. About the Gillespies. About Brodie's involvement with them,' Logan spat. 'You told him everything months ago. Didn't you?'

Down on the floor, Jinkies said nothing. Logan lunged at him, forcing Ben aside and grabbing the Chief Inspector by his tie. '*Didn't you?*'

'No! No!' Jinkies protested. 'I mean, not like that.' He shot Ben and the others a pleading look. 'He makes it sound worse than it is. It wasn't like that. He's just, Fulton Randall, he's just…'

'A friend of the station. Deserves to be kept in the loop,' Logan said, finishing the sentence for him. He released his grip, letting Jinkies sink back to the floor, then turned to DS Lowrey. 'You were worried there was a leak? Well, good news. We found it. There it is right there. So do us all a favour, will you?'

He sneered down at the snivelling shitebag on the floor. 'Plug the bastard up.'

While Logan had been dealing with Jinkies, Hamza had been processing the ramifications of the new information, and had quickly come to the same conclusion that Logan had.

'If Fulton Randall knew that Brodie and the Gillespies were dealing…'

'Oh, that's not the half of it,' Logan said. 'He also knew about the domestics. He knew all along that Brodie had been kicking the shite out of his wee girl. When he heard about it yesterday, he seemed surprised, but it was an act. It was all an act.'

'You don't think…' Ben began.

'Aye, I think,' Logan said. He pointed through the glass to where Sandy Gillespie and his solicitor were sitting in silence. 'You two get back in there. See what you can get out of them. Hamza, give DS Whatever-His-Name-Is a hand with the soon-to-be-former Chief Inspector Pickering, will you?'

'Uh, aye, sir,' Hamza said, briefly locking eyes with the CID man.

'What about you, Jack?' Ben asked. 'What are you going to do?'

'I'm going to sort this mess out,' Logan said. He flexed and tightened his fingers, imagining them back around Jinkies' throat. 'One way or another.'

# Chapter 44

The driveway leading up to Fulton Randall's house was steep and uneven. It zig-zagged as it climbed the hill, forcing Logan to creep the Volvo around the corners in low gear.

At the top, it opened onto a wide driveway. Fulton's four-by-four had been neatly reversed in so it was facing down the hill. The car was reasonably new, but the paintwork was currently faded by the veneer of dusty white that coated most local cars when the temperature dropped and the gritters came out.

Logan parked beside the big Range Rover, peeked in through one of the car's side windows, then went striding towards the house.

He was at the door when he spotted the big plastic chest stationed just along the wall. A hatch on top and another on the front gave easy access to the contents.

Salt and grit, for keeping the driveway clear. The driveway was long, which meant the container was large. Large enough to hide a body in, with room to spare.

He was about to knock when he heard the thudding of little feet go running past, followed by a shout.

'Come here, you wee monkey!'

A giggle followed, then a squeal of delight.

It all stopped when Logan rapped his knuckles on the glass panel of the front door.

Fulton Randall looked surprised to see him. He spent a few seconds staring at the detective through the glass, then hurriedly opened the door.

'DCI Logan. Hello. I wasn't expecting… well, anyone,' he said.

'Sorry to intrude like this,' Logan said. 'Mind if I have a word?'

Fulton glanced back into the house. 'Uh, aye. Sure. No problem. Hannah's not here, though, if you're looking for her. She and her mother nipped out. I'm left babysitting again.'

'Actually, Mr Randall, it's you I wanted to talk to.' Logan gestured past the man at the hallway beyond. 'Do you mind?'

Fulton's hand was still on the door, his arm blocking Logan's path. His expression didn't change, but the texture of it seemed to shift, like he was deliberately holding his features in place.

'Of course. Aye. In you come,' he said, stepping aside. He waited until Logan had entered, then closed the door and squeezed past the detective into the hall. 'Carrie! I'll just be a minute, all right?'

A couple of coats hanging from a rack on the wall rustled as they were pushed aside to reveal the girl hiding behind them. 'OK,' she said, then she let them fall back until only her legs were visible at the bottom.

'Tea? Coffee?' Fulton asked, leading Logan in the direction of the kitchen.

'No. Thank you.'

'Sure? I'm having one.'

'I'll be fine,' Logan reiterated.

The kitchen was old-fashioned, but fresh-looking, like it had been done recently in a deliberate, if not entirely convincing, farmhouse style. Logan waited while Fulton filled the kettle from an ornate copper-coloured tap.

Only when the kettle had been plugged in and switched on did Fulton turn around. 'I heard one of your officers was injured. By Sandy Gillespie. Is that right?' he asked, concern troubling his brow.

'She died,' Logan said.

'Oh. God. I'm so sorry,' Fulton said, covering his mouth with a hand. 'I mean... God. You got Gillespie, though, right? You caught him?'

Logan nodded. 'Questioning him now.'

'Right. Right. Well, that's something, I suppose,' Fulton said. The kettle rolled closer to the boil behind him. He turned to a cupboard and took out a mug. The words 'Grandpa's Tea' were printed on it, and he half-smiled as he read them. 'Do you think he could've been responsible for Brodie? For his murder, I mean?'

'The thought did occur,' Logan confirmed.

'Makes sense, I suppose,' Fulton said. 'It's what happens, isn't it? In that, I don't know, world, or what-have-you. You get involved in something like that, chances are there are going to be consequences.'

'Aye. It happens,' Logan said. 'We see it all the time. And, you know, for a minute there, I almost believed it. Nearly convinced myself that it was Sandy Gillespie or his sister who had murdered Brodie.'

Fulton set the mug down on the counter. The water rumbled inside the kettle.

'But it wasn't. Was it, Fulton?'

'Wasn't it?' Fulton asked. His voice was high, elevated by an artificial lightness. 'Are you sure? If he was involved with them in some sort of drugs thing, then I'd have thought it was obvious, given his injuries, that they—'

'Aye. That's what we were all meant to think. It was staged, you see? All orchestrated to make it look like it was drug-related. Killing him. Cutting him open. Even removing his teeth and fingers. It was carefully planned to make us think it was connected to Brodie's drug trafficking.'

Logan let that hang in the air between them for a moment, before continuing.

'But it wasn't.'

'Wasn't it?' Fulton asked. The tremble in his voice was unmissable.

'It's over, Fulton,' Logan told him. 'I know what happened. I know what you did.'

Both men stood in silence, Fulton's hands splayed flat on the kitchen worktop, the mug filling the space between them.

There was a loud click as the kettle came to the boil. The sound was a starting pistol that drew Logan's gaze for a split-second and kicked Fulton into life.

He shifted, spun. The mug exploded against Logan's left temple, filling his skull with pain and noise and swirling lights.

The floor lurched. Logan staggered, grabbing at Fulton. He found only thin air, and then felt a crack as his forehead met the edge of the kitchen worktop. He saw blood, tasted it, too, and then the floor came up to meet him, and he was dragged down, down, down into a stifling, smothering darkness.

–

Logan awoke to a woman screaming at him. It was the sound he heard first, his eyes stuck fast with blobs of drying blood. She was somewhere close, right in his face, and he shoved her away before rolling onto his front and heaving himself up onto his feet.

'What the hell's going on? Where's Dad? Where's Carrie?'

Logan thumbed the crusts from his eyes, and opened them to see Hannah Randall practically squaring up to him, panic etched across the freckles of her face. From elsewhere in the house, he heard an older woman shouting Fulton's name, but receiving no answer.

'Shite,' Logan spat. He staggered to the window, the world bobbing and weaving around him like it was trying to get out of his way. 'His car's gone.'

'We know! What happened? What are you doing here?' Hannah demanded.

'He's not here,' said her mother, scurrying into the kitchen. Sandra rushed over to Logan and turned him with a yank on his arm. 'Where is he? Where's my husband?'

'Where's Carrie?' Hannah demanded. 'Who did this to you? Was someone here?'

Her face crumpled. Tears rushed in. Sandra caught the girl around the shoulders, sensing an imminent collapse. 'Did someone take her?' Hannah whispered.

'What's the car reg?' Logan asked, fishing into his pocket for his phone. He opened the text messaging app, then barked out the question again. 'His car reg. What is it?'

Sandra shut her eyes in concentration, then recited the plate.

Logan thumbed the characters into a message, rattled off a couple of instructions, then sent it to Ben, Tyler, and Hamza.

'What's going on?' Hannah pleaded. Her eyes flicked to the spot on his forehead that was currently throbbing like a bastard. From the way she flinched, he reckoned it was a bad one. 'Who did this?'

'Fulton did. Your dad,' Logan said.

Both women exchanged looks of disbelief.

'What? No. Fulton?' Sandra said. 'What are you talking about? What do you mean?'

'There's no time to explain,' Logan told them. 'I need you to think where he might be. Where he might have gone.'

'Gone?' Sandra said, her pitch rising. 'What do you mean? Why would he have gone anywhere? What are you talking about?'

Logan had lost enough time. He wasn't about to throw away any more.

'I have reason to believe Fulton killed Brodie.'

'*What*?' Sandra spat. 'Have you lost your mind?'

'When I started to question him, he did this.' Logan pointed to his head injuries. 'Now he's gone, and he's taken your daughter with him, Hannah. He's taken Carrie. I need you to think where he might have gone.'

Hannah's hands fumbled for the worktop, searching for support. 'Mum?' she said. 'What's he talking about?'

'I don't know. I don't know. It's nonsense. It's all nonsense!'

Logan shook his head, trying to clear away the cobwebs. The effect was almost exactly the opposite, and the world went blurry around the edges. He ignored it, and focused on the parts in the middle.

'Hannah, listen to me,' he urged. 'Whether he's guilty or not, your dad did this to me. He panicked. He's out there now somewhere, scared. Not thinking straight. And he's got your little girl with him.'

Hannah covered her mouth with a trembling hand. 'He wouldn't hurt her. He won't.'

'Not deliberately, maybe,' Logan said. 'But she's out there with him now, and she'll be scared, and confused, just like he will be. But she won't understand what's going on. She won't understand what's happening.'

He stepped in closer. 'So I need you to think, Hannah. I need you to think about where he might go. Where he might've taken her.'

Hannah shook her head, like she didn't want to think about it, didn't want to face up to the reality of what Logan was telling her.

For a moment, she looked like she was going to burst into tears, but then she sucked it up and swallowed it down. Her voice, when it came, was stronger than Logan had been expecting.

'He'd have headed down the road. Glasgow way, probably. He knows a lot of people down there.'

'We've got a holiday rental,' Sandra added. 'Near Largs.'

Logan's phone buzzed in his hand. He glanced at the message from Hamza.

'Right, well, we're on the lookout for the car. If he does head down that way, he'll get picked up on the cameras, if not before.'

'I'm sure it's all just a… a misunderstanding,' Sandra said. 'Why would he kill Brodie? It's ridiculous! It doesn't make sense!'

'Aye, well, what matters right now is finding him. Everything else we can sort out after that, OK?' Logan said. 'We've got eyes on the roads in all directions. Whichever way he goes, we'll find him, and then we can get to the bottom of it all once Carrie's back home safe. All right?'

'Unless…' Hannah began.

She fell silent again, only continuing when Logan prompted her with a raised eyebrow, and an, 'Unless what?'

Hannah met his gaze. Her eyes were wet with tears, and heavy with worry. 'Unless he doesn't take the road.'

# Chapter 45

He could feel the girl shivering in his arms, her wee body trembling under the blanket he'd grabbed from the back of the car.

'It's cold, Grandpa,' she said, her chin wobbling as her teeth chattered together. 'It's *fleezing*.'

'I know, sweetheart. I know it's *fleezing*,' Fulton said. His breath came out as a cloud of white mist, illuminated in the glow of his head torch. He rubbed her back through the blanket as he picked his way across the scree that covered this stretch of the mountainside. 'We'll get you inside soon, OK? We'll get all warmed up.'

'When?'

'Soon, OK?'

'How soon?'

'Just *soon*, Carrie, all right?'

He regretted his tone immediately, tried to make up for it by jiggling her in his arms and plastering on a smile. 'It's an adventure! Just you and me, off on an adventure together. It's going to be fun. Won't it?'

He heard her sob beneath the blanket. *No, no, no.*

'How about a song, eh? Will we sing a song? What's that one you like? The wheels on the bus go…'

The voice that emerged from under the blanket was small and strained. 'Round an' round.'

'That's it! Round and round, round and round. The wheels on the bus go—'

His boot slipped on the loose stone shards, and he yelped as a leg went skiting out from under him. Twisting, he managed to land on his back, instead of his front, but the jarring impact brought a gasp, then tears from the girl in his arms.

'I'm sorry, I'm sorry, you're all right, you're OK,' he soothed, rocking her back and forth. 'I've got you, Carrie. We're all right.'

Her cries settled down into sniffles, as Fulton got back to his feet. His back and shoulder ached from carrying her, and she clung to him as he swapped her from one arm to the other.

How long had they been walking for now? Two hours? Three? He'd left his watch and his phone back at the house, so he couldn't say for sure. The sun had dipped below the horizon a few miles back, though. If he hadn't had the head torch in the car, they'd be wandering blind by now.

The bothy had to be nearby. Ten minutes of trudging. Less, if he hurried. They could get a fire started in there, get them warm. Once he was warm, he could plan. He could figure out what to do. Figure out how to fix this mess.

But the girl was so heavy, and the fall had hurt his back. And ten minutes might as well have been a lifetime.

'I want to go home, Grandpa.'

'Well, we can't right now, darling. All right? Not yet. But we're going to somewhere even better. Just me and you. We'll get warm, you can have some chocolate—'

'I want home.'

Anger bubbled up inside him, sharply tightening his grip on the girl. 'Well, you can't go home, Carrie! Not yet. So stop complaining, all right?'

More tears came then. More wailing. Fulton marched on, the circle of torchlight sweeping across the scree, Carrie wrestling against him like she wanted to break free.

'Stop it! Stop it, you'll fall. Is that what you want? Is it? To fall? Because it's a long way down from here, and you won't like what happens when you get to the bottom!'

The crying intensified. The struggling, too. His arms burned like they were on fire. She was so heavy, and he'd been carrying her for so long.

'Shh. Stop. Stop it!'

She twisted in his grip. An elbow was driven into his throat. He felt her slip beneath the blanket, realised too late that she was going to fall. He grabbed for her, but found only the rough, woollen material.

There was a thack from the stones at his feet.

The crying stopped, and silence rushed in to fill the space it had left behind. The circle of light from the head torch picked out the lifeless shape on the scree, one arm folded in beneath her, one leg bent atop the other.

Fulton snatched her up, shook her, hugged her against him. She felt tiny and limp against him. And cold. So very cold.

'Carrie? Sweetheart. Come on. Come on, wake up,' he whimpered. 'Wake up, come on, darling, come on. Please. Wake up for Grandpa, all right? Wake up for—'

She screamed. It was simultaneously the best and worst noise Fulton had ever heard. He kept her pinned against him as she howled and wailed and screeched in his ear. She was cold, she was terrified, and she was hurting.

But she was alive. Thank God, she was alive.

It took her a good few minutes to run out of energy. The adrenaline spike that had fuelled the screaming session was exhausted, and she sagged in Fulton's arms.

With the crying over, the silence returned. Only, it wasn't silence this time. Not quite. There was another sound in there, too. A *whum-whum-whum* that he was only too familiar with.

Hugging Carrie closer to him, Fulton clicked off his torch and began to run just as the helicopter crested the top of the mountain ahead of them, its spotlight slicing through the darkness. The roar of the rotors was deafening, their downdraft flattening the heather and bracken further up the mountainside.

Down there, on the scree, they were too low for the spotlight to reach them. If they could make it past, get to the next ridge without being seen, they could still make it to the bothy.

They couldn't stay there now, of course. Not for long. But he could take a few minutes to rest. He could find a way to get Carrie on his back, make her easier to carry. He could think. For a minute, he could just stop and think.

A bundle of stone fragments slipped out from beneath his feet. He was ready for it this time and kept his balance as they slid a few dozen feet down the hillside, further away from the beam of the helicopter's spotlight.

There were trees ahead. Not many, but enough to offer some cover. Slipping and skidding across the scree, he stumbled into the bracken, and went scurrying through the copse of trees.

The thundering of the rotor blades faded as Fulton emerged from the thicket and rounded the shoulder of the mountain. Clinging to his granddaughter with one arm, he kicked and pulled them up the steep incline, making hand-holds from whatever foliage he could reach.

They were both breathing heavily when he finally got them to the ridge. The helicopter was half a mile away and still going, and Fulton felt safe enough switching his head torch back on.

The circle of light immediately picked out the old stone wall of the bothy. It had been a hill crofter's house, once upon a time, but was now open to climbers and walkers passing through the area. A place for rest and respite from the unforgiving terrain.

There was no smoke from the chimney, and no signs of movement from inside. Fulton hurried to the front door and shouldered it open, then turned and closed it behind him, before wedging it shut with the back of one of the bothy's rickety wooden chairs.

'Here we are, here we go. What did I tell you?' Fulton whispered, rubbing the warmth back into Carrie's shivering body. She hadn't said anything since the fall. Barely made a sound since she'd stopped crying, in fact.

She was probably tired, that was all. Tired, and cold, and hungry. Half an hour here would see them both right. Half an hour with the fire on, and they'd both be ready to set off again.

He found a box of matches on the mantle. There was a candle, too, the wax mostly melted until it was little more than a stumpy little stub with a blackened wick. It wouldn't be bright enough to see from outside—not from the helicopter, certainly—but a bit of light might help set Carrie at ease.

He wasted a couple of matches before he was able to get the thing lit. The flame burned tall and bright for a few

319

seconds, before settling down. In that moment, though, he saw the shadow dancing across the wall.

'Well, well, well. Fancy seeing you here, Mr Randall.'

Fulton tightened his grip on the girl as Logan stepped forward into the shallow pool of the candlelight.

'I was starting to think you weren't going to show.'

Fulton's mouth flapped open and closed. 'I don't... it's not what it looks like. None of this. I don't know what you think happened, but it's, it's, it's not that.'

Logan pointed to his face. One side of it was a mess of bruising, swelling, and blood that had dried almost black.

'You didn't wallop me with a mug?' he said. 'You didn't put your granddaughter at risk by fleeing with her into the mountains?'

The floorboards creaked as Logan came to a stop. 'You didn't murder Brodie Welsh?'

'No, I... it's not like that. You've got it all wrong!'

'Enlighten me then, Mr Randall,' Logan said. 'Tell me what happened. Explain it to me.'

Carrie wriggled in Fulton's arms. He rubbed her back and rocked from foot to foot, trying to soothe her. 'I don't... I can't...'

'How about I tell you what I think happened? Make it easier,' Logan said. 'I think you found out exactly who and what Brodie was. I think you were so angry with him, so disgusted by him, that you decided to get rid of him. For Hannah's sake. And Carrie's.'

Fulton flinched at the sound of the girl's name and hugged her so tightly she whimpered beneath the blanket.

'I think you thought you could pin it on the Gillespies. Make it look like a drugs thing by cutting him open. Shift the blame to them, kill two birds with one stone,' Logan continued. 'But for that to work, he had to be found, didn't he? You kept him in your grit bin until you could move him, and then, once you'd buried him and left a few Gillespie-sized footprints around the place, you made the call to the mountain rescue, knowing someone would find his body.'

The windows of the bothy shook, and a trickle of dust fell from the rafters as the helicopter came circling back towards the building.

'That's about the size of it, isn't it, Mr Randall? That's pretty close.'

Fulton's throat was tight and narrow, and barely able to get the words out.

'He was hitting her. He was hurting my daughter.'

'Aye. I know,' Logan said.

'What if he'd hurt Carrie, too? Hmm? What if he'd started hitting her? Or worse! What then?'

'I understand your concerns, Fulton. I do. I've a daughter myself. If I found out someone was hurting her. Causing her pain. Well...' Logan's eyes briefly glazed over, like some internal realisation was drawing power from the rest of him. 'Well, I'd never forgive them. I'd hate them for it.'

Fulton shook his head, sending tears plopping to the dusty wooden floor. 'I didn't hate him. Not really. I didn't want him to suffer. I just... when I found out what he'd done. What he was doing. I couldn't just let it go on. I couldn't. I had to do something. For Carrie's sake. I didn't want to, but I had to. I had to!'

The whumming of the helicopter rotors grew louder overhead. Outside, the beam of the searchlight came sweeping across the heather.

'Aye, well, let's go get you both warmed up, Fulton,' Logan said. 'We can talk about this somewhere a bit less…' He gestured around at the bothy. '…grim.'

Fulton rocked the child in his arms. She had stopped struggling now. He could hear her breathing, soft and slow, feel its warmth against his neck.

He'd never have this again. Never have this closeness. Never have another moment like this one, with her holding him, trusting him, loving him.

He'd killed her daddy. She'd never forgive him. He might not even see her again.

The thought of it kicked his weary legs into life and he raced for the door, Carrie clutched to him like a rugby ball as he went barrelling outside into the blinding bright storm of the helicopter.

'Fulton, wait!'

Logan's voice was right behind him. Close. Too close. Fulton slammed the door on him and broke into a run, tripping and stumbling through the spotlight's beam.

They were going to take her. Take Carrie. Take her away from him forever.

He couldn't let them. He couldn't lose her. Wouldn't. Not here. Not now. Not like this.

The edge of the ridge came up quickly, catching him by surprise. He skidded to a stop just inches from where the ground fell away, and heard the distant clatter of sliding rocks on the mountainside far below.

The chopper's downdraft was like a hand on his back, forcing him closer to the edge, and the long drop beyond it. He was a step away, that was all. One step. Just one, and he'd never have to see the look of betrayal on his granddaughter's face. He'd never have to hear Hannah tell him he'd never get to see either of them again.

He'd never have to face up to what he'd done.

One step.

Just one.

Fulton's foot trembled as he raised it off the ground.

'Don't you fucking dare!'

The tone and the wording of the shout took him by surprise. He wobbled for a moment, then his foot returned to join the other on the ground.

He shuffled around in a tight half-circle to find Logan silhouetted against the spotlight's beam, his coat billowing around him like a cape.

'What the hell do you think you're playing at, you daft bastard?' the detective demanded.

It was not the sort of negotiation strategy that Fulton had been expecting, and his brain struggled to formulate any sort of response.

'You're going to jump. Is that it?' Logan asked. 'You're going to jump off there with your granddaughter in your arms?'

Fulton glanced back at the drop. Six inches behind his heels, the world fell away into darkness. It would be quick. She'd never even know.

'They won't let me see her again,' he sobbed, raising his voice over the thunder of the rotor blades. 'I'll go to jail, and they'll all hate me, and I won't get to see her again.'

'Aye, well, can you blame them? You're threatening to kill her, Fulton,' Logan said. 'Does that sound like the sort of person that should be involved in her life? Honestly?'

Fulton tightened his grip on the girl. She groaned in her sleep, or her exhaustion, but otherwise didn't react.

'You say you care about her—'

'I do! Of course, I do! I did all this for her! I love her!'

'Not from where I'm standing, you don't,' Logan said. 'From where I'm standing, you're a selfish bastard who'd rather end her life here and now than have her find out what you did. If you can't have her, no one can. Is that it, Fulton?'

'No! No, it's not like that!'

Logan sighed. 'Look, if you want to jump, be my guest.'

Fulton blinked. 'What?'

'I mean it. I'd rather you didn't, but honestly? I don't care. Jump. Don't. It's up to you,' Logan said. He took a step forward and held out a hand. 'But give me the girl, Fulton. Give me Carrie. She doesn't deserve this. She deserves to go to school, make friends, fall in love. She deserves to have a life.'

He shuffled forward a step. Fulton didn't flinch or draw back.

'Are you really going to take that from her?' Logan pressed. 'Or are you going to be her grandfather, and do what's right?'

Fulton rocked the girl, whispering to her, as tears cut tracks down his cheeks. She was cold. So cold. Her breathing so shallow.

What was he doing? What had he done?

He pulled the blanket aside, just a fraction, and kissed the top of her head. He inhaled her, breathing in the smell of her for what he knew would be the very last time.

She stirred, opened her eyes, and looked up into his. She smiled, just for a moment, then her eyelids grew heavy again, and her head fell against his chest.

Fulton nodded, just once, and held the precious bundle out. 'Here. Take her,' he said. 'Hurry.'

Logan approached quickly but cautiously, one hand outstretched, the other emerging from his coat pocket.

He took the girl, blanket and all, and hugged her against him.

Fulton opened his mouth, and something primal emerged. Fear, and angst, and anger, and shame, all mixed up in one desperate, pitiful cry.

He turned away. Took a step. His foot found nothing but empty air.

And then, metal dug into his wrist, pain shot up his arm, and he was dragged back from the edge of the abyss.

Fulton stared in disbelief at the handcuff around his wrist. At the other end of it, DCI Logan drew himself up to his full, terrifying height.

'Fulton Randall,' he began. 'I am arresting you on suspicion of the murder of Brodie Welsh.'

# Chapter 46

Four days later, Logan muttered to himself as he readjusted his tie for the fifth time in as many minutes. He hated the bloody things, and this one seemed determined to be as difficult as possible. It was either too long or too short, or all twisted at the knot.

He'd tried everything—using the mirror, not using the mirror, tying it first then pulling it on over his head, calling it an arsehole and throwing it across the room. You name it, he'd done it, and still the thing wasn't sitting right.

'You no' ready yet?' asked Ben.

'It's this bastarding tie,' Logan said. He grimaced as he tried to flatten down the twisted knot. 'It's broken.'

'It's a tie. How can it be broken?' Ben asked. He swatted Logan's hands away and stretched up, adjusting the tie for him. 'Here. Let me have a look.'

Logan tilted his head back, giving the DI free rein.

'Maybe if you didn't have such a fat neck,' Ben muttered.

'It's no' a fat neck, it's a boxer's neck,' Logan insisted.

'Aye, and I suppose they're boxer's chins, too, are they?'

Logan started to protest, but a sudden tightening of the tie choked him into silence.

'There,' Ben said, stepping back. 'How's that?'

Logan tucked a finger into his shirt collar and loosened the tie a fraction, then checked his reflection in the hotel mirror. 'Aye. Fine.'

His phone dinged, and he searched the pockets of his suit until he found it. Ben watched him as he checked the screen.

'Anything exciting?'

'Email from Hoon,' Logan said, scrolling through the message. 'Fulton Randall's court date has been set.'

'That was quick.'

'Aye, well, he's confessed to everything. Murdering Brodie, trying to frame the Gillespies. The works.'

Back at the station, Fulton had been quick to sing, and slow to stop. He'd confirmed that Sergeant Jaffray had let slip about the domestic assault. Once he'd heard about that, he'd gone straight to Jinkies, who'd revealed Brodie's connection to the Gillespies. He'd done it 'one friend to another', Fulton insisted, but that would make no difference to the internal investigation, Logan knew. Jaffray might get through it with a demotion, but Jinkies was done for.

Good riddance.

It hadn't all tied up neatly, though. Fulton insisted he had nothing to do with Maureen Gillespie's murder, and there was no evidence to connect him to it. He also hadn't found any drugs when he'd cut Brodie open, so there was very probably some sort of missing shipment out there somewhere. Whose hands it was in, if anyone's, remained a mystery.

Sandy Gillespie wasn't talking, either. He claimed that Maureen had been the mastermind behind their little drug empire, and that he'd never even heard the names of the people she was working with, never mind met them.

He was scared. That much was obvious. Someone had to have told him about Maureen's death, and unless they had some sort of psychic sibling link that extended beyond the grave, it was likely that the 'someone' in question was directly involved in her murder.

Still, they would have plenty of time to work on him. They had him bang to rights on Caitlyn's murder. He wasn't going anywhere for a long, long time.

'You spoken to the family again?' Ben asked, as he unhooked his suit jacket from the hanger on the back of the door.

'Bit snug that, Benjamin,' Logan remarked, as the DI squeezed himself into it. 'And aye. Yesterday. Just briefly.'

'How's the wee one?' Ben asked. He started fastening a button, then realised it was a bridge too far, and decided just to let the jacket hang open.

'Full of the cold. Confused. Wondering where her dad and her granddad are.'

Ben sucked air in through his teeth. 'They've not told her?'

'How do you explain it to someone her age?' Logan asked.

'Aye. Rather them than me, right enough,' Ben said. 'How are the wife and daughter?'

'About how you'd expect,' Logan said. 'It won't be easy for them.'

He fiddled with his tie again, earning himself a slap on the arm from the older man.

'Leave that. It's fine.'

Logan rubbed a hand across his chin. For once, it was completely smooth. Well, mostly. He'd found a tiny patch he'd missed between his chin and his neck, and it had been annoying him ever since. Not enough for him to go dig out his shaving gear again, but enough that he kept feeling it with his thumb and tutting.

There was a knock at the door. Ben checked his watch, adjusted his own tie, then gave Logan the look both of them had been quietly dreading.

'You ready, then?' he asked.

Logan wasn't ready. He never was for these things. Not really.

'Aye. Ready,' he lied, then he pulled on his coat as Ben opened the door.

Hamza, Tyler, and Sinead stood out in the corridor, sombre and silent, all dressed up in shades of black.

Logan adjusted his collar, shoved his hands deep down in his pockets, and checked his reflection one more time. He nodded, accepting that his reflection was as good as it was likely to get.

'Right, then. We fit?' he asked.

'Ready, boss,' Tyler said, and the others murmured their agreement.

Ben joined them in the corridor. Logan stepped out, letting the door close behind him.

'Nice day for it,' Ben remarked, as they stepped out of the hotel and into the bracing Orkney air a couple of minutes later.

Logan looked up. The sky was lined with shades of grey. A blanket of thick cloud hung over everything, dark, and heavy, and oppressive.

'Aye. Pretty much perfect, I'd say,' he observed.

His phone buzzed in his pocket. He checked the screen.

'Unknown Caller'.

He regarded it impassively for a few moments, letting it vibrate in his hand.

'Everything all right, Jack?' Ben asked.

Logan thumbed the button to reject the call and switched the handset off.

'Aye. Everything's fine,' he said.

And with that, they joined the slow procession heading to the church, and set off to say their final farewells.

Together.

# CANELOCRIME

Do you love crime fiction and are always on the lookout for brilliant authors?

Canelo Crime is home to some of the most exciting novels around. Thousands of readers are already enjoying our compulsive stories. Are you ready to find your new favourite writer?

Find out more and sign up to our newsletter at canelocrime.com